The NEW
EDGAR
WINNERS

· THE MYSTERY ·
WRITERS *of* AMERICA

The NEW
EDGAR
WINNERS

Edited by
Martin H. Greenberg

Introduction by
Donald E. Westlake

WYNWOOD™ Press
New York, New York

Library of Congress Cataloging-in-Publication Data

The New Edgar winners / Mystery Writers of America ; edited by Martin
  H. Greenberg.
        p.   cm.
    ISBN 0-922066-35-3 : $17.95
    1. Detective and mystery stories, American.   I. Greenberg, Martin
Harry.   II. Mystery Writers of America.
PS648.D4N5   1990
813'.087208—dc20   90-30680
                                                                         CIP

Copyright © 1990 by Mystery Writers of America, Inc.
Published by WYNWOOD™ Press
New York, New York
Printed in the United States of America

Acknowledgments

Grateful acknowledgment is made by Mystery Writers of America, Inc., and WYNWOOD™ Press for permission to include the following:

"Armed and Dangerous" by Geoffrey Norman. Copyright © 1979 by Geoffrey Norman. Reprinted by permission of the author.

"Horn Man" by Clark Howard. Copyright © 1980 by Clark Howard. Reprinted by permission of the author.

"The Absence of Emily" by Jack Ritchie. Copyright © 1981 by Davis Publications, Inc. Reprinted by permission of the Larry Sternig Literary Agency.

"There Are No Snakes in Ireland" by Frederick Forsyth. Copyright © 1982 by Frederick Forsyth. Reprinted by permission of Curtis Brown, Ltd.

"The New Girl Friend" by Ruth Rendell. Copyright © 1983 by Ruth Rendell. Reprinted by permission of the author.

"By the Dawn's Early Light" by Lawrence Block. Copyright © 1984 by Lawrence Block. Reprinted by permission of the author.

"Ride the Lightning" by John Lutz. Copyright © 1985 by John Lutz. Reprinted by permission of the author.

Contents

Introduction: The New Edgar Winners

by DONALD E. WESTLAKE

Most storytellers in our time have begun their careers by writing short stories, as though short stories were easy, the literary equivalent of a finger exercise on the piano. (Which would, of course, make the novel a symphony.) But the analogy breaks down, because finally every story, of whatever length, is a *story*; which is to say, it's a series of manufactured events leading to a point or conclusion. And that means that any story of whatever length must provide possible human beings as characters, have them operate from believable motivations in a world whose reality we can accept, and lead them toward a conclusion or stopping-point that will satisfy us. To do all that at five thousand words is not easier than to do it at one hundred thousand. To do it right in such cramped quarters is a lot harder.

This is a volume of stories by people who did it right. They did it so very right, in fact, that their work was recognized by their peers; each of them has been awarded the best short story of the year Edgar award by the membership of the Mystery Writers of America, most of whom, almost by definition, will have at some point in their careers turned their own hands to the same form and therefore will know just how much a piece of cake it isn't.

And particularly is the short story a tricky form in the mystery genre, which by the nature of the beast can't be a slice of life or plotless vignette or tone poem. At the very least, the mystery story requires an event that involves conflict, plus its resolution, and that's what's delivered in the Edgar winners, every time. Here is the best of what our people do, the mystery writers collectively say, year by year these are the best short stories that were published in a genre that demands clear detail and psychological accuracy and plausible event from *all* its stories, at whatever length and in whatever medium.

Given the problems that constricted space creates, why would anyone want to tell a story short when it would apparently be so much easier to tell it long? (For those who would answer, because a particular story doesn't have enough incident or complexity to sustain a novel, I would point immediately to the Howard and Forsyth and Block stories herein, which certainly do. And Ruth Rendell's full-length works have often hinged on just the kind of strange on-off relationship between individuals that motors "The New Girl Friend.")

So the reason these stories exist can't be because they're easier than anything else to write. And it can't be for fame, either; no mystery writer of the last generation has built a wide reputation on the basis of short stories alone, a fact which always plagued that consummate miniaturist, the late Jack Ritchie, whose typical spare attack you'll find represented here by "The Absence of Emily." Nor can money be the reason, since the short story—in every field—is just about the only escapee from inflation I can think of. The genre magazines that paid a nickel a word fifty years ago pay a nickel a word (or less) today. The slick magazines of the thirties paid around three thousand dollars for a story; so do the slick magazines published now.

So if neither fame nor fortune is the spur, what is it that keeps our best writers returning to the short story time after time? (Two of the contributors to this volume, Ruth Rendell and Harlan Ellison, are represented by their *second* Edgar-winning stories.) I think one answer may be the challenge itself, and here I'd like to adapt the musical analogy I started out with. If the novel is a symphony, then a short story is a concerto, say for the piano or violin. The full orchestra is still there, sawing away, but the point has become the skill and flair and personal vision of the soloist. The short story refines the skills and talents of its soloist, the writer, into concentrated form, lets him toy with technique, stretch his muscles, demonstrate his bravura skill in swift arpeggio.

The short story also permits the writer to deal interestingly with subjects that concern him, without losing the reader by being preachy or tendentious. Frederick Forsyth takes this opportunity in "There Are No Snakes in Ireland" and Geoffrey Norman does something similar (yet vastly different) in "Armed and Dangerous."

Taking another tack, the writer might use the short story to comment obliquely on the whole concept of popular fiction, as Robert Sampson's "Rain in Pinton County" sums up and comments on the history of the tough pulp crime story, and Bill Crenshaw's "Flicks" plays (with great originality) with the question of why audiences go to be frightened at horror films.

Are there similarities among these stories, repetitions, familial resemblances, given that they were all written in the same genre and all appealed to the same award-proffering organization? Not at all. They range in this volume from the brisk tongue-in-cheek approach of Jack Ritchie to the coiled violent emotion of Robert Sampson to the diamond-hard fatalism of Lawrence Block to the evocative poetry of Harlan Ellison. Only one plot element, it seems to me, appears more than once in all of these stories: both Clark Howard in "Horn Man" and John

Lutz in "Ride the Lightning" deal with a man who keeps silence for the sake of a woman; but how different are the two uses of that idea!

Where did these stories originally appear? Three come from the redoubtable *Ellery Queen's Mystery Magazine*, that amazing source of the highest quality short fiction consistently for over half a century, and two more were first published in EQMM's kid brother, *Alfred Hitchcock's Mystery Magazine*. One each are from much more recent additions to the world of crime-fiction publication: *The New Black Mask* and the *Black Lizard Anthology of Crime Fiction*. Two come from the wider world of general-interest magazines, one from *Esquire* and one from *Playboy*. And Frederick Forsyth's story appeared in his own collection, making it one of the rarest of all creatures, a mystery short story that has been on the best-seller list.

Wherever these stories came from, they caught the eye of the Mystery Writers of America judges, and it is to all our benefit that they did. A decade of fine—the finest—short stories. Enjoy.

The NEW
EDGAR
WINNERS

GEOFFREY NORMAN

Armed and Dangerous

1979

Calloway found Sandra's note Scotch-taped on the refrigerator door, and it said for him to meet her at the police station. He drove furiously and found her sitting in an office with glass walls. She looked composed, almost serene, except that she was biting her lower lip.

"What happened?" he said, out of breath.

"I was raped, Dan."

The news took a few seconds to penetrate his shock, like a stone settling into ice. He walked over to her, lifted her from the chair and held her.

"Are you all right?"

"I've been raped. I've been tested over at the hospital. You know ... for *evidence*. I've had to tell my story to five different cops who didn't believe me. But on the whole I'd say I'm all right."

Her face was pressed into his shoulder, and he could feel her crying and fighting each sob.

"Jesus, I'm sorry. Take it easy ... don't worry, it will be all right. Why didn't you call me?"

"Because I wanted to handle it myself," she said, pushing away from him and looking directly into his face. "What could you do? Go kill the guy?"

"I just wanted to help."

"Then tell these cops that I generally don't go around making up stories about being raped and that I don't screw every man I meet."

A thin man in shirt sleeves looked at Calloway from across a desk cluttered with files and loose-leaf binders. He shrugged. "We don't mean any offense, Mr. Calloway . . . Mrs. Calloway," he said. "We have to do this. It'll be a lot worse in court."

"I didn't rape anybody," Sandra said loudly. "I don't know why you treat me like a suspect."

"No offense."

"Have you got what you need?" Calloway said to the man. "Can she go now?"

"Yes. We'll be calling you."

They did not talk on the drive home, and once she was inside, Sandra went straight into the bathroom. Calloway could hear the toilet flush and the water running in the tub. He poured a glass of bourbon.

She took an hour. When she came out, she was wearing a terry cloth robe and her skin was flushed and pink from hot water and scrubbing. She sat down across from him.

"Can I get you something?" he said.

"No."

"You want to go to bed? Take something to make you sleep?"

"No. I just want to sit here for a while."

"Okay. I'll do anything I can."

"There isn't anything. It happened. You can't change that."

"All right. If you do want something, you tell me."

She sat in her chair with her bare feet flat on the floor and her arms folded across her body. She looked straight ahead. Her eyes were blank. She looked like somebody who had just come from a family funeral: spent, numb, and deep in grief.

"You just couldn't imagine it," she said finally. "He was an animal. He put his arm around my neck and started to squeeze. I knew he was going to kill me. And he would have done it. He really would have. I *know* he would have."

"Who was he, Sandra?"

"An animal." She looked away. "He was head of some youth program. He put an ad in the paper for an assistant, and I wanted to go to work. I called and got an appointment."

"Why didn't you tell me about it, baby?"

"Why should I? Do I have to get your permission to work?"

"No. But I could have talked to you about it. That's all. And gone along with you, maybe."

"Great world, isn't it? I can't go to a job interview without taking my husband along because some other man might rape me," she said. "*Might*, hell."

She stopped and waited a few seconds. "You know what the worst of it was? It wasn't being afraid that he was going to kill me. I mean, I was afraid. For sure, I was afraid. But the worst part was that he just forced himself inside of me when I was still totally dry. You just can't imagine. That was the most painful and humiliating part. He didn't care a single thing about me. He didn't even mind hurting me in that one more way. He liked it, you know. Really liked it."

"Baby, who was the guy?"

"Just a dude. Said his name was Irvine. Pronounced it 'Irvine.'"

"Where is he?"

"Oh, come on."

"I mean it."

"The police have him by now."

"Maybe not."

"What are you going to do? Kill him because he wronged your woman?"

"Maybe," he said. He could feel his jaw tightening like a twisted rope.

"Dan, I'm the one he raped. Let me handle it. My way."

"The police?"

"Yes. I'm going to point to him in court, and he is going to know who sent him to prison."

"I hope it works out that way."

She was crying. Two glittering wet tracks ran down her cheeks, and she blinked trying to stop them. He stood up to go to her and hold her, but she got up and walked out of the room.

The police arrested the man. His real name was R. Johnson, and he had been arrested a half-dozen times before. Never for rape. He was still in his office when the police got there, and he did not resist. "You boys are making a mistake," he said when they put the handcuffs on and explained his rights. "A mistake you are purely going to regret when this gets in the papers."

One of the police officers found an appointment book, and on one page there were the names of all the people who had answered his job advertisement. There were fifteen of them, all women's names.

"We took all of them names," a detective said to Calloway, "and looked them up in the phone book. Went by and talked to every one of those women. Sent around one of our best men with a lady cop to do the talking. If she thought it would help, she'd ask the man to leave the room while she talked to the woman in private. She'd explain how we had the guy, but we needed all the evidence and testimony we could get to help send him up where he belongs. Then she'd ask each of them women to help us put this turkey away. Tell them there wasn't any shame in it and that it would be a real service to mankind and like that. Half of them women just wouldn't say a thing. It was , 'Job interview? Let me see. Oh, yes, I seem to remember going for a job interview at that address. But nothing *unusual* happened. Nothing at all.'

"But the other half, every one of them, had been raped by this gentleman. Every one. And after they talked to the lady cop for a while, they told her everything. But not one of them would have come in on her own."

"Why not?" Calloway said. "I don't understand that."

"Your wife may be the one making the mistake, the way things work these days."

"Sandra is pretty tough," Calloway said. They were sitting in his kitchen. The detective had come by to ask Sandra some questions, but she was out. It was after hours, so the detective accepted Calloway's offer of a beer.

"No doubt about it," he said. "She's a gutsy lady. None of those other women would even report that guy. Shit, I think he raped them all. Half of them wouldn't even admit it after we had the guy in the pound and told them there were other witnesses." The detective paused. "But by the time that dude goes to trial . . . if he goes to trial . . . we'll be lucky if we can get even one or two of those other girls to testify against him."

Calloway went to the refrigerator for more beer. "Embarrassed or scared?" he said.

"Both. That creep is already back on the streets. Made bail the first day. Knowing that probably doesn't help any of the women sleep better at night. Then, just about all women know what they're in for at a rape trial. Defense attorney is going to try to make them look like whores . . . like they wanted it . . . led the guy on. He'll ask a lot of really evil questions . . . make them talk about their sex

lives . . . make it all seem like their fault . . . or something
they made up. Most women just don't want to go through
all that. And I can't say as I blame them.''

"Sandra isn't going to quit."

"Well, I'd understand if she did," the detective said.
"You should too."

Calloway resented the advice but didn't say anything.

The detective went on. If he noticed that Calloway was
irritated, he didn't care. "That guy is going to have a slick
lawyer whose only idea is to get his man off. He's going to
make sure there are at least a couple of old church ladies
on the jury, and he is going to make your wife sound like
some kind of slut. He'll try to get those jurors to believe
that she went down there looking for action." The detective stopped and sighed. He swallowed half a can of beer
and stood up. "It's going to be rough. That's all I can tell
you. Try to help her out. And good luck."

Sandra met four times with the prosecutor. She told
him her story in detail each time, and he tried, each time,
to find the flaws in it, to anticipate the defense attorney's
line of attack. After each meeting, she came home gray
and shaken.

At the last meeting, he told her how to dress and how
much makeup to wear to court and to make sure that she
got a good night's sleep.

Before the case was called, Sandra and Calloway stood
in a monotonous courthouse corridor where clerks
walked from room to room carrying documents. She had
been up since before sunrise, and twice she had gone into
the bathroom to vomit.

"Are you okay? You want me to call a doctor?" Calloway asked her.

"Don't worry about me, Dan," she said. "I'm just getting psyched up. Just like you used to do before a tough
game."

The prosecutor found them in the hallway and told them there had been a postponement. "Judge ruled in favor of a defense motion. I had four of the other women down here ready to testify. It took a lot to get them here. I'll be lucky if any of them show up again. And with this judge, there will be another delay anyway."

"How long?" Calloway asked.

"The new date is two months from now. Defense will move for another postponement, and they'll probably get it. This judge gives you two free ones just for asking. We won't start jury selection for six months. I'm sorry, Mrs. Calloway. I told you it was going to be tough."

"I'll still be around when the trial starts," she said. "You can count on that."

"Good."

"So in the meantime," Calloway said, "this ape just keeps up with business?"

"Yes. He's out on bail. The presumption of innocence still applies."

"Also the presumption that he just won't take a hike," Calloway said.

"Yes, that too," the prosecutor said. He was a thin man and very precise. His clothes were perfectly tailored and pressed; his hair was perfectly styled, almost engineered; and he spoke in perfectly modulated tones. He sounded sincere, concerned, and professional. Calloway guessed he had large ambitions.

"That's one of the most significant difficulties we face with this system of bail and long delays," he said. "One problem is that if the defendant has been out on the streets for six months or a year after he was charged and if he comes in voluntarily for trial after that and he hasn't gotten into trouble again . . . well, judges and juries think that alone is evidence that he should not be dealt with too harshly. It shows he is not a likely repeater."

"The point isn't whether he'll do it again," Calloway said. He could feel all his hatred of routine and officials and orderly procedure burning in him like gas. "He did it, and he ought to pay for it. Or does he get a freebie?"

"I know it's very frustrating. For you as well as for us."

"Except we aren't on salary," Calloway said. "This is your system."

Sandra inhaled with a hissing sound and stiffened. A stocky man with a wide, flat face walked by. He was talking to a young, slender man. "That's him," Sandra said.

Calloway looked. The two men were careful not to look back in his direction. They stood, hands in their pockets, looking at the floor and talking in low voices. They were less than thirty feet away. The whole situation was so ordinary, Calloway thought, that they could have been waiting for a table at a restaurant, talking about a stock deal or a man with good tickets to the Falcons' game. They were just two men in suits, studying their options and trying to come up with a winning plan.

The moment was so ordinary that it seemed obscene to Calloway. It reminded him of the men who flew in on choppers after a firefight and walked around kicking bodies and talking to survivors and taking down notes on their clipboards. They were there to impose a neat, logical order on what had been a random collision: chaos and panic and blundering men trying to kill but mostly trying to stay alive. The visitors would get back on their chopper and go back to Da Nang, where they would write it all up and call it a battle. What had happened to Sandra had happened. Now these two men were going to make some kind of sense out of it and call it a legal defense. It would be their version, and their job would be to sell it.

"Hey, fatso," Calloway said almost without wanting to. "Let me have a word with you outside."

Calloway saw the prosecutor signal to a policeman. He

felt a grip on his shoulder and when he tried to break away from it, he felt the nightstick under his chin, tightening and cutting off his air.

As he staggered backward, choking, he could see the man's face . . . the face of the man who had raped his wife and was now busy cooking up his public excuse with another man who didn't even know Sandra. It was a sullen and malevolent face, but there was no real anger in it. Just thick, scowling lips, and heavy, scornful eyes. The face was full of irritation; it didn't like putting up with this bullshit. Then Calloway did not see the face any longer.

"Don't you ever do anything like that again," Sandra said.

They were in the car, driving home, and she was staring straight ahead. "I'm not going to have you defend my honor . . . if I can't take care of myself, then I don't deserve to be taken care of."

"What makes you think you've got a chance? You heard the man. Six-month delay, if you're lucky. All the witnesses bugging out. Some lawyer trying to prove you asked for it."

"I'll do it my way."

Calloway said nothing the rest of the way home. He slowly lost his angry edge and felt a sort of pity for her, pity mingled with admiration that he was careful to conceal, since he was sure she wouldn't understand.

"Mrs. Calloway, where did you meet your husband?"

"Objection."

"Your Honor, the defense wonders if there is any question the prosecution will not object to."

"And the people wonder, Your Honor, if the defense knows how to conduct a proper cross-examination."

Calloway sat in the third row hating it all. Sandra had

been on the witness stand for over an hour. The whole time, the man who had raped her sat slouched and indifferent in a chair a few feet away. He was not paying attention. He was bored.

Calloway had looked over at him two or three times while the prosecutor carefully took Sandra through her account of the rape. The man would not look back. Once, his lawyer whispered something to him, and he shrugged elaborately. Calloway felt sick with rage.

It was worse when the defense attorney began his cross-examination.

"Mrs. Calloway," he said with formal politeness, "what is your occupation?"

"I'm a housewife," Sandra said weakly. The lawyer had forced the most humiliating confession on the first question.

"Do you have any children?"

"No."

"I see. And have you ever been employed? In a full-time capacity, that is?"

"No."

"But you are a college graduate . . . isn't that right?"

"Yes."

"And what sort of degree do you have?"

"B.A."

"From what institution?"

"Randolph-Macon."

"And in what subject?"

"English."

"I see. Have you ever had any training in social work?"

"No."

"Have you ever done any community work? In a voluntary capacity . . . for the Red Cross, say? Or Planned Parenthood?"

"No."

"But you felt qualified to answer an advertisement for a staff job in a community program with funding in the several millions of dollars . . . a full-time job working in some of the most neglected neighborhoods of the city, with some of the most deprived people in those neighborhoods . . . isn't that correct?"

"Yes."

"Do you *really* feel qualified?"

"Yes."

"Oh, come now," the man said, turning on her quickly. "You've told us that you are an English major with no experience in community work . . . that you've never held a job and that you've never had any children. Isn't it true that you were simply bored and looking for excitement? For a few kicks, as it were?"

"Your Honor," the prosecutor stood and was speaking in a tone of patience stretched into exasperation. It was as studied as the defense attorney's tone of incredulity. "Aside from the planted insult, the question is irrelevant. The witness is not on trial. It is not a crime to answer a want ad, even if you are unqualified. Her motives in answering that ad are not the concern of this court."

"Your Honor," the defense attorney said, "the charge is rape. The witness made the charge, and the defense is trying to establish her motive for making that charge. We do not deny that sexual relations took place . . . merely that force was involved. Our contention—and the truth of the matter is—that the plaintiff was not job hunting but thrill seeking."

"Object, Your Honor."

"Gentlemen," the judge said, "that's enough. We will recess for lunch, and I will make my ruling when we return."

Sandra stepped off the witness stand, and Calloway walked over to meet her. She was trembling.

"Bastard," she said. "Bastard."

"Easy," Calloway said. "Take it easy."

"That's the first thing any man thinks, that the woman was asking for it."

"Come on. Let's get something to eat."

"I hate that lawyer as much as I hate the pig who did it."

"Come on, Sandra. Let's go."

"I'd like to kill them both," she said, and walked out ahead of him.

They ate in a small place that served large hamburgers and mugs of beer. There were peanut shells on the floor and regimental posters on the wall. Two men played darts in the back of the room.

"Who is that creep, anyway?" Sandra asked.

"Which one?"

"The lawyer. The one who thinks it's my own fault."

"I don't know. Some guy named Scoggins. Graduate of Washington and Lee who likes trial work. Hangs around politics a little."

"Who told you that?"

"One of the guys in the prosecutor's office. He said Scoggins was good. That he'd rolled up a pretty big score since he came to Atlanta."

"It wouldn't bother me so much if he was some old, over-the-hill, whiskey-faced cracker. But this guy is somebody I could know. I could have gone out with him at school. He doesn't have any reason to do this to me. He doesn't even believe in it. He doesn't care what happened to me or what he is doing to me. He is doing this for his own reasons."

"He's a lawyer, Sandra. You have to be a shithead to be a lawyer. The really good ones enjoy being shitheads."

"What will happen if he wins?"

"The guy who did it will walk out. And Scoggins will have a little celebration. Champagne, probably."

"So it will be my fault?"

"Some people will believe that. Your friends will know better."

"What about you?"

"What about me?"

"Will you believe it was rape?"

"I believe what you tell me. You're my wife, and I couldn't operate any other way."

The defense attorney was allowed to continue with his line of questioning, and he quickly established that Sandra had never gone out looking for a job before the day she was raped.

"What were you wearing, Mrs. Calloway?" he asked. He was a small man who wore vested suits that made him look bird-chested. He reminded Calloway of the pugnacious little men he had seen strutting around gyms and locker rooms. Competitive and loud and always ready to fight, they made up for their size by staying on the attack.

"I don't remember exactly," Sandra said.

"Well, were you wearing a dress?"

"No, pants."

"And on top? A blouse? Sweater?"

"Blouse."

"What sort of material?"

"I don't remember."

"Were you wearing a bra?"

"I don't remember."

"Do you always wear a bra?"

"No."

"How often, then? Half the time?"

"Maybe a little less."

"So there is a better-than-even chance that you were not wearing a bra?"

Sandra did not say anything.

"In fact, Mrs. Calloway, I can produce witnesses who will swear you were not wearing a bra when you went in for your interview."

"All right," Sandra said. She no longer seemed angry to Calloway. Only defeated.

The defense attorney continued. He was working toward a sort of dramatic climax, and the earlier questions were all prelude, part of the necessary buildup. He had established a notion of Sandra's character. Now he would prove that there had been no rape, merely some bored and tawdry sex.

"Mrs. Calloway, did you go to a hospital for an examination after the episode in question?"

"Yes, I did."

"For tests?"

"Yes."

"What kind of tests?"

"Well, to see if I . . . to see if there had been any intercourse."

"And the results of the test were positive?"

"Yes."

"Did you receive any medical treatment at the hospital?"

"I don't understand."

"Were any bones splintered? Any cuts stitched? Bruises treated?"

"No."

"But you had been in a struggle, hadn't you?"

"Yes."

"And you resisted."

"Yes."

"But you received no injuries that required treatment at the hospital?"

"No."

"Mrs. Calloway, what did you do between the time you

left the defendant's office and your arrival at the hospital?"

"I drove home."

"How long did that take?"

"Fifteen minutes, I guess."

"What did you do when you got home?"

"I called the police."

"Right away?"

"No."

"How long after you got home did you call the police?"

"Maybe an hour."

"Why so long?"

"I was trying to decide what to do. I was confused."

It went on, but Calloway could not follow it. Everything was incomprehensible: the words, the people, the courtroom, the entire event. The impulse to take the little man and beat him into a bloody sponge was all that Calloway could feel. The strutting, cocky little lawyer might just as well have been doing pantomime for all the sense Calloway could make of his words.

The little man said, "Thank you. That will be all." Sandra got up and walked to where Calloway was sitting. They gripped each other's hands. He was trembling, but he noticed that her hands were cold.

When the prosecutor tried to call one of the other women, the defense objected. Her name had been obtained by illegal search. The police would not have known about her if they had not gone through the defendant's appointment book, which they had no warrant to do.

The judge recessed the court for ten minutes to hear the arguments in his chambers. Sandra did not want to leave the courtroom, so she and Calloway sat like solitary worshippers in a deserted church. Sandra chewed her lip and picked at her hands. Calloway did not say anything to her. Her face was the color of soot.

The judge ruled in favor of the defense, so the prosecution's entire case came down to Sandra's testimony. Neither side called any more witnesses, and court was adjourned. In the morning, the lawyers would make their closing arguments and the case would go to the jury. Sandra took two Seconals and went to bed as soon as she got home. Her doctor had prescribed the pills after the rape, and she had been taking them every night to go to sleep. This was the earliest she had ever taken them: five-thirty in the afternoon.

Calloway sat in the living room drinking bourbon and trying to think. It had been six months. He had not made love to Sandra in all that time. He had barely touched her. Things had gotten worse lately. Much worse. She had lost weight and had settled into a cone of gloom that nothing seemed to penetrate. They would go out to dinner and everything would seem fine. She would order a scotch sour and say, "It's a real suburban drink, don't you think? It takes me back to my roots." He would tell her about his day and about the latest Lester Maddox blunder. He had been a political consultant in Atlanta for two years, and he had learned to mimic Maddox almost perfectly. He could almost always make her laugh when he did it. "The people of Georgia," he would say in that peculiar high-pitched voice, "are going to have to pull together if we are going to lick this VD problem. And it is not just a colored problem or a white problem. And it is not just a problem here, in Atlanta, or out in the country. It is everybody's problem, everywhere. Now I say let's show the world what we are made of, and let's run VD clean out of the state of Georgia."

But somewhere along the way, she would fall silent, go almost mute. And before long she would start crying softly, almost to herself, as if she had suddenly remembered an old buried regret.

They had gone to a few parties, but she had always come to him in less than an hour and said she wanted to go home. She told him at home after one of those parties that she saw pity in every face. Some of the men looked at her differently and there was something animal in their eyes that turned her flesh cold.

They had tried the mountains for a weekend. They went to the Chattooga River to a cabin in the hills, in a small fold of earth almost a mile from the main road and just above a dazzling stretch of the river.

They used a Jeep to get down the old trail to the cabin. Once they had unloaded and stopped to relax, they realized just how far away they were from everything familiar in their lives. The only sounds came from the river, the wind, and the small animals and birds. Calloway built a fire and went down to the river, where he caught a few small trout that he brought back for dinner.

When they were washing the dishes, she said, without looking at him, "I can't stand it. I just can't stand it. I know why we are here. I'm a patient . . . poor Sandra . . . maybe she'll get better if we just take her out to the country, where there is nothing to remind her. But it won't work. I don't think about anything out here *except* being raped. It's the thing I'm not supposed to think about . . . so it is the only thing I *can* think about." She paused and lowered her voice. "Dan, I want to go home tonight."

He put out the fire and loaded the Jeep. It took almost two hours to drive the narrow, rutted, overgrown logging road, the headlights showing the faint tracks that he followed, never sure they would not just disappear in some impassable bog. Sandra sat stiffly next to him and did not say a thing all the way home. She had been asleep when he finished unloading.

A few days after the failed trip to the woods, she had left the table suddenly in the middle of dinner. He caught her by the arm before she reached the bedroom and shouted at her that it just had to stop.

Then he said some of what he had been thinking, that she was beginning to like the part she was playing, that it was cowardly and selfish, that she could dig herself a hole too deep to climb out of. She looked at him tolerantly and waited for him to finish. It was a set speech that he had worked on for hours, running it over and over in his head like a song lyric that would not go away.

But the words had no effect. When he finished, she told him placidly, "Forget it, Dan. It's not going to be that easy. I won't just 'come to my senses' because somebody gives me a good talking to. It doesn't work that way. I might grow out of it. But it will take time." She smiled wanly. "Lots of time."

Calloway had put his hopes on the trial. But now that was a shambles. There was no way the prosecutor could convince all twelve jurors to vote for a conviction in the morning. At least one of them—and probably all of them—would believe that Sandra had brought it on herself. Or that she had not done enough to resist. She was going to lose in court, and everything would get worse.

Calloway felt the whiskey at work, and he had a sure and dreadful sense that something permanent had been done to Sandra's life and to his. Things would never be the same again. This whole thing was like an unhealing wound, a hideous mutilation. And there was nothing he could do. Nothing at all.

In his closing argument, the defense attorney sneered at this "supposed rape that was not reported by the victim for over an hour. During that hour we must imagine that she was assessing her psychic wounds. I say 'psychic' because there don't appear to be any other kinds of wounds. No broken bones. No cuts. Not even any bruises. If this was indeed a rape, then it must have been one of the gentlest rapes in history. So gentle, I submit, that it took the defendant an hour to decide that it was a rape at all."

The jury decided quickly on a verdict of "not guilty." Sandra sagged when the words were spoken, but she seemed to expect it. She said nothing on the way home, took Seconal again, and went to bed. For almost a week, Calloway did not see her out of her bathrobe. She never put on makeup and barely combed her hair. It was unwashed, and it clung to the contours of her skull like it had been pasted there. She looked gaunt and defeated, and Calloway was afraid he would have to find a place to send her. A hospital or sanitarium. He didn't know where to begin.

Then one day he came home from work, and she was dressed. Her hair was washed and combed, she was wearing makeup. She looked almost cheerful.

"You feeling better?" he said warily.

"Much better. It just took some time. I told you it would. But I can't let this thing destroy me."

"That's what I like to hear."

"I'm going to do my best to get through this. I can't let it get any worse."

She tried that night in bed, too, but broke down sobbing after a few minutes. Calloway rubbed her back and waited for her to say something. Finally, she said, "It's all men now. He was a man and every time, I'll think of him."

"Sandra, don't start thinking that way."

"I can't help it."

But for the next few weeks things were better; then one night she asked him if he would teach her to shoot.

"Why?"

"So nothing like that will ever happen to me again."

"I don't have a gun."

"I do."

She showed him a squat, ugly, snub-nosed .38, so new that the bluing glistened like the skin of a snake.

"Yes," he said. "Yes, you *do* have a gun. A real sure enough belly pistol. Where in hell did you get it?"

"I bought it. I did it this morning, and it made me feel better than anything I've done since this whole business started."

"Are you going to just run that dude down and waste him?"

"No. It's too late for that. I'm not going to have any more of my life ruined by him. I'm sure not going to be tried for murdering him. But no other man will ever do that to me, and I won't spend the rest of my life in fear."

"Don't you think it would be more sensible to learn karate? I thought that's what women were doing for self-defense."

"I'm small, and I'm not very athletic. I'd never be sure of my ability with karate. With this," she said, nodding toward the evil-looking pistol, "I'd only have to pull the trigger. And I know I could do that."

"Sandra, are you sure this is a good idea?"

"I'm going to do it, Dan. It's done. I own that gun, and I'm going to learn how to shoot it. I thought since you were a Marine and all, you could teach me. But if you don't want to, I'll find somebody else."

"You could probably do a lot better. It was all I could do to qualify with a pistol. But I'll teach you."

She learned quickly. They shot one hundred rounds a day, every day for a month. They would leave the indoor range in the early evening just as other couples in Atlanta were going from drinks after work to dinner. Calloway felt odd going home at this time of day with his ears ringing from gunfire and his hands stinking of cordite. He wanted to be joining those other couples for dinner. Sandra loved the shooting.

At night, she would carefully clean the pistol before bed, oiling it and wrapping it securely in a silicone cloth. "You're going to be taking the goddamned thing to bed with you soon," Calloway said one night.

"They are awfully seductive, don't you think?" she said.

"How so?"

"The way the design suits the function. True efficiency."

"They don't do much for me."

"I can't believe that. Everybody reacts to guns."

They began going to the woods, where she practiced firing from the hip and instinct shooting. She would stand facing a wall of gravel in an old borrow pit, the pistol hanging at her side, gripped loosely in her small hand. Without warning, he would throw a tin can in front of her. As soon as the can hit the ground, Sandra would fire. If the first snap shot from the hip did not hit the can, she would raise the pistol, aim, and shoot until she hit the can. Within a few days, she was hitting half of her targets on the first shot. She almost never needed a third.

"You ready to go?" she asked one afternoon when he got home.

"Sandra, you can shoot the eyes off a gnat. You don't need any more practice."

"I guess you're right. You're a pretty good teacher."

"You are a determined student," he said. "Do you carry that damned thing with you in your purse?"

"Everywhere I go," she said.

"Jesus. Be careful, will you. Most people who get shot are not the people who are supposed to get shot."

"I won't make any mistakes."

Calloway had carried an M16 for eighteen months, until it was nothing more than an eight-pound plastic-and-steel extension of his arm. He had watched while a machine gunner had burned the barrel out of an M60 one night at Gia Dinh. He didn't think anything about going into a dove field full of half-drunk men with twelve-gauge shotguns or walking in a woods full of eager deer hunters. He had even taken a military .45 away from an angry gunnery sergeant at Da Nang one night. A gun held less terror for him than an ax. But the thought of his wife walking around town with a snub-nosed .38 in her purse made him nearly physically sick.

He ran into Scoggins at a party. It was a benefit for Herman Talmadge. "A little get-together," Calloway's partner had said, "to show 'Humun' how much folks in Atlanta appreciate his work on the Watergate committee. That . . . and to raise a few thousand dollars. I hope the cheap bastard doesn't line his pockets with it."

He had not wanted to go, but Sandra insisted. She watched the hearings every day, and the senators were as important to her as the regular actors were to soap opera fans. "I don't care that much for Herman," she said. "Maybe it's just because he's the local boy. I like Senator Sam and that cute little assistant of his. That Rufus Edmiston. And I adore Montoya. I'm probably his only groupie."

So they went to the huge ballroom at the Hyatt Regency. Calloway got a drink from one of the ten different bars. The drink came in a glass the size of a baby-food jar. Calloway joined a conversation with the first people he encountered and made no effort to circulate.

Most of the people in the room were from political Atlanta. Some were full-time political, and he knew most of them. This party was their work. They were bored and attentive at the same time. Some of the people were sincere political enthusiasts who genuinely cared and could be counted on for the most tedious volunteer work. Calloway tried to avoid them, since they all wanted to talk issues. There were a few big-money contributors in the room, and they stood a little apart and aloof, taking in the party with a proprietary gaze. For all the talk about a new South, Calloway thought, the obsession with politics remained. It was less sweaty than before, but no less real and no less corrupt.

Calloway skipped the receiving line, but Sandra wanted to touch the stars of her favorite program and lined up. Calloway said he would see her later and went back to the bar.

Scoggins was right in front of him. Calloway did not recognize the little man at first. He merely looked over his head and tried to catch the harassed bartender's eye. Then Scoggins turned around, and Calloway was looking directly down on a man he had wanted to murder.

"Hello, dickhead," he said. "How's the practice?"

"Do I know you?" Scoggins said, irritated and thinking, perhaps, that he was dealing with a drunk.

"You know my wife," Calloway said.

"I'm afraid there is some sort of misunderstanding," Scoggins said and tried to go around him.

"No misunderstanding, little man," Calloway said. He grabbed Scoggins's tie and yanked it like the starter cord on a chain saw. Scoggins spun and dropped his drink. People parted all around them. Calloway slapped Scoggins twice across the face with his open hand, as though he was trying to revive him. "You did some work for the man who raped my wife. It involved making her look like a slut."

"Look here," Scoggins said. "There's going to be some real trouble—"

Calloway hit him in the ribs with a short punch that

was grooved perfectly as a piston stroke. Then he drew his hand back and hit him again in the same place. In a few seconds he had hit the little man ten times in exactly the same spot. It was like working on a heavy bag. When Scoggins's legs give out, Calloway jerked him upright by his tie and hit him again.

The color was flushed from Scoggins's face, leaving a blank, gray look of fear. He knew that he was hurt. In his fear that Calloway might not stop, he thought that he might be killed. A look of real desperation crossed his face. A look of complete pleading.

It was all over in less than ten seconds, and Calloway let the little man drop when he heard a woman scream. There were a few men on the verge of stepping in, but they backed away when they saw Calloway's face. Calloway had seen the same thing happen one day when an old man hit a young Marine in the ear with a baseball bat. The man was too grim for the Marine's six buddies, even though any one of them outweighed him and he was as old as any three of them put together.

Calloway walked out the door and to his car without anyone saying a thing to him. The room was so big that only a few people at the party had seen the beating. Sandra was on the other side of the room, but Calloway knew that somebody would tell her about it. He sat on the hood of his car and waited for her.

"Why did you have to interfere like some goddamned cowboy?" she said. "I don't want it. I don't need it. It's something you're doing for yourself, and if you don't stop, I'm going to leave."

She put her hands on her hips and glared at him. "I mean that," she said.

Calloway stood up and said, "Okay. Now let's go home." The rage had passed him, and now he felt calm.

He opened the door for her, but before she could slide

into the seat Scoggins was standing at his car thirty feet away, embracing himself around his broken ribs and trying to shout.

"Okay, mister, I'm going to the hospital now, and whatever it cost is just going to be the first bill you'll pay. I'm going to sue you for the whole fifty dollars you're worth. Then your old lady will really have to go to work."

Calloway started for him. Sandra said, "Do it, Dan, and I won't be around for you to defend anymore."

"You better listen to her, hot rod. Or you'll end up in jail, and you don't want her out where you can't keep an eye on her."

"I don't think you got enough, ass face," Calloway said.

"Dan, get in the car. This is your last chance."

"Better do what she says," Scoggins said. He was trying to shout, but he could not. The effort was too much. Pain flashed across his face and he winced.

"Next time," Calloway said, and got in the car. He started the engine.

"Wait," Sandra said.

She watched while Scoggins lowered himself into his Corvette, started it, and put it into gear. As he started down the exit lane of the parking lot, she opened her door and stepped onto the asphalt. She was holding her pistol and aimed it at Scoggins's car.

"Sandra!" Calloway yelled.

Her feet were spread and planted, and her arms were extended in front of her body, elbows locked. The pistol was steady, and her aiming eye was sighting calmly down the barrel.

She fired and the pistol bucked. Calloway's ears rang.

Scoggins's Corvette swerved as one of the huge rear tires was hit. Sandra fired again and hit another tire. The Corvette fishtailed and was facing her. She calmly shot out both front tires as Scoggins flung himself under the steering wheel, wailing in terror. Four shots, Calloway thought, and four blown tires. Not bad.

Sandra looked at Calloway and smiled. "You know, if this was a .357, I could put one clean through that turkey's engine block."

Calloway laughed with the kind of relief he had not felt in years, since he'd once thought he was certain to die and had not. "Well," he said finally, "we can wait here for them to arrest us or go home first and have a drink. Either way I suppose they'll use the cuffs."

"They won't arrest us," Sandra said, and walked over to the Corvette. "You won't say anything, will you, little man?" she said to Scoggins, who was sitting straight up again. There were tears on his face. "If you say anything, we'll hurt you again. Maybe even shoot you."

Sandra was smiling as she said it.

Scoggins muttered something, then said very loudly, "You're crazy. Both of you."

"How about it?" Sandra said grimly. She still had the gun in her hand.

"Go away, please."

"You've never seen us, have you?"

"No. Never."

"Well, then," Sandra said as sweetly as a hostess seeing her guest off after supper, "bye-bye, Mr. Scoggins."

They drove home without noticing the thousands of points of light that made up the city at night and signaled the existence of other souls. Everything they cared about was inside their own car, and they felt alone and together as they had not since the rape and could not even a few weeks before in the deepest Georgia woods.

"I thought you were going to shoot him."

"No. He's not worth it. I just wanted to get even, that's all."

"Scared me to death."

"Dan, why don't you drive faster? I want to get home before it wears off. I don't want to leave this feeling in the car."

"We'll get a speeding and reckless driving to go along with assault and attempted murder."

"Just hurry."

No flashing blue lights appeared behind them, and they pulled into the drive feeling unstoppable.

Just before they got into bed, Sandra said, "I'm not glad I got raped or anything stupid like that, but I'll tell you this, it feels good to know that I'm never going to be afraid again."

Calloway knew better, and he also knew better than to argue with her.

CLARK HOWARD

Horn Man

1980

When Dix stepped off the Greyhound bus in New Orleans, old Rainey was waiting for him near the terminal entrance. He looked just the same as Dix remembered him. Old Rainey had always looked old, since Dix had known him, ever since Dix had been a little boy. He had skin like black saddle leather and patches of cotton-white hair, and his shoulders were round and stooped. When he was contemplating something, he chewed on the inside of his cheeks, pushing his pursed lips in and out as if he were revving up for speech. He was doing that when Dix walked up to him.

"Hey, Rainey."

Rainey blinked surprise and then his face split into a wide smile of perfect, gleaming teeth. "Well, now. Well, well, well, now." He looked Dix up and down. "They give you that there suit of clothes?"

Dix nodded. "Everyone gets a suit of clothes if they done more than a year." Dix's eyes, the lightest blue possible without being gray, hardened just enough for Rainey to notice. "And I sure done more than a year," he added.

"That's the truth," Rainey said. He kept the smile on his face and changed the subject as quickly as possible. "I got you a room in the Quarter. Figured that's where you'd want to stay."

Dix shrugged. "It don't matter no more."

"It will," Rainey said with the confidence of years. "It will when you hear the music again."

Dix did not argue the point. He was confident that none of it mattered. Not the music, not the French Quarter, none of it. Only one thing mattered to Dix.

"Where is she, Rainey?" he asked. "Where's Madge?"

"I don't rightly know," Rainey said.

Dix studied him for a moment. He was sure Rainey was lying. But it didn't matter. There were others who would tell him.

They walked out of the terminal, the stooped old black man and the tall, prison-hard white man with a set to his mouth and a canvas zip-bag containing all his worldly possessions. It was late afternoon: the sun was almost gone and the evening coolness was coming in. They walked toward the Quarter, Dix keeping his long-legged pace slow to accommodate old Rainey.

Rainey glanced at Dix several times as they walked, chewing inside his mouth and working up something. Finally he said, "You been playing at all while you was in?"

Dix shook his head. "Not for a long time. I did a little the first year. Used to dry play, just with my mouthpiece. After a while, though, I gave it up. They got a different kind of music over there in Texas. Stompin' music. Not my style." Dix forced a grin at old Rainey. "I ever kill a man again, I'll be sure I'm on *this* side of the Louisiana line."

Rainey scowled. "You know you ain't never killed nobody, boy," he said harshly. "You know it wudn't you that done it. It was *her.*"

Dix stopped walking and locked eyes with old Rainey. "How long have you knowed me?" he asked.

"Since you was eight months old," Rainey said. "You

know that. Me and my sistuh, we worked for your grand-mamma, Miz Jessie DuChatelier. She had the finest gen-tlemen's house in the Quarter. Me and my sistuh, we cleaned and cooked for Miz Jessie. And took care of you after your own poor mamma took sick with the consump-tion and died—"

"Anyway, you've knowed me since I was less than one, and now I'm *forty*-one."

Rainey's eyes widened. "Naw," he said, grinning again, "you ain't that old. Naw."

"Forty-one, Rainey. I been gone sixteen years. I got twenty-five, remember? And I done sixteen."

Sudden worry erased Rainey's grin. "Well, if you forty-one how old that make *me*?"

"About two hundred. I don't know. You must be sev-enty or eighty. Anyway, listen to me now. In all the time you've knowed me, have I ever let anybody make a fool out of me?"

Rainey shook his head. "Never. No way."

"That's right. And I'm not about to start now. But if word got around that I done sixteen years for a killing that was somebody else's, I'd look like the biggest fool that ever walked the levee, wouldn't I?"

"I reckon so," Rainey allowed.

"Then don't ever say again that I didn't do it. Only one person alive knows for certain positive that I didn't do it. And I'll attend to her myself. Understand?"

Rainey chewed the inside of his cheeks for a moment, then asked, "What you fixin' to do about her?"

Dix's light-blue eyes hardened again. "Whatever I have to do, Rainey," he replied.

Rainey shook his head in slow motion. "Lord, Lord, Lord," he whispered.

*   *   *

Old Rainey went to see Gaston that evening at Tradition Hall, the jazz emporium and restaurant that Gaston owned in the Quarter. Gaston was slick and dapper. For him, time had stopped in 1938. He still wore spats.

"How does he look?" Gaston asked old Rainey.

"He *look* good," Rainey said. "He *talk* bad." Rainey leaned close to the white club owner. "He fixin' to kill that woman. Sure as God made sundown."

Gaston stuck a sterling-silver toothpick in his mouth. "He know where she is?"

"I don't think so," said Rainey. "Not yet."

"*You* know where she is?"

"Lastest I heard, she was living over on Burgundy Street with some doper."

Gaston nodded his immaculately shaved and lotioned chin. "Correct. The doper's name is LeBeau. He's young. I think he keeps her around to take care of him when he's sick." Gaston examined his beautifully manicured nails. "Does Dix have a lip?"

Rainey shook his head. "He said he ain't played in a while. But a natural like him, he can get his lip back in no time a'tall."

"Maybe," said Gaston.

"He can," Rainey insisted.

"Has he got a horn?"

"Naw. I watched him unpack his bag and I didn't see no horn. So I axed him about it. He said after a few years of not playing, he just give it away. To some cowboy he was in the Texas pen with."

Gaston sighed. "He should have killed that fellow on this side of the state line. If he'd done the killing in Louisiana, he would have went to the pen at Angola. They play good jazz at Angola. Eddie Lumm is up there. You remember Eddie Lumm? Clarinetist. Learned to play from Frank Teschemacher and Jimmie Noone. Eddie killed his old lady. So now he blows at Angola. They play good jazz at Angola."

Rainey didn't say anything. He wasn't sure if Gaston thought Dix had really done the killing or not. Sometimes Gaston *played* like he didn't know a thing, just to see if somebody *else* knew it. Gaston was smart. Smart enough to help keep Dix out of trouble if he was a mind. Which was what old Rainey was hoping for.

Gaston drummed his fingertips silently on the table where they sat. "So. You think Dix can get his lip back with no problem, is that right?"

"Tha's right. He can."

"He planning to come around and see me?"

"I don't know. He probably set on finding that woman first. Then he might not be *able* to come see you."

"Well, see if you can get him to come see me first. Tell him I've got something for him. Something I've been saving for him. Will you do that?"

"You bet." Rainey got up from the table. "I'll go do it right now."

George Tennell was big and beefy and mean. Rumor had it that he had once killed two men by smashing their heads together with such force that he literally knocked their brains out. He had been a policeman for thirty years, first in the colored section, which was the only place he could work in the old days, and now in the *Vieux Carré*, the Quarter, where he was detailed to keep the peace to whatever extent it was possible. He had no family, claimed no friends. The Quarter was his home as well as his job. The only thing in the world he admitted to loving was jazz.

That was why, every night at seven, he sat at a small corner table in Tradition Hall and ate dinner while he listened to the band tune their instruments and warm up.

Most nights, Gaston joined him later for a liqueur. Tonight he joined him before dinner.

"Dix got back today," he told the policeman. "Remember Dix?"

Tennell nodded. "Horn man. Killed a fellow in a motel
room just across the Texas line. Over a woman named
Madge Noble."

"That's the one. Only there's some around don't think
he did it. There's some around think *she* did it."

"Too bad he couldn't have found twelve of those people for his jury."

"He didn't have no jury, George. Quit laying back on
me. You remember it as well as I do. One thing you'd
never forget is a good horn man."

Tennell's jaw shifted to the right a quarter of an inch,
making his mouth go crooked. The band members were
coming out of the back now and moving around on
the bandstand, unsnapping instrument cases, inserting
mouthpieces, straightening chairs. They were a mixed
lot—black, white, and combinations; clean-shaven and
goateed; balding and not; clear-eyed and strung out. None
of them was under fifty—the oldest was the trumpet
player, Luther Dodd, who was eighty-six. Like Louis Armstrong, he had learned to blow at the elbow of Joe "King"
Oliver, the great cornetist. His Creole-styled trumpet playing was unmatched in New Orleans. Watching him near
the age when he would surely die was agony for the jazz
purists who frequented Tradition Hall.

Gaston studied George Tennell as the policeman
watched Luther Dodd blow out the spit plug of his gleaming Balfour trumpet and loosen up his stick-brittle fingers
on the valves. Gaston saw in Tennell's eyes that odd look
of a man who truly worshipped traditional jazz music,
who felt it down in the pit of himself just like the old men
who played it, but who had never learned to play himself.

It was a look that had the mix of love and sadness and
years gone by. It was the only look that ever turned Tennell's eyes soft.

"You know how long I been looking for a horn man to
take Luther's place?" Gaston asked. "A straight year. I've
listened to a couple dozen guys from all over. Not a one of
them could play traditional. Not a one." He bobbed his
chin at Luther Dodd. "His fingers are like old wood, and
so's his heart. He could go on me any night. And if he
does, I'll have to shut down. Without a horn man, there's
no Creole sound, no tradition at all. Without a horn, this
place of mine, which is the last of the great jazz empori-
ums, will just give way to"—Gaston shrugged helplessly,
"—whatever. Disco music, I suppose."

A shudder circuited George Tennell's spine, but he gave
no outward sign of it. His body was absolutely still, his
hands resting motionlessly on the snow-white tablecloth,
eyes steadily fixed on Luther Dodd. Momentarily the band
went into its first number, *Layfayette*, played Kansas City
style after the way of Bennie Moten. The music pulsed
out like spurts of water, each burst overlapping the one
before it to create an even wave of sound that flooded the
big room. Because Kansas City style was so rhythmic and
highly danceable, some of the early diners immediately
moved onto the dance floor and fell in with the music.

Ordinarily, Tennell liked to watch people dance while
he ate; the moving bodies lent emphasis to the music he
loved so much, music he had first heard from the window
of the St. Pierre Colored Orphanage on Decatur Street
when he had been a boy; music he had grown up with
and would have made his life a part of if he had not been
so completely talentless, so inept that he could not even
read sharps and flats. But tonight he paid no attention to
the couples out in front of the bandstand. He concentrated only on Luther Dodd and the old horn man's breath

intake as he played. It was clear to Tennell that Luther
was struggling for breath, fighting for every note he blew,
utilizing every cubic inch of lung power that his old body
could marshal.

After watching Luther all the way through *Lafayette*,
and halfway through *Davenport Blues*, Tennell looked
across the table at Gaston and nodded.

"All right," he said simply. "All right."

For the first time ever Tennell left the club without
eating dinner.

As Dix walked along with old Rainey toward Gaston's
club, Rainey kept pointing out places to him that he had
not exactly forgotten, but had not remembered in a long
time.

"That house there," Rainey said, "was where Paul
Mares was born back in nineteen-and-oh-one. He's the
one formed the original New Orleans Rhythm Kings. He
only lived to be forty-eight but he was one of the best horn
men of all time."

Dix would remember, not necessarily the person himself but the house and the story of the person and how
good he was. He had grown up on those stories, gone to
sleep by them as a boy, lived the lives of the men in them
many times over as he himself was being taught to blow
trumpet by Rozell "The Lip" Page when Page was already
past sixty and he, Dix, was only eight. Later, when Page
died, Dix's education was taken over by Shepherd Norden and Blue Johnny Meadows, the two alternating as his
teacher between their respective road tours. With Page,
Norden, and Meadows in his background, it was no wonder that Dix could blow traditional.

"Right up the street there," Rainey said as they walked,
"is where Wingy Manone was born in nineteen-and-oh-
four. His given name was Joseph, but after his accident

ever'body taken to calling him 'Wingy.' The accident was, he fell under a streetcar and lost his right arm. But that boy didn't let a little thing like that worry him none, no sir. He learned to play trumpet *left-handed*, and *one-handed*. And he was *good*. Lord, he was good."

They walked along Dauphin and Chartres and Royal. All around them were the French architecture and grille-work and statuary and vines and moss that made the *Vieux Carré* a world unto itself, a place of subtle sights, sounds, and smells—black and white and fish and age— that no New Orleans tourist, no Superdome visitor, no casual observer, could ever experience, because to expe-rience was to understand, and understanding of the Quar-ter could not be acquired, it had to be lived.

"Tommy Ladnier, he used to live over there," Rainey said, "right up on the second floor. He lived there when he came here from his hometown of Mandeville, Loozey-ana. Poor Tommy, he had a short life too, only thirty-nine years. But it was a good life. He played with King Oliver and Fletcher Henderson and Sidney Bechet. Yessir, he got in some good licks."

When they got close enough to Tradition Hall to hear the music, at first faintly, then louder, clearer, Rainey stopped talking. He wanted Dix to hear the music, to *feel* the sound of it as it wafted out over Pirate's Alley and the Café du Monde and Congo Square (they called it Beaure-gard Square now, but Rainey refused to recognize the new name). Instinctively, Rainey knew that it was important for the music to get back into Dix, to saturate his mind and catch in his chest and tickle his stomach. There were some things in Dix that needed to be washed out, some bad things, and Rainey was certain that the music would help. A good purge was always healthy.

Rainey was grateful, as they got near enough to define

melody, that *Sweet Georgia Brown* was being played. It was a good melody to come home to.

They walked on, listening, and after a while Dix asked, "Who's on horn?"

"Luther Dodd."

"Don't sound like Luther. What's the matter with him?"

Rainey waved one hand resignedly. "Old. Dying. I'spect."

They arrived at the Hall and went inside. Gaston met them with a smile. "Dix," he said, genuinely pleased, "it's good to see you." His eyes flicked over Dix. "The years have been good to you. Trim. Lean. No gray hair. How's your lip?"

"I don't have a lip no more, Mr. Gaston," said Dix. "Haven't had for years."

"But he can get it back quick enough," Rainey put in. "He gots a natural lip."

"I don't play no more, Mr. Gaston," Dix told the club owner.

"That's too bad," Gaston said. He bobbed his head toward the stairs. "Come with me. I want to show you something."

Dix and Rainey followed Gaston upstairs to his private office. The office was furnished the way Gaston dressed—old-style, roaring Twenties. There was even a windup Victrola in the corner.

Gaston worked the combination of a large, ornate floor vault and pulled its big-tiered door open. From somewhere in its dark recess he withdrew a battered trumpet case, one of the very old kind with heavy brass fittings on the corners and, one knew, real velvet, not felt, for a lining. Placing it gently in the center of his desk, Gaston carefully opened the snaplocks and lifted the top. Inside, indeed on real velvet, deep-purple real velvet, was a gleaming, silver, hand-etched trumpet. Dix and Rainey stared at it in unabashed awe.

"Know who it once belonged to?" Gaston asked.

Neither Dix nor Rainey replied. They were mesmerized by the instrument. Rainey had not seen one like it in fifty years. Dix had *never* seen one like it; he had only heard stories about the magnificent silver horns that the quadroons made of contraband silver carefully hidden away after the War Between the States. Because the silver cache had not, as it was supposed to, been given over to the Federal army as part of the reparations levied against the city, the quadroons, during the Union occupation, had to be very careful what they did with it. Selling it for value was out of the question. Using if for silver service, candlesticks, walking canes, or any other of the more obvious uses would have attracted the notice of a Union informer. But letting it lie dormant, even though it was safer as such, was intolerable to the quads, who refused to let a day go by without circumventing one law or another.

So they used the silver to plate trumpets and cornets and slide trombones that belonged to the tabernacle musicians who were just then beginning to experiment with the old *Sammsamounn* tribal music that would eventually mate with work songs and prison songs and gospels, and evolve into traditional blues, which would evolve into traditional, or Dixie-style, jazz.

"Look at the initials," Gaston said, pointing to the top of the bell. Dix and Rainey peered down at three initials etched in the silver: BRB.

"Lord have mercy," Rainey whispered. Dix's lips parted as if he too intended to speak, but no words sounded.

"That's right," Gaston said. "Blind Ray Blount. The first, the best, the *only*. Nobody has ever touched the sounds he created. That man hit notes nobody ever heard before—or since. He was the master."

"Amen," Rainey said. He nodded his head toward Dix. "Can he touch it?"

"Go ahead," Gaston said to Dix.

Like a pilgrim to Mecca touching the holy shroud, Dix ever so lightly placed the tips of three fingers on the silver horn. As he did, he imagined he could feel the touch left there by the hands of the amazing blind horn man who had started the great blues evolution in a patch of town that later became Storyville. He imagined that—

"It's yours if you want it," Gaston said. "All you have to do is pick it up and go downstairs and start blowing."

Dix wet his suddenly dry lips. "Tomorrow I—"

"Not tomorrow," Gaston said, "Tonight. Now."

"Take it, boy," Rainey said urgently.

Dix frowned deeply, his eyes narrowing as if he felt physical pain. He swallowed, trying to push an image out of his mind; an image he had clung to for sixteen years. "I can't tonight—"

"Tonight or never," Gaston said firmly.

"For God's sake, boy, take it!" said old Rainey.

But Dix could not. The image of Madge would not let him.

Dix shook his head violently, as if to rid himself of devils, and hurried from the room.

Rainey ran after him and caught up with him a block from the Hall. "Don't do it," he pleaded. "Hear me now. I'm an old man and I know I ain't worth nothin' to nobody, but I'm begging you, boy, please, please, please don't do it. I ain't never axed you for nothing in my whole life, but I'm axing you for this: please don't do it."

"I got to," Dix said quietly. "It ain't that I want to; I got to."

"But why, boy? *Why?*"

"Because we made a promise to each other," Dix said. "That night in that Texas motel room, the man Madge was with had told her he was going to marry her. He'd been telling her that for a long time. But he was already married and kept putting off leaving his wife. Finally Madge had enough of it. She asked me to come to her room between sets. I knew she was doing it to make him jealous, but it didn't matter none to me. I'd been crazy about her for so long that I'd do anything she asked me to, and she knew it.

"So between sets I slipped across the highway to where she had her room. But he was already there. I could hear through the transom that he was roughing her up some, but the door was locked and I couldn't get in. Then I heard a shot and everything got quiet. A minute later Madge opened the door and let me in. The man was laying across the bed dying. Madge started bawling and saying how they would put her in the pen and how she wouldn't be able to stand it, she'd go crazy and kill herself.

"It was then I asked her if she'd wait for me if I took the blame for her. She promised me she would. And I promised her I'd come back to her." Dix sighed quietly. "That's what I'm doing, Rainey—keeping my promise."

"And what going to happen if she ain't kept *hers?*" Rainey asked.

"Mamma Rulat asked me the same thing this afternoon when I asked her where Madge was at." Mamma Rulat was an octaroon fortuneteller who always knew where everyone in the Quarter lived.

"What did you tell her?"

"I told her I'd do what I had to do. That's all a man *can* do, Rainey."

Dix walked away, up a dark side street. Rainey, watch-

ing him go, shook his head in the anguish of the aged and
helpless.

"Lord, Lord, Lord—"

The house on Burgundy Street had once been a grand
mansion with thirty rooms and a tiled French courtyard
with a marble fountain in its center. It had seen nobility
and aristocracy and great generals come and go with elegant, genteel ladies on their arms. Now the thirty rooms
were rented individually with hotplate burners for light
cooking, and the only ladies who crossed the courtyard
were those of the New Orleans night.

A red light was flashing atop a police car when Dix got
there, and uniformed policemen were blocking the gate
into the courtyard. There was a small curious crowd talking about what happened.

"A doper named LeBeau," someone said. "He's been
shot."

"I heared it," an old man announced. "I heared the
shot."

"There's where it happened, that window right up
there—"

Dix looked up, but as he did another voice said, "They're
bringing him out now!"

Two morgue attendants wheeled a sheet-covered gur-
ney across the courtyard and lifted it into the back of a
black panel truck. Several policemen, led by big beefy
George Tennell, brought a woman out and escorted her to
the car with the flashing red light. Dix squinted, focusing
on her in the inadequate courtyard light. He frowned.
Madge's mother, he thought, his mind going back two
decades. What's Madge's mother got to do with this?

Then he remembered. Madge's mother was dead. She
had died five years after he had gone to the pen.

Then who—?

Madge?

Yes, it *was* her. It was Madge. Older, as he was. Not a girl anymore, as he was not a boy anymore. For a moment he found it difficult to equate the woman in the courtyard with the memory in his mind. But it was Madge, all right.

Dix tried to push forward, to get past the gate into the courtyard, but two policemen held him back. George Tennell saw the altercation and came over.

"She's under arrest, mister," Tennell told Dix. "Can't nobody talk to her but a lawyer right now."

"What's she done anyhow?" Dix asked.

"Killed her boyfriend," said Tennell. "Shot him with this."

He showed Dix a pearl-handled over-and-under Derringer two-shot.

"Her boyfriend?"

Tennell nodded. "Young feller. 'Bout twenty-five. Neighbors say she was partial to young fellers. Some women are like that."

"Who says she shot him?"

"I do. I was in the building at the time, on another matter. I heard the shot. Matter of fact, I was the first one to reach the body. Few minutes later she come waltzing in. Oh, she put on a good act, all right, like she didn't even know what happened. But I found the gun in her purse myself."

By now the other officers had Madge Noble in the police car and were waiting for Tennell. He slipped the Derringer into his coat pocket and hitched up his trousers. Jutting his big jaw out an inch, he fixed Dix in a steady gaze.

"If she's a friend of yours, don't count on her being around for a spell. She'll do a long time for this."

Tennell walked away, leaving Dix still outside the gate.

Dix waited there, watching, as the police car came through to the street. He tried to catch a glimpse of Madge as it passed, but there was not enough light in the backseat where they had her. As soon as the car left, the people who had gathered around began to leave too.

Soon Dix was the only one standing there.

At midnight George Tennell was back at his usual table in Tradition Hall for the dinner he had missed earlier. Gaston came over and joined him. For a few minutes they sat in silence, watching Dix up on the bandstand. He was blowing the silver trumpet that had once belonged to Blind Ray Blount; sitting next to the aging Luther Dodd; jumping in whenever he could as they played *Tailspin Blues*, then *Tank Town Bump*, then *Everybody Loves My Baby*.

"Sounds like he'll be able to get his lip back pretty quick," Tennell observed.

"Sure," said Gaston. "He's a natural. Rozell Page was his first teacher, you know."

"No, I didn't know that."

"Sure," Gaston adjusted the celluloid collar he wore, and turned the diamond stickpin in his tie. "What about the woman?" he asked.

Tennell shrugged. "She'll get twenty years. Probably do ten or eleven."

Gaston thought for a moment, then said. "That should be time enough. After ten or eleven years nothing will matter to him except the music. Don't you think?"

"It won't even take that long." Tennell guessed. "Not for him."

Up on the bandstand the men who played traditional went into *Just a Closer Walk with Thee*.

And sitting on the sawdust floor behind the bandstand, old Rainey listened with happy tears in his eyes.

JACK RITCHIE

The Absence of Emily

1981

The phone rang and I picked up the receiver. "Yes?"

"Hello, darling, this is Emily."

I hesitated. "Emily who?"

She laughed lightly. "Oh, come now, darling. Emily, your wife."

"I'm sorry, you must have a wrong number." I hung up, fumbling a bit as I cradled the phone.

Millicent, Emily's cousin, had been watching me. "You look white as a sheet."

I glanced covertly at a mirror.

"I don't mean in actual *color*, Albert. I mean figuratively. In attitude. You seem frightened. Shocked."

"Nonsense."

"Who phoned?"

"It was a wrong number."

Millicent sipped her coffee. "By the way, Albert, I thought I saw Emily in town yesterday, but, of course, that was impossible."

"Of course it was impossible. Emily is in San Francisco."

"Yes, but *where* in San Francisco?"

"She didn't say. Just visiting friends."

"I've known Emily all her life. She has very few secrets from me. She doesn't *know* anybody in San Francisco. When will she be back?"

"She might be gone a rather long time."

"How long?"

"She didn't know."

Millicent smiled. "You have been married before, haven't you, Albert?"

"Yes."

"As a matter of fact, you were a widower when you met Emily?"

"I didn't try to keep that fact a secret."

"Your first wife met her death in a boating accident five years ago? She fell overboard and drowned?"

"I'm afraid so. She couldn't swim a stroke."

"Wasn't she wearing a life preserver?"

"No. She claimed they hindered her movements."

"It appears that you were the only witness to the accident."

"I believe so. At least no one else ever came forward."

"Did she leave you any money, Albert?"

"That's none of your business, Millicent."

Cynthia's estate had consisted of a fifty-thousand-dollar life insurance policy, of which I was the sole beneficiary, some forty-thousand dollars in sundry stocks and bonds, and one small sailboat.

I stirred my coffee. "Millicent, I thought I'd give you first crack at the house."

"First crack?"

"Yes. We've decided to sell this place. It's really too big for just the two of us. We'll get something smaller. Perhaps even an apartment. I thought you might like to pick up a bargain. I'm certain we can come to satisfactory terms."

She blinked. "Emily would never sell this place. It's her home. I'd have to hear the words from her in person."

"There's no need for that. I have her power of attorney.

She has no head for business, you know, but she trusts me implicitly. It's all quite legal and aboveboard."

"I'll think it over." She put down her cup. "Albert, what did you do for a living before you met Emily? Or Cynthia, for that matter?"

"I managed."

When Millicent was gone, I went for my walk on the back grounds of the estate. I went once again to the dell and sat down on the fallen log. How peaceful it was here. Quiet. A place to rest. I had been coming here often in the last few days.

Millicent and Emily. Cousins. They occupied almost identical large homes on spacious grounds next to each other. And, considering that fact, one might reasonably have supposed that they were equally wealthy. Such, however, was not the case, as I discovered after my marriage to Emily.

Millicent's holdings must certainly reach far into seven figures, since they require the full-time administrative services of Amos Eberly, her attorney and financial advisor.

Emily, on the other hand, owned very little more than the house and the grounds themselves and she had borrowed heavily to keep them going. She had been reduced to two servants, the Brewsters. Mrs. Brewster, a surly creature, did the cooking and desultory dusting, while her husband, formerly the butler, had been reduced to a man-of-all-work, who pottered inadequately about the grounds. The place really required the services of two gardeners.

Millicent and Emily. Cousins. Yet it was difficult to imagine two people more dissimilar in either appearance or nature.

Millicent is rather tall, spare, and determined. She fancies herself an intellect and she has the tendency to rule and dominate all those about her, and that had certainly included Emily. It is obvious to me that Millicent deeply resents the fact that I removed Emily from under her thumb.

Emily. Shorter than average. Perhaps twenty-five pounds overweight. An amiable disposition. No claim to blazing intelligence. Easily dominated, yes, though she had a surprising stubborn streak when she set her mind to something.

When I returned to the house, I found Amos Eberly waiting. He is a man in his fifties and partial to gray suits.

"Where is Emily?" he asked.

"In Oakland." He gave that thought.

"I meant San Francisco. Oakland is just across the bay, isn't it? I usually think of them as one, which, I suppose, is unfair to both."

He frowned. "San Francisco? But I saw her in town just this morning. She was looking quite well."

"Impossible."

"Impossible for her to be looking well?"

"Impossible for you to have seen her. She is still in San Francisco."

He sipped his drink. "I know Emily when I see her. She wore a lilac dress with a belt. And a sort of gauzy light-blue scarf."

"You were mistaken. Besides, women don't wear gauzy light-blue scarves these days."

"Emily did. Couldn't she have come back without letting you know?"

"No."

Eberly studied me. "Are you ill or something, Albert? Your hands seem to be shaking."

"Touch of the flu," I said quickly. "Brings out the jitters in me. What brings you here anyway, Amos?"

"Nothing in particular, Albert. I just happened to be in the neighborhood and thought I'd drop in and see Emily."

"Damn it, I told you she isn't here."

"All right, Albert," he said soothingly. "Why should I doubt you? If you say she isn't here, she isn't here."

It has become my habit on Tuesday and Thursday afternoons to do the household food shopping, a task which I preempted from Mrs. Brewster when I began to suspect her arithmetic.

As usual, I parked in the supermarket lot and locked the car. When I looked up, I saw a small, slightly stout woman across the street walking toward the farther end of the block. She wore a lilac dress and a light-blue scarf. It was the fourth time I'd seen her in the last ten days.

I hurried across the street. I was still some seventy-five yards behind her when she turned the corner.

Resisting the temptation to shout at her to stop, I broke into a trot.

When I reached the corner, she was nowhere in sight. She could have disappeared into any one of a dozen shop fronts.

I stood there, trying to regain my breath, when a car pulled to the curb.

It was Millicent. "Is that you, Albert?"

I regarded her without enthusiasm. "Yes."

"What in the world are you doing? I saw you running and I've never seen you run before."

"I was not running. I was merely trotting to get my blood circulating. A bit of jogging is supposed to be healthy, you know."

I volunteered my adieu and strode back to the supermarket.

The next morning when I returned from my walk to the dell, I found Millicent in the drawing room, pouring herself coffee and otherwise making herself at home—a habit from the days when only Emily occupied the house.

"I've been upstairs looking over Emily's wardrobe," Millicent said. "I didn't see anything missing."

"Why should anything be missing? Has there been a thief in the house? I suppose you know every bit and parcel of her wardrobe?"

"Not every bit and parcel, but almost. Almost. And very little, if anything, seems to be missing. Don't tell me that Emily went off to San Francisco without any luggage."

"She had luggage. Though not very much."

"What was she wearing when she left?"

Millicent had asked that question before. This time I said, "I don't remember."

Millicent raised an eyebrow. "You don't remember?" She put down her cup. "Albert, I'm holding a séance at my place tonight. I thought perhaps you'd like to come."

"I will not go to any damn séance."

"Don't you want to communicate with any of your beloved dead?"

"I believe in letting the dead rest. Why bother them with every trifling matter back here?"

"Wouldn't you want to speak with your first wife?"

"Why the devil would I want to communicate with Cynthia? I have absolutely nothing to say to her anyway."

"But perhaps she has something to say to you."

I wiped my forehead. "I'm not going to your stupid séance and that's final."

That evening, as I prepared for bed, I surveyed the contents of Emily's closet. How would I dispose of her clothes? Probably donate them to some worthy charity, I thought.

I was awakened at two A.M. by the sound of music.

I listened. Yes, it was plainly Emily's favorite sonata being played on the piano downstairs.

I stepped into my slippers and donned my dressing robe. In the hall, I snapped on the lights.

I was halfway down the stairs when the piano-playing ceased. I completed my descent and stopped at the music room doors. I put my ear to one of them. Nothing. I slowly opened the door and peered inside.

There was no one at the piano. However, two candles in holders flickered on its top. The room seemed chilly. Quite chilly.

I found the source of the draft behind some drapes and closed the French doors to the terrace. I snuffed out the candles and left the room.

I met Brewster at the head of the stairs.

"I thought I heard a piano being played, sir," he said. "Was that you?"

I wiped the palms of my hands on my robe. "Of course."

"I didn't know you played the piano, sir."

"Brewster, there are a lot of things you don't know about me and never will."

I went back to my room, waited half an hour, and then dressed. In the bright moonlight outside, I made my way to the garden shed. I unbolted its door, switched on the lights, and surveyed the gardening equipment. My eyes went to the tools in the wall racks.

I pulled down a long-handled irrigating shovel and knocked a bit of dried mud from its tip. I slung the implement over my shoulder and began walking toward the dell.

I was nearly there when I stopped and sighed heavily. I shook my head and returned to the shed. I put the shovel back into its place on the rack, switched off the lights, and returned to bed.

The next morning, Millicent dropped in as I was having breakfast.

"How are you this morning, Albert?"

"I have felt better."

Millicent sat down at the table and waited for Mrs. Brewster to bring her a cup.

Mrs. Brewster also brought the morning mail. It included a number of advertising fliers, a few bills, and one small blue envelope addressed to me.

I examined it. The handwriting seemed familiar and so did the scent. The postmark was torn.

I slit open the envelope and pulled out a single sheet of notepaper.

Dear Albert:
   You have no idea how much I miss you. I shall return home soon, Albert. Soon.
                                        Emily

I put the note back into the envelope and slipped both into my pocket.

"Well?" Millicent asked.

"Well, what?"

"I thought I recognized Emily's handwriting on the envelope. Did she say when she'd be back?"

"That is not Emily's handwriting. It is a note from my aunt in Chicago."

"I didn't know you had an aunt in Chicago."

"Millicent, rest assured. I do have an aunt in Chicago."

That night I was in bed, but awake, when the phone on my night table rang. I picked up the receiver.

"Hello, darling. This is Emily."

I let five seconds pass. "You are not Emily. You are an imposter."

"Now, Albert, why are you being so stubborn? Of course this is me, Emily."

"You couldn't be."

"Why couldn't I be?"

"*Because.*"

"Because why?"

"Where are you calling from?"

She laughed. "I think you'd be surprised."

"You couldn't be Emily. I *know* where she is and she couldn't—*wouldn't*—make a phone call at this hour of the night just to say hello. It's well past midnight."

"You think you know where I am, Albert? No, I'm not there anymore. It was so uncomfortable, so dreadfully uncomfortable. And so I left, Albert. I left."

I raised my voice. "Damn you, I can *prove* you're still there."

She laughed. "Prove? How can you prove anything like that, Albert? Good night." She hung up.

I got out of bed and dressed. I made my way downstairs and detoured into the study. I made myself a drink, consumed it slowly, and then made another.

When I consulted my watch for the last time it was nearly one A.M. I put on a light jacket against the chill of the night and made my way to the garden shed. I opened the doors, turned on the lights, and pulled the long-handled shovel from the rack.

This time I went all the way to the dell. I paused beside a huge oak and stared at the moonlit clearing.

I counted as I began pacing. "One, two, three, four—" I stopped at sixteen, turned ninety degrees, and then paced off eighteen more steps.

I began digging.

I had been at it for nearly five minutes when suddenly I heard the piercing blast of a whistle and immediately I became the focus of perhaps a dozen flashlight beams and approaching voices.

I shielded my eyes against the glare and recognized Millicent. "What the devil is this?"

She showed cruel teeth. "You had to make sure she was really dead, didn't you, Albert? And the only way you could do that was to return to her grave."

I drew myself up. "I am looking for Indian arrowheads. There's an ancient superstition that if one is found under the light of the moon it will bring luck for the finder for several weeks."

Millicent introduced the people gathered about me. "Ever since I began suspecting what really has happened to Emily you've been under twenty-four-hour surveillance by private detectives."

She indicated the others. "Miss Peters. She is quite a clever mimic and was the voice of Emily you heard over the phone. She also plays piano. And Mrs. McMillan. She reproduced Emily's handwriting and was the woman in the lilac dress and the blue scarf."

Millicent's entire household staff seemed to be present. I also recognized Amos Eberly and the Brewsters. I would fire them tomorrow.

The detectives had brought along their own shovels and spades, and two of them superseded me in my shallow depression. They began digging.

"See here," I said, exhibiting indignation. "You have no right to do that. This is my property. At the very least you need a search warrant."

Millicent found that amusing. "This is not your property, Albert. It is mine. You stepped over the dividing line six paces back."

I wiped my forehead. "I'm going back to the house."

"You are under arrest, Albert."

"Nonsense, Millicent. I do not see a proper uniformed policeman among these people. And in this state private detectives do not have the right to arrest anyone at all."

For a moment she seemed stymied, but then saw light. "You are under citizen's arrest, Albert. Any citizen has the power to make a citizen's arrest and I am a citizen."

Millicent twirled the whistle on its chain. "We knew we were getting to you, Albert. You almost dug her up last night, didn't you? But then you changed your mind. But that was just as well. Last night I couldn't have produced as many witnesses. Tonight we were ready and waiting."

The detectives dug for some fifteen minutes and then paused for a rest. One of them frowned. "You'd think the digging would be easier. This ground looks like it's never been dug up before."

They resumed their work and eventually reached a depth of six feet before they gave up. The spade man climbed out of the excavation. "Hell, nothing's been buried here. The only thing we found was an Indian arrowhead."

Millicent had been glaring at me for the last half hour.

I smiled. "Millicent, what makes you think that I *buried* Emily?"

With that I left them and returned to the house.

When had I first become aware of Millicent's magnificent maneuverings and the twenty-four-hour surveillance? Almost from the very beginning, I suspect. I'm rather quick on the uptake.

What had been Millicent's objective? I suppose she envisioned reducing me to such a state of fear that eventually I'd break down and confess to the murder of Emily.

Frankly, I would have regarded the success of such a scheme as farfetched, to say the least. However, once I was aware of what Millicent was attempting, I got into the spirit of the venture.

Millicent may have initiated the enterprise, the play, but it is I who led her to the dell.

There were times when I thought I overdid it just a bit—wiping at nonexistent perspiration, trotting after the elusive woman in the lilac dress, that sort of thing—but on the other hand I suppose these reactions were rather expected of me and I didn't want to disappoint any eager watchers.

Those brooding trips to the dell had been quite a good touch, I thought. And the previous night's halfway journey there, with the shovel over my shoulder, had been intended to assure a large audience at the finale twenty-four hours later.

I had counted eighteen witnesses, excluding Millicent.

I pondered. Defamation of character? Slander? Conspiracy? False arrest? Probably a good deal more.

I would threaten to sue for a large and unrealistic amount. That was the fashion nowadays, wasn't it? Twenty million? It didn't really matter, of course, because I doubted very much if the matter would ever reach court.

No, Millicent wouldn't be able to endure the publicity. She couldn't let the world know what a total fool she'd made of herself. She couldn't bear to be the laughingstock of her circle, her peers.

She would, of course, attempt to hush it up as best she could. A few dollars here and a few there to buy the silence of the witnesses. But could one seriously hope to buy the total silence of eighteen individual people? Probably not. However, when the whispers began to circulate, it would be a considerable help to Millicent if the principal player involved would join her in vehemently denying that any such ridiculous event had ever taken place at all.

And I would do that for Millicent. For a consideration. A *large* consideration.

At the end of the week, my phone rang.

"This is Emily. I'm coming home now, dear."

"Wonderful."

"Did anyone miss me?"

"You have no idea."

"You haven't told anyone where I've been these last four weeks, have you, Albert? Especially not Millicent?"

"Especially not Millicent."

"What *did* you tell her?"

"I said you were visiting friends in San Francisco."

"Oh, dear. I don't *know* anybody in San Francisco. Do you suppose she got suspicious?"

"Well, maybe just a little bit."

"She thinks I have absolutely no will power, but I really have. But just the same, I didn't want her laughing at me if I didn't stick it out. Oh, I suppose going to a health farm is cheating, in a way. I mean you can't be tempted because they control all of the food. But I really stuck it out. I could have come home any time I wanted to."

"You have marvelous will power, Emily."

"I've lost *thirty* pounds, Albert! And it's going to *stay* off. I'll bet I'm every bit as slim now as Cynthia ever was."

I sighed. There was absolutely no reason for Emily to keep comparing herself to my first wife. The two of them are separate entities and each has her secure compartment in my affections.

Poor Cynthia. She had insisted on going off by herself in that small craft. I had been at the yacht-club window sipping a martini and watching the cold gray harbor.

Cynthia's boat seemed to have been the only one on the water on that inhospitable day and there had apparently been an unexpected gust of wind. I had seen the boat heel over sharply and Cynthia thrown overboard. I'd raised the alarm immediately, but by the time we got out there it had been too late.

Emily sighed too. "I suppose I'll have to get an entire new wardrobe. Do you think we can really afford one, Albert?"

We could now. And then some.

FREDERICK FORSYTH

There Are No Snakes in Ireland

1982

McQueen looked across his desk at the new applicant for a job with some skepticism. He had never employed such a one before. But he was not an unkind man, and if the job seeker needed the money and was prepared to work, McQueen was not averse to giving him a chance.

"You know it's damn hard work?" he said in his broad Belfast accent.

"Yes, sir," said the applicant.

"It's a quick in-and-out job, ye know. No questions, no pack drill. You'll be working on the lump. Do you know what that means?"

"No, Mr. McQueen."

"Well, it means you'll be paid well but you'll be paid in cash. No red tape. Geddit?"

What he meant was there would be no income tax paid, no National Health contributions deducted at source. He might also have added that there would be no National Insurance cover and that the Health and Safety standards would be completely ignored. Quick profits for all were the order of the day, with a fat slice off the top for himself as the contractor. The job seeker nodded his head to indicate he had "goddit" though in fact he had not. McQueen looked at him speculatively.

"You say you're a medical student, in your last year at the Royal Victoria?" Another nod. "On the summer vacation?"

Another nod. The applicant was evidently one of those students who needed money over and above his grant to put himself through medical school. McQueen, sitting in his dingy Bangor office running a hole-and-corner business as a demolition contractor with assets consisting of a battered truck and a ton of second-hand sledgehammers, considered himself a self-made man and heartily approved of the Ulster Protestant work ethic. He was not one to put down another such thinker, whatever he looked like.

"All right," he said, "you'd better take lodgings here in Bangor. You'll never get from Belfast and back in time each day. We work from seven in the morning until sundown. It's work by the hour, hard but well paid. Mention one word to the authorities and you'll lose the job like shit off a shovel. OK?"

"Yes, sir. Please, when do I start and where?"

"The truck picks the gang up at the main station yard every morning at six-thirty. Be there Monday morning. The gang foreman is Big Billie Cameron. I'll tell him you'll be there."

"Yes, Mr. McQueen." The applicant turned to go.

"One last thing," said McQueen, pencil poised. "What's your name?"

"Harkishan Ram Lal," said the student. McQueen looked at his pencil, the list of names in front of him and the student.

"We'll call you Ram," he said, and that was the name he wrote down on the list.

The student walked out into the bright July sunshine of Bangor, on the north coast of County Down, Northern Ireland.

By that Saturday evening he had found himself cheap lodgings in a dingy boarding house halfway up Railway View Street, the heart of Bangor's bed-and-breakfast land. At least it was convenient to the main station from which the works truck would depart every morning just after sunup. From the grimy window of his room he could look straight at the side of the shored embankment that carried the trains from Belfast into the station.

It had taken him several tries to get a room. Most of those houses with a B-and-B notice in the window seemed to be fully booked when he presented himself on the doorstep. But then it was true that a lot of casual labor drifted into the town in the height of summer. True also that Mrs. McGurk was a Catholic and she still had rooms left.

He spent Sunday morning bringing his belongings over from Belfast, most of them medical textbooks. In the afternoon he lay on his bed and thought of the bright hard light on the brown hills of his native Punjab. In one more year he would be a qualified physician, and after another year of intern work he would return home to cope with the sicknesses of his own people. Such was his dream. He calculated he could make enough money this summer to tide himself through to his finals and after that he would have a salary of his own.

On the Monday morning he rose at a quarter to six at the bidding of his alarm clock, washed in cold water, and was in the station yard just after six. There was time to spare. He found an early-opening café and took two cups of black tea. It was his only sustenance. The battered truck, driven by one of the demolition gang, was there at a quarter past six and a dozen men assembled near it. Harkishan Ram Lal did not know whether to approach them and introduce himself, or wait at a distance. He waited.

At twenty-five past the hour the foreman arrived in his own car, parked it down a side road and strode up to the truck. He had McQueen's list in his hand. He glanced at the dozen men, recognized them all and nodded. The Indian approached. The foreman glared at him.

"Is youse the darkie McQueen has put on the job?" he demanded.

Ram Lal stopped in his tracks. "Harkishan Ram Lal," he said. "Yes."

There was no need to ask how Big Billie Cameron had earned his name. He stood 6 feet and 3 inches in his stockings but was wearing enormous nail-studded steel-toed boots. Arms like tree trunks hung from huge shoulders and his head was surmounted by a shock of ginger hair. Two small, pale-lashed eyes stared down balefully at the slight and wiry Indian. It was plain he was not best pleased. He spat on the ground.

"Well, get in the fecking truck," he said.

On the journey out to the work site Cameron sat up in the cab which had no partition dividing it from the back of the lorry, where the dozen laborers sat on two wooden benches down the sides. Ram Lal was near the tailboard next to a small, nut-hard man with bright blue eyes, whose name turned out to be Tommy Burns. He seemed friendly.

"Where are youse from?" he asked with genuine curiosity.

"India," said Ram Lal. "The Punjab."

"Well, which?" said Tommy Burns.

Ram Lal smiled. "The Punjab is a part of India," he said.

Burns thought about this for a while. "You Protestant or Catholic?" he asked at length.

"Neither," said Ram Lal patiently. "I am a Hindu."

"You mean you're not a Christian?" asked Burns in amazement.

"No. Mine is the Hindu religion."

"Hey," said Burns to the others, "your man's not a Christian at all." He was not outraged, just curious, like a small child who has come across a new and intriguing toy.

Cameron turned from the cab up front. "Aye," he snarled, "a heathen."

The smile dropped off Ram Lal's face. He stared at the opposite canvas wall of the truck. By now they were well south of Bangor, clattering down the motorway towards Newtownards. After a while Burns began to introduce him to the others. There was a Craig, a Munroe, a Patterson, a Boyd and two Browns. Ram Lal had been long enough in Belfast to recognize the names as being originally Scottish, the sign of the hard Presbyterians who make up the backbone of the Protestant majority of the Six Counties. The men seemed amiable and nodded back to him.

"Have you not got a lunch box, laddie?" asked the elderly man called Patterson.

"No," said Ram Lal, "it was too early to ask my landlady to make one up."

"You'll need lunch," said Burns, "aye, and breakfast. We'll be making tay ourselves on a fire."

"I will make sure to buy a box and bring some food tomorrow," said Ram Lal.

Burns looked at the Indian's rubber-soled soft boots. "Have you not done this kind of work before?" he asked.

Ram Lal shook his head.

"You'll need a pair of heavy boots. To save your feet, you see."

Ram Lal promised he would also buy a pair of heavy

ammunition boots from a store if he could find one open late at night. They were through Newtownards and still heading south on the A21 towards the small town of Comber. Craig looked across at him.

"What's your real job?" he asked.

"I'm a medical student at the Royal Victoria in Belfast," said Ram Lal. "I hope to qualify next year."

Tommy Burns was delighted. "That's near to being a real doctor," he said. "Hey, Big Billie, if one of us gets a knock young Ram could take care of it."

Big Billie grunted. "He's not putting a finger on me," he said.

That killed further conversation until they arrived at the work site. The driver had pulled northwest out of Comber, and two miles up the Dundonald road he bumped down a track to the right until they came to a stop where the trees ended and saw the building to be demolished.

It was a huge old whiskey distillery, a sheer-sided, long derelict. It had been one of two in these parts that had once turned out good Irish whiskey but had gone out of business years before. It stood beside the River Comber, which had once powered its great waterwheel as it flowed down from Dundonald to Comber and on to empty itself in Strangford Lough. The malt had arrived by horse-drawn cart down the track and the barrels of whiskey had left the same way. The sweet water that had powered the machines had also been used in the vats. But the distillery had stood alone, abandoned and empty for years.

Of course the local children had broken in and found it an ideal place to play. Until one had slipped and broken a leg. Then the county council had surveyed it, declared it a hazard, and the owner found himself with a compulsory demolition order.

He, scion of an old family of squires who had known

better days, wanted the job done as cheaply as possible. That was where McQueen came in. It could be done faster but more expensively with heavy machinery; Big Billie and his team would do it with sledges and crowbars. McQueen had even lined up a deal to sell the best timbers and the hundreds of tons of mature bricks to a jobbing builder. After all, the wealthy nowadays wanted their new houses to have "style" and that meant looking old. So there was a premium on antique sun-bleached old bricks and genuine ancient timber beams to adorn the new-look-old "manor" houses of the top executives. Mc-Queen would do all right.

"Right lads," said Big Billie as the truck rumbled away back to Bangor. "There it is. We'll start with the roof tiles. You know what to do."

The group of men stood beside their pile of equipment. There were great sledgehammers with 7-pound heads; crowbars 6 feet long and over an inch thick; nailbars a yard long with curved split tips for extracting nails; short-handled, heavy-headed lump hammers and a variety of timber saws. The only concessions to human safety were a number of webbing belts with dogclips and hundreds of feet of rope. Ram Lal looked up at the building and swallowed. It was four storeys high and he hated heights. But scaffolding is expensive.

One of the men unbidden went to the building, prized off a plank door, tore it up like a playing card and started a fire. Soon a billycan of water from the river was boiling away and tea was made. They all had their enamel mugs except Ram Lal. He made a mental note to buy that also. It was going to be thirsty, dusty work. Tommy Burns finished his own mug and offered it, refilled, to Ram Lal.

"Do they have tea in India?" he asked.

Ram Lal took the proffered mug. The tea was ready-mixed, sweet and off-white. He hated it.

They worked through the first morning perched high on the roof. The tiles were not to be salvaged, so they tore them manually and hurled them to the ground away from the river. There was an instruction not to block the river with falling rubble. So it all had to land on the other side of the building, in the long grass, weeds, broom and gorse which covered the area round the distillery. The men were roped together so that if one lost his grip and began to slither down the roof, the next man would take the strain. As the tiles disappeared, great yawning holes appeared between the rafters. Down below them was the floor of the top storey, the malt store.

At ten they came down the rickety internal stairs for breakfast on the grass, with another billycan of tea. Ram Lal ate no breakfast. At two they broke for lunch. The gang tucked into their piles of thick sandwiches. Ram Lal looked at his hands. They were nicked in several places and bleeding. His muscles ached and he was very hungry. He made another mental note about buying some heavy work gloves.

Tommy Burns held up a sandwich from his own box. "Are you not hungry, Ram?" he asked. "Sure, I have enough here."

"What do you think you're doing?" asked Big Billie from where he sat across the circle round the fire.

Burns looked defensive. "Just offering the lad a sandwich," he said.

"Let the darkie bring his own fecking sandwiches," said Cameron. "You look after yourself."

The men looked down at their lunch boxes and ate in silence. It was obvious no one argued the toss with Big Billie.

"Thank you, I am not hungry," said Ram Lal to Burns. He walked away and sat by the river where he bathed his burning hands.

By sundown when the truck came to collect them half the tiles on the great roof were gone. One more day and they would start on the rafters, work for saw and nailbar.

Throughout the week the work went on, and the once proud building was stripped of its rafters, planks and beams until it stood hollow and open, its gaping windows like open eyes staring at the prospect of its imminent death. Ram Lal was unaccustomed to the arduousness of this kind of labor. His muscles ached endlessly, his hands were blistered, but he toiled on for the money he needed so badly.

He had acquired a tin lunch box, enamel mug, hard boots and a pair of heavy gloves, which no one else wore. Their hands were hard enough from years of manual work. Throughout the week Big Billie Cameron needled him without letup, giving him the hardest work and positioning him on the highest points once he had learned Ram Lal hated heights. The Punjabi bit on his anger because he needed the money. The crunch came on the Saturday.

The timbers were gone and they were working on the masonry. The simplest way to bring the edifice down away from the river would have been to plant explosive charges in the corners of the side wall facing the open clearing. But dynamite was out of the question. It would have required special licenses in Northern Ireland of all places, and that would have alerted the tax man. McQueen and all his gang would have been required to pay substantial sums in income tax, and McQueen in National Insurance contributions. So they were chipping the walls down in square-yard chunks, standing hazardously on sagging floors as the supporting walls splintered and cracked under the hammers.

During lunch Cameron walked round the building a couple of times and came back to the circle round the fire.

He began to describe how they were going to bring down a sizable chunk of one outer wall at third-floor level. He turned to Ram Lal.

"I want you up on the top there," he said. "When it starts to go, kick it outwards."

Ram Lal looked up at the section of wall in question. A great crack ran along the bottom of it.

"That brickwork is going to fall at any moment," he said evenly. "Anyone sitting on top there is going to come down with it."

Cameron stared at him, his face suffusing, his eyes pink with rage where they should have been white. "Don't you tell me my job; you do as you're told, you stupid fecking nigger." He turned and stalked away.

Ram Lal rose to his feet. When his voice came, it was in a hard-edged shout. *"Mister Cameron . . ."*

Cameron turned in amazement. The men sat open-mouthed. Ram Lal walked slowly up to the big ganger.

"Let us get one thing plain," said Ram Lal, and his voice carried clearly to everyone else in the clearing. "I am from the Punjab in northern India. I am also a Kshatriya, member of the warrior caste. I may not have enough money to pay for my medical studies, but my ancestors were soldiers and princes, rulers and scholars, two thousand years ago when yours were crawling on all fours dressed in skins. Please do not insult me any further."

Big Billie Cameron stared down at the Indian student. The whites of his eyes had turned a bright red. The other laborers sat in stunned amazement.

"Is that so?" said Cameron quietly. "Is that so, now? Well, things are a bit different now, you black bastard. So what are you going to do about that?"

On the last word he swung his arm, open-palmed, and his hand crashed into the side of Ram Lal's face. The youth was thrown bodily to the ground several feet away. His head sang. He heard Tommy Burns call out, "Stay down, laddie. Big Billie will kill you if you get up."

Ram Lal looked up into the sunlight. The giant stood over him, fists bunched. He realized he had not a chance in combat against the big Ulsterman. Feelings of shame and humiliation flooded over him. His ancestors had ridden, sword and lance in hand, across plains a hundred times bigger than these six counties, conquering all before them.

Ram Lal closed his eyes and lay still. After several seconds he heard the big man move away. A low conversation started among the others. He squeezed his eyes tighter shut to hold back the tears of shame. In the blackness he saw the baking plains of the Punjab and men riding over them; proud, fierce men, hook-nosed, bearded, turbaned, black-eyed, the warriors from the land of Five Rivers.

Once, long ago in the world's morning, Iskander of Macedon had ridden over these plains with his hot and hungry eyes; Alexander, the young god, whom they called The Great, who at twenty-five had wept because there were no more worlds to conquer. These riders were the descendants of his captains, and the ancestors of Harkishan Ram Lal.

He was lying in the dust as they rode by, and they looked down at him in passing. As they rode, each of them mouthed one single word to him. Vengeance.

Ram Lal picked himself up in silence. It was done, and what still had to be done had to be done. That was the way of his people. He spent the rest of the day working in complete silence. He spoke to no one and no one spoke to him.

That evening in his room he began his preparations as night was about to fall. He cleared away the brush and comb from the battered dressing table and removed also the soiled doily and the mirror from its stand. He took his book of the Hindu religion and from it cut a page-sized portrait of the great goddess Shakti, she of power and justice. This he pinned to the wall above the dressing table to convert it into a shrine.

He had bought a bunch of flowers from a seller in front of the main station, and these had been woven into a garland. To one side of the portrait of the goddess he placed a shallow bowl half-filled with sand, and in the sand stuck a candle which he lit. From his suitcase he took a cloth roll and extracted half a dozen joss sticks. Taking a cheap, narrow-necked vase from the bookshelf, he placed them in it and lit the ends. The sweet, heady odor of the incense began to fill the room. Outside, big thunderheads rolled up from the sea.

When his shrine was ready he stood before it, head bowed, the garland in his fingers, and began to pray for guidance. The first rumble of thunder rolled over Bangor. He used not the modern Punjabi but the ancient Sanskrit, language of prayer. "*Devi Shakti . . . Maa . . .* Goddess Shakti . . . great mother. . . ."

The thunder crashed again and the first raindrops fell. He plucked the first flower and placed it in front of the portrait of Shakti.

"I have been grievously wronged. I ask vengeance upon the wrongdoer. . . ." He plucked the second flower and put it beside the first.

He prayed for an hour while the rain came down. It drummed on the tiles above his head, streamed past the window behind him. He finished praying as the storm subsided. He needed to know what form the retribution should take. He needed the goddess to send him a sign.

When he had finished, the joss sticks had burned themselves out and the room was thick with their scent. The candle guttered low. The flowers all lay on the lacquered surface of the dressing table in front of the portrait. Shakti stared back at him unmoved.

He turned and walked to the window to look out. The rain had stopped but everything beyond the panes dripped water. As he watched, a dribble of rain sprang from the guttering above the window and a trickle ran down the dusty glass, cutting a path through the grime. Because of the dirt it did not run straight but meandered sideways, drawing his eye farther and farther to the corner of the window as he followed its path. When it stopped he was staring at the corner of his room, where his dressing gown hung on a nail.

He noticed that during the storm the dressing-gown cord had slipped and fallen to the floor. It lay coiled upon itself, one knotted end hidden from view, the other lying visible on the carpet. Of the dozen tassels only two were exposed, like a forked tongue. The coiled dressing-gown cord resembled nothing so much as a snake in the corner. Ram Lal understood. The next day he took a train to Belfast to see the Sikh.

Ranjit Singh was also a medical student, but he was more fortunate. His parents were rich and sent him a handsome allowance. He received Ram Lal in his well-furnished room at the hotel.

"I have received word from home," said Ram Lal. "My father is dying."

"I am sorry," said Ranjit Singh, "you have my sympathies."

"He asks to see me. I am his first born. I should return."

"Of course," said Singh. "The first-born son should always be by his father when he dies."

"It is a matter of the air fare," said Ram Lal. "I am working and making good money. But I do not have enough. If you will lend me the balance I will continue working when I return and repay you."

Sikhs are no strangers to moneylending if the interest is right and repayment secure. Ranjit Singh promised to withdraw the money from the bank on Monday morning.

That Sunday evening Ram Lal visited Mr. McQueen at his home at Groomsport. The contractor was in front of his television set with a can of beer at his elbow. It was his favorite way to spend a Sunday evening. But he turned the sound down as Ram Lal was shown in by his wife.

"It is about my father," said Ram Lal. "He is dying."

"Oh, I'm sorry to hear that, laddie," said McQueen.

"I should go to him. The first-born son should be with his father at this time. It is the custom of our people."

McQueen had a son in Canada whom he had not seen for seven years.

"Aye," he said, "that seems right and proper."

"I have borrowed the money for the air fare," said Ram Lal. "If I went tomorrow I could be back by the end of the week. The point is, Mr. McQueen, I need the job more than ever now; to repay the loan and for my studies next term. If I am back by the weekend, will you keep the job open for me?"

"All right," said the contractor. "I can't pay you for the time you're away. Nor keep the job open for a further week. But if you're back by the weekend, you can go back to work. Same terms, mind."

"Thank you," said Ram, "you are very kind."

He retained his room in Railway View Street but spent the night at his hotel in Belfast. On the Monday morning he accompanied Ranjit Singh to the bank where the Sikh withdrew the necessary money and gave it to the Hindu. Ram took a taxi to Aldergrove airport and the shuttle to London where he bought an economy-class ticket on the next flight to India. Twenty-four hours later he touched down in the blistering heat of Bombay.

On the Wednesday he found what he sought in the teeming bazaar at Grant Road Bridge. Mr. Chatterjee's Tropical Fish and Reptile Emporium was almost deserted when the young student, with his textbook on reptiles under his arm, wandered in. He found the old proprietor sitting near the back of his shop in half-darkness, surrounded by his tanks of fish and glass-fronted cases in which his snakes and lizards dozed through the hot day.

Mr. Chatterjee was no stranger to the academic world. He supplied several medical centers with samples for study and dissection, and occasionally filled a lucrative order from abroad. He nodded his white-bearded head knowledgeably as the student explained what he sought.

"Ah yes," said the old Gujerati merchant, "I know the snake. You are in luck. I have one, but a few days arrived from Rajputana."

He led Ram Lal into his private sanctum and the two men stared silently through the glass of the snake's new home.

Echis carinatus, said the textbook, but of course the book had been written by an Englishman, who had used the Latin nomenclature. In English, the saw-scaled viper, smallest and deadliest of all his lethal breed.

Wide distribution, said the textbook, being found from West Africa eastwards and northwards to Iran, and on to India and Pakistan. Very adaptable, able to acclimatize to almost any environment, from the moist bush of western Africa to the cold hills of Iran in winter to the baking hills of India.

Something stirred beneath the leaves in the box.

In size, said the textbook, between 9 and 13 inches long and very slim. Olive brown in color with a few paler spots, sometimes hardly distinguishable, and a faint undulating darker line down the side of the body. Nocturnal in dry, hot weather, seeking cover during the heat of the day.

The leaves in the box rustled again and a tiny head appeared.

Exceptionally dangerous to handle, said the textbook, causing more deaths than even the more famous cobra, largely because of its size which makes it so easy to touch unwittingly with hand or foot. The author of the book had added a footnote to the effect that the small but lethal snake mentioned by Kipling in his marvelous story "Rikki-Tikki-Tavi" was almost certainly not the krait, which is about two feet long, but more probably the saw-scaled viper. The author was obviously pleased to have caught out the great Kipling in a matter of accuracy.

In the box, a little black forked tongue flickered towards the two Indians beyond the glass.

Very alert and irritable, the long-gone English natural-ist had concluded his chapter on *Echis carinatus*. Strikes quickly without warning. The fangs are so small they make a virtually unnoticeable puncture, like two tiny thorns. There is no pain, but death is almost inevitable, usually taking between two and four hours, depending on the body weight of the victim and the level of his physical exertions at the time and afterwards. Cause of death is invariably a brain hemorrhage.

"How much do you want for him?" whispered Ram Lal.

The old Gujerati spread his hands helplessly. "Such a prime specimen," he said regretfully, "and so hard to come by. Five hundred rupees."

Ram Lal clinched the deal at 350 rupees and took the snake away in a jar.

For his journey back to London, Ram Lal purchased a box of cigars, which he emptied of their contents and in

whose lid he punctured twenty small holes for air. The
tiny viper, he knew, would need no food for a week and
no water for two or three days. It could breathe on an
infinitesimal supply of air, so he wrapped the cigar box,
resealed and with the viper inside it among his leaves, in
several towels whose thick sponginess would contain
enough air even inside a suitcase.

He had arrived with a handgrip, but he bought a cheap
fiber suitcase and packed it with clothes from market
stalls, the cigar box going in the center. It was only minutes before he left his hotel for Bombay airport that he
closed and locked the case. For the flight back to London
he checked the suitcase into the hold of the Boeing air-
liner. His hand baggage was searched, but it contained
nothing of interest.

The Air India jet landed at London Heathrow on Friday
morning and Ram Lal joined the long queue of Indians
trying to get into Britain. He was able to prove he was a
medical student and not an immigrant, and was allowed
through quite quickly. He even reached the luggage car-
ousel as the first suitcases were tumbling onto it, and saw
his own in the first two dozen. He took it to the toilet,
where he extracted the cigar box and put it in his handgrip.

In the Nothing-to-Declare channel he was stopped all
the same, but it was his suitcase that was ransacked. The
customs officer glanced in his shoulder bag and let him
pass. Ram Lal crossed Heathrow by courtesy bus to Number One Building and caught the midday shuttle to Belfast. He was in Bangor by teatime and able at last to
examine his import.

He took a sheet of glass from the bedside table and
slipped it carefully between the lid of the cigar box and
its deadly contents before opening wide. Through the
glass he saw the viper going round and round inside. It

paused and stared with angry black eyes back at him. He pulled the lid shut, withdrawing the pane of glass quickly as the box top came down.

"Sleep, little friend," he said, "if your breed ever sleep. In the morning you will do Shakti's bidding for her."

Before dark he bought a small screw-top jar of coffee and poured the contents into a china pot in his room. In the morning, using his heavy gloves, he transferred the viper from the box to the jar. The enraged snake bit his glove once, but he did not mind. It would have recovered its venom by midday. For a moment he studied the snake, coiled and cramped inside the glass coffee jar, before giving the top a last, hard twist and placing it in his lunch box. Then he went to catch the works truck.

Big Billie Cameron had a habit of taking off his jacket the moment he arrived at the work site, and hanging it on a convenient nail or twig. During the lunch break, as Ram Lal had observed, the giant foreman never failed to go to his jacket after eating, and from the right-hand pocket extract his pipe and tobacco pouch. The routine did not vary. After a satisfying pipe, he would knock out the dottle, rise and say, "Right, lads, back to work," as he dropped his pipe back into the pocket of his jacket. By the time he turned round everyone had to be on their feet.

Ram Lal's plan was simple but foolproof. During the morning he would slip the snake into the right-hand pocket of the hanging jacket. After his sandwiches the bullying Cameron would rise from the fire, go to his jacket and plunge his hand into the pocket. The snake would do what great Shakti had ordered that he be brought halfway across the world to do. It would be he, the viper, not Ram Lal, who would be the Ulsterman's executioner.

Cameron would withdraw his hand with an oath from the pocket, the viper hanging from his finger, its fangs deep in the flesh. Ram Lal would leap up, tear the snake away, throw it to the ground and stamp upon its head. It would by then be harmless, its venom expended. Finally, with a gesture of disgust he, Ram Lal, would hurl the dead viper far into the River Comber, which would carry all evidence away to the sea. There might be suspicion, but that was all there would ever be.

Shortly after eleven o'clock, on the excuse of fetching a fresh sledgehammer, Harkishan Ram Lal opened his lunch box, took out the coffee jar, unscrewed the lid and shook the contents into the right-hand pocket of the hanging jacket. Within sixty seconds he was back at his work, his act unnoticed.

During lunch he found it hard to eat. The men sat as usual in a circle round the fire; the dry old timber balks crackled and spat, the billycan bubbled above them. The men joshed and joked as ever, while Big Billie munched his way through the pile of doorstep sandwiches his wife had prepared for him. Ram Lal had made a point of choosing a place in the circle near to the jacket. He forced himself to eat. In his chest his heart was pounding and the tension in him rose steadily.

Finally Big Billie crumpled the paper of his eaten sandwiches, threw it in the fire and belched. He rose with a grunt and walked towards his jacket. Ram Lal turned his head to watch. The other men took no notice. Billie Cameron reached his jacket and plunged his hand into the right-hand pocket. Ram Lal held his breath. Cameron's hand rummaged for several seconds and then withdrew his pipe and pouch. He began to fill the bowl with fresh tobacco. As he did so he caught Ram Lal staring at him.

"What are youse looking at?" he demanded belligerently.

"Nothing," said Ram Lal, and turned to face the fire. But he could not stay still. He rose and stretched, contriving to half turn as he did so. From the corner of his eye he saw Cameron replace the pouch in the pocket and again withdraw his hand with a box of matches in it. The foreman lit his pipe and pulled contentedly. He strolled back to the fire.

Ram Lal resumed his seat and stared at the flames in disbelief. Why, he asked himself, why had great Shakti done this to him? The snake had been her tool, her instrument brought at her command. But she had held it back, refused to use her own implement of retribution. He turned and sneaked another glance at the jacket. Deep down in the lining at the very hem, on the extreme left-hand side, something stirred and was still. Ram Lal closed his eyes in shock. A hole, a tiny hole in the lining, had undone all his planning. He worked the rest of the afternoon in a daze of indecision and worry.

On the truck ride back to Bangor, Big Billie Cameron sat up front as usual, but in view of the heat folded his jacket and put it on his knees. In front of the station Ram Lal saw him throw the still-folded jacket onto the back seat of his car and drive away. Ram Lal caught up with Tommy Burns as the little man waited for his bus.

"Tell me," he asked, "does Mr. Cameron have a family?"

"Sure," said the little laborer innocently, "a wife and two children."

"Does he live far from here?" said Ram Lal. "I mean, he drives a car."

"Not far," said Burns, "up on the Kilcooley estate. Ganaway Gardens, I think. Going visiting are you?"

"No, no," said Ram Lal, "see you Monday."

Back in his room Ram Lal stared at the impassive image of the goddess of justice.

"I did not mean to bring death to his wife and children," he told her. "They have done nothing to me."

The goddess from far away stared back and gave no reply.

Harkishan Ram Lal spent the rest of the weekend in an agony of anxiety. That evening he walked to the Kilcooley housing estate on the ring road and found Ganaway Gardens. It lay just off Owenroe Gardens and opposite Woburn Walk. At the corner of Woburn Walk there was a telephone kiosk, and here he waited for an hour, pretending to make a call, while he watched the short street across the road. He thought he spotted Big Billie Cameron at one of the windows and noted the house.

He saw a teenage girl come out of it and walk away to join some friends. For a moment he was tempted to accost her and tell her what demon slept inside her father's jacket, but he dared not.

Shortly before dusk a woman came out of the house carrying a shopping basket. He followed her down to the Clandeboye shopping center, which was open late for those who took their wage packets on a Saturday. The woman he thought to be Mrs. Cameron entered Stewarts supermarket and the Indian student trailed round the shelves behind her, trying to pluck up the courage to approach her and reveal the danger in her house. Again his nerve failed him. He might, after all, have the wrong woman, even be mistaken about the house. In that case they would take him away as a madman.

He slept ill that night, his mind racked by visions of the saw-scaled viper coming out of its hiding place in the jacket lining to slither, silent and deadly, through the sleeping council house.

On the Sunday he again haunted the Kilcooley estate, and firmly identified the house of the Cameron family. He saw Big Billie clearly in the back garden. By mid-afternoon he was attracting attention locally and knew he must either walk boldly up to the front door and admit what he had done, or depart and leave all in the hands of the goddess. The thought of facing the terrible Cameron with the news of what deadly danger had been brought so close to his children was too much. He walked back to Railway View Street.

On Monday morning the Cameron family rose at a quarter to six, a bright and sunny August morning. By six the four of them were at breakfast in the tiny kitchen at the back of the house, the son, daughter and wife in their dressing gowns, Big Billie dressed for work. His jacket was where it had spent the weekend, in a closet in the hallway.

Just after six his daughter Jenny rose, stuffing a piece of marmaladed toast into her mouth.

"I'm away to wash," she said.

"Before ye go, girl, get my jacket from the press," said her father, working his way through a plate of cereal. The girl reappeared a few seconds later with the jacket, held by the collar. She proffered it to her father. He hardly looked up.

"Hang it behind the door," he said. The girl did as she was bid, but the jacket had no hanging tab and the hook was no rusty nail but a smooth chrome affair. The jacket hung for a moment, then fell to the kitchen floor. Her father looked up as she left the room.

"Jenny," he shouted, "pick the damn thing up."

No one in the Cameron household argued with the head of the family. Jenny came back, picked up the jacket and hung it more firmly. As she did, something thin and dark slipped from its folds and slithered into the corner with a dry rustle across the linoleum. She stared at it in horror.

"Dad, what's that in your jacket?"

Big Billie Cameron paused, a spoonful of cereal half-way to his mouth. Mrs. Cameron turned from the cooker. Fourteen-year-old Bobby ceased buttering a piece of toast and stared. The small creature lay curled in the corner by the row of cabinets, tight-bunched, defensive, glaring back at the world, tiny tongue flickering fast.

"Lord save us, it's a snake," said Mrs. Cameron.

"Don't be a bloody fool, woman. Don't you know there are no snakes in Ireland? Everyone knows that," said her husband. He put down the spoon. "What is it, Bobby?"

Though a tyrant inside and outside his house, Big Billie had a grudging respect for the knowledge of his young son, who was good at school and was being taught many strange things. The boy stared at the snake through his owlish glasses.

"It must be a slowworm, Dad," he said. "They had some at school last term for the biology class. Brought them in for dissection. From across the water."

"It doesn't look like a worm to me," said his father.

"It isn't really a worm," said Bobby. "It's a lizard with no legs."

"Then why do they call it a worm?" asked his truculent father.

"I don't know," said Bobby.

"Then what the hell are you going to school for?"

"Will it bite?" asked Mrs. Cameron fearfully.

"Not at all," said Bobby. "It's harmless."

"Kill it," said Cameron senior, "and throw it in the dustbin."

His son rose from the table and removed one of his slippers, which he held like a flyswat in one hand. He was advancing, bare-ankled towards the corner, when his father changed his mind. Big Billie looked up from his plate with a gleeful smile.

"Hold on a minute, just hold on there, Bobby," he said, "I have an idea. Woman, get me a jar."

"What kind of a jar?" asked Mrs. Cameron.

"How should I know what kind of a jar? A jar with a lid on it."

Mrs. Cameron sighed, skirted the snake and opened a cupboard. She examined her store of jars.

"There's a jamjar, with dried peas in it," she said.

"Put the peas somewhere else and give me the jar," commanded Cameron. She passed him the jar.

"What are you going to do, Dad?" asked Bobby.

"There's a darkie we have at work. A heathen man. He comes from a land with a lot of snakes in it. I have in mind to have some fun with him. A wee joke, like. Pass me that oven glove, Jenny."

"You'll not need a glove," said Bobby. "He can't bite you."

"I'm not touching the dirty thing," said Cameron.

"He's not dirty," said Bobby. "They're very clean creatures."

"You're a fool, boy, for all your school learning. Does the Good Book not say: 'On thy belly shalt thou go, and dust shalt thou eat . . .'? Aye, and more than dust, no doubt. I'll not touch him with me hand."

Jenny passed her father the oven glove. Open jamjar in his left hand, right hand protected by the glove, Big Billie Cameron stood over the viper. Slowly his right hand descended. When it dropped, it was fast; but the small snake was faster. It's tiny fangs went harmlessly into the padding of the glove at the center of the palm. Cameron did not notice, for the act was masked from his view by his own hands. In a trice the snake was inside the jamjar and the lid was on. Through the glass they watched it wriggle furiously.

"I hate them, harmless or not," said Mrs. Cameron. "I'll thank you to get it out of the house."

"I'll be doing that right now," said her husband, "for I'm late as it is."

He slipped the jamjar into his shoulder bag, already containing his lunch box, stuffed his pipe and pouch into the right-hand pocket of his jacket and took both out to the car. He arrived at the station yard five minutes late and was surprised to find the Indian student staring at him fixedly.

"I suppose he wouldn't have the second sight," thought Big Billie as they trundled south to Newtownards and Comber.

By mid-morning all the gang had been let into Big Billie's secret joke on pain of a thumping if they let on to "the darkie." There was no chance of that; assured that the slowworm was perfectly harmless, they too thought it a good leg-pull. Only Ram Lal worked on in ignorance, consumed by his private thoughts and worries.

At the lunch break he should have suspected something. The tension was palpable. The men sat in a circle around the fire as usual, but the conversation was stilted and had he not been so preoccupied he would have noticed the half-concealed grins and the looks darted in his direction. He did not notice. He placed his own lunch box between his knees and opened it. Coiled between the sandwiches and the apple, head back to strike, was the viper.

The Indian's scream echoed across the clearing, just ahead of the roar of laughter from the laborers. Simultaneously with the scream, the lunch box flew high in the air as he threw it away from himself with all his strength. All the contents of the box flew in a score of directions, landing in the long grass, the broom and gorse all around them.

Ram Lal was on his feet, shouting. The gangers rolled helplessly in their mirth, Big Billie most of all. He had not had such a laugh in months.

"It's a snake," screamed Ram Lal, "a poisonous snake. Get out of here, all of you. It's deadly."

The laughter redoubled; the men could not contain themselves. The reaction of the joke's victim surpassed all their expectations.

"Please, believe me. It's a snake, a deadly snake."

Big Billie's face was suffused. He wiped tears from his eyes, seated across the clearing from Ram Lal, who was standing looking wildly round.

"You ignorant darkie," he gasped, "don't you know? There are no snakes in Ireland. Understand? There aren't any."

His sides ached with laughing and he leaned back in the grass, his hands behind him to support him. He failed to notice the two pricks, like tiny thorns, that went into the vein on the inside of the right wrist.

The joke was over and the hungry men tucked into their lunches. Harkishan Ram Lal reluctantly took his seat, constantly glancing round him, a mug of steaming tea held ready, eating only with his left hand, staying clear of the long grass. After lunch they returned to work. The old distillery was almost down, the mountains of rubble and savable timbers lying dusty under the August sun.

At half past three Big Billie Cameron stood up from his work, rested on his pick and passed a hand across his forehead. He licked at a slight swelling on the inside of his wrist, then started work again. Five minutes later he straightened up again.

"I'm not feeling so good," he told Patterson, who was next to him. "I'm going to take a spell in the shade."

He sat under a tree for a while and then held his head in his hands. At a quarter past four, still clutching his splitting head, he gave one convulsion and toppled side-

ways. It was several minutes before Tommy Burns noticed him. He walked across and called to Patterson.

"Big Billie's sick," he called. "He won't answer me."

The gang broke and came over to the tree in whose
shade the foreman lay. His sightless eyes were staring at
the grass a few inches from his face. Patterson bent over
him. He had been long enough in the laboring business to
have seen a few dead ones.

"Ram," he said, "you have medical training. What do
you think?"

Ram Lal did not need to make an examination, but he
did. When he straightened up he said nothing, but Patterson understood.

"Stay here all of you," he said, taking command. "I'm
going to phone an ambulance and call McQueen." He set
off down the track to the main road.

The ambulance got there first, half an hour later. It re-
versed down the track and two men heaved Cameron onto
a stretcher. They took him away to Newtownards General
Hospital, which has the nearest casualty unit, and there
the foreman was logged in as DOA—dead on arrival. An
extremely worried McQueen arrived thirty minutes after
that.

Because of the unknown circumstance of the death an
autopsy had to be performed and it was, by the North
Down area pathologist, in the Newtownards municipal
mortuary to which the body had been transferred. That
was on the Tuesday. By that evening the pathologist's
report was on its way to the office of the coroner for North
Down, in Belfast.

The report said nothing extraordinary. The deceased
had been a man of forty-one years, big-built and im-
mensely strong. There were upon the body various minor
cuts and abrasions, mainly on the hands and wrists, quite
consistent with the job of navvy, and none of these were

in any way associated with the cause of death. The latter, beyond a doubt, had been a massive brain hemorrhage, itself probably caused by extreme exertion in conditions of great heat.

Possessed of this report, the coroner would normally not hold an inquest, being able to issue a certificate of death by natural causes to the registrar at Bangor. But there was something Harkishan Ram Lal did not know.

Big Billie Cameron had been a leading member of the Bangor council of the outlawed Ulster Volunteer Force, the hard-line Protestant paramilitary organization. The computer at Lurgan, into which all deaths in the province of Ulster, however innocent, are programmed, threw this out and someone in Lurgan picked up the phone to call the Royal Ulster Constabulary at Castlereagh.

Someone there called the coroner's office in Belfast, and a formal inquest was ordered. In Ulster death must not only be accidental; it must be seen to be accidental. For certain people, at least. The inquest was in the Town Hall at Bangor on the Wednesday. It meant a lot of trouble for McQueen, for the Inland Revenue attended. So did two quiet men of extreme Loyalist persuasion from the UVF council. They sat at the back. Most of the dead man's workmates sat near the front, a few feet from Mrs. Cameron.

Only Patterson was called to give evidence. He related the events of the Monday, prompted by the coroner, and as there was no dispute none of the other laborers was called, not even Ram Lal. The coroner read the pathologist's report aloud and it was clear enough. When he had finished, he summed up before giving his verdict.

"The pathologist's report is quite unequivocal. We have heard from Mr. Patterson of the events of that lunch break, of the perhaps rather foolish prank played by the deceased upon the Indian student. It would seem that Mr.

Cameron was so amused that he laughed himself almost to the verge of apoplexy. The subsequent heavy labor with pick and shovel in the blazing sun did the rest, provoking the rupture of a large blood vessel in the brain or, as the pathologist puts it in more medical language, a cerebral hemorrhage. This court extends its sympathy to the widow and her children, and finds that Mr. William Cameron died of accidental causes."

Outside on the lawns that spread before Bangor Town Hall McQueen talked to his navvies.

"I'll stand fair by you, lads," he said. "The job's still on, but I can't afford not to deduct tax and all the rest, not with the Revenue breathing down my neck. The funeral's tomorrow, you can take the day off. Those who want to go on can report on Friday."

Harkishan Ram Lal did not attend the funeral. While it was in progress at the Bangor cemetery he took a taxi back to Comber and asked the driver to wait on the road while he walked down the track. The driver was a Bangor man and had heard about the death of Cameron.

"Going to pay your respects on the spot, are you?" he asked.

"In a way," said Ram Lal.

"That the manner of your people?" asked the driver.

"You could say so," said Ram Lal.

"Aye, well, I'll not say it's any better or worse than our way, by the graveside," said the driver, and prepared to read his paper while he waited.

Harkishan Ram Lal walked down the track to the clearing and stood where the camp fire had been. He looked around at the long grass, the broom and the gorse in its sandy soil.

"Visha serp," he called out to the hidden viper. "O venomous snake, can you hear me? You have done what I brought you so far from the hills of Rajputana to achieve.

But you were supposed to die. I should have killed you myself, had it all gone as I planned, and thrown your foul carcass in the river.

"Are you listening, deadly one? Then hear this. You may live a little longer but then you will die, as all things die. And you will die alone, without a female with which to mate, because there are no snakes in Ireland."

The saw-scaled viper did not hear him, or if it did, gave no hint of understanding. Deep in its hole in the warm sand beneath him, it was busy, totally absorbed in doing what nature commanded it must do.

At the base of a snake's tail are two overlapping plate-scales which obscure the cloaca. The viper's tail was erect, the body throbbed in ancient rhythm. The plates were parted, and from the cloaca, one by one, each an inch long in its transparent sac, each as deadly at birth as its parent, she was bringing her dozen babies into the world.

RUTH RENDELL

The New Girl Friend

1983

You know what we did last time?" he said.

She had waited for this for weeks. "Yes?"

"I wondered if you'd like to do it again."

She longed to but she didn't want to sound too keen. "Why not?"

"How about Friday afternoon then? I've got the day off and Angie always goes to her sister's on Friday."

"Not *always*, David." She giggled.

He also laughed a little. "She will this week. Do you think we could use your car? Angie'll take ours."

"Of course. I'll come for you about two, shall I?"

"I'll open the garage doors and you can drive straight in. Oh, and Chris, could you fix it to get back a bit later? I'd love it if we could have the whole evening together."

"I'll try," she said, and then, "I'm sure I can fix it. I'll tell Graham I'm going out with my new girl friend."

He said goodbye and that he would see her on Friday. Christine put the receiver back. She had almost given up expecting a call from him. But there must have been a grain of hope still, for she had never left the receiver off the way she used to.

The last time she had done that was on a Thursday three weeks before, the day she had gone round to Angie's and found David there alone. Christine had got into the

habit of taking the phone off the hook during the middle
part of the day to avoid getting calls for the Midland Bank.
Her number and the Midland Bank's differed by only one
digit. Most days she took the receiver off at nine-thirty
and put it back at three-thirty. On Thursday afternoons
she nearly always went round to see Angie and never
bothered to phone first.

Christine knew Angie's husband quite well. If she
stayed a bit later on Thursdays she saw him when he
came home from work. Sometimes she and Graham and
Angie and David went out together as a foursome. She
knew that David, like Graham, was a salesman or sales
executive, as Graham always described himself, and she
guessed from her friend's lifestyle that David was rather
more successful at it. She had never found him particularly attractive, for, although he was quite tall, he had
something of a girlish look and very fair wavy hair.

Graham was a heavily built, very dark man with a swar-
thy skin. He had to shave twice a day. Christine had
started going out with him when she was fifteen and they
had got married on her eighteenth birthday. She had
never really known any other man at all intimately and
now if she ever found herself alone with a man she felt
awkward and apprehensive. The truth was that she was
afraid a man might make an advance to her and the
thought of that frightened her very much. For a long while
she carried a penknife in her handbag in case she should
need to defend herself. One evening, after they had been
out with a colleague of Graham's and had had a few
drinks, she told Graham about this fear of hers.

He said she was silly but he seemed rather pleased.

"When you went off to talk to those people and I was
left with John I felt like that. I felt terribly nervous. I
didn't know how to talk to him."

Graham roared with laughter. "You don't mean you

thought old John was going to make a pass at you in the middle of a crowded restaurant?''

"I don't know," Christine said. "I never know what they'll do."

"So long as you're not afraid of what I'll do," said Graham, beginning to kiss her, "that's all that matters."

There was no point in telling him now, ten years too late, that she was afraid of what he did and always had been. Of course she had got used to it, she wasn't actually terrified, she was resigned and sometimes even quite cheerful about it. David was the only man she had ever been alone with when it felt all right.

That first time, that Thursday when Angie had gone to her sister's and hadn't been able to get through on the phone and tell Christine not to come, that time it had been fine. And afterwards she had felt happy and care-free, though what had happened with David took on the coloring of a dream next day. It wasn't really believable. Early on he had said:

"Will you tell Angie?"

"Not if you don't want me to."

"I think it would upset her, Chris. It might even wreck our marriage. You see—" He had hesitated. "You see, that was the first time I—I mean, anyone ever—" And he had looked into her eyes. "Thank God it was you."

The following Thursday she had gone round to see Angie as usual. In the meantime there had been no word from David. She stayed late in order to see him, beginning to feel a little sick with apprehension, her heart beating hard when he came in.

He looked quite different from how he had when she had found him sitting at the table reading, the radio on. He was wearing a gray flannel suit and a gray striped tie. When Angie went out of the room and for a minute she

was alone with him, she felt a flicker of that old wariness
that was the forerunner of her fear. He was getting her a
drink. She looked up and met his eyes and it was all right
again. He gave her a conspiratorial smile, laying a finger
on his lips.

"I'll give you a ring," he had whispered.

She had to wait two more weeks. During that time she
went twice to Angie's and twice Angie came to her. She
and Graham and Angie and David went out as a foursome
and while Graham was fetching drinks and Angie was in
the Ladies, David looked at her and smiled and lightly
touched her foot with his foot under the table.

"I'll phone you. I haven't forgotten."

It was a Wednesday when he finally did phone. Next
day Christine told Graham she had made a new friend, a
girl she had met at work. She would be going out somewhere with this new friend on Friday and she wouldn't
be back till eleven. She was desperately afraid he would
want the car—it was *his* car or his firm's—but it so happened he would be in the office that day and would go by
train. Telling him these lies didn't make her feel guilty. It
wasn't as if this were some sordid affair, it was quite
different.

When Friday came she dressed with great care. Normally, to go round to Angie's, she would have worn jeans
and a T-shirt with a sweater over it. That was what she
had on the first time she found herself alone with David.
She put on a skirt and blouse and her black velvet jacket.
She took the heated rollers out of her hair and brushed it
into curls down on her shoulders. There was never much
money to spend on clothes. The mortgage on the house
took up a third of what Graham earned and half what she
earned at her part-time job. But she could run to a pair of
sheer black tights to go with the highest-heeled shoes
she'd got, her black pumps.

The doors of Angie and David's garage were wide open and their car was gone. Christine turned into their driveway, drove into the garage, and closed the doors behind her. A door at the back of the garage led into the yard and garden. The kitchen door was unlocked as it had been that Thursday three weeks before and always was on Thursday afternoons. She opened the door and walked in.

"Is that you, Chris?"

The voice sounded very male. She needed to be reassured by the sight of him. She went into the hall as he came down the stairs.

"You look lovely," he said.

"So do you."

He was wearing a suit. It was of navy silk with a pattern of pink-and-white flowers. The skirt was very short, the jacket clinched into his waist with a wide navy patent-leather belt. The long golden hair fell to his shoulders. He was heavily made-up and this time he had painted his fingernails. He looked far more beautiful than he had that first time.

Then, that first time, three weeks before, the sound of her entry drowned in loud music from the radio, she had come upon this girl sitting at the table reading *Vogue*. For a moment she had thought it must be David's sister. She had forgotten Angie had said David was an only child. The girl had long fair hair and was wearing a red summer dress with white spots on it, white sandals, and around her neck a string of white beads. When Christine saw that it was not a girl but David himself she didn't know what to do.

He stared at her in silence and without moving, and then he switched off the radio. Christine said the silliest and least relevant thing. "What are you doing home at this time?"

That made him smile. "I'd finished, so I took the rest of the day off. I should have locked the back door. Now you're here you may as well sit down."

She sat down. She couldn't take her eyes off him. He didn't look like a man dressed up as a girl, he looked like a girl—and a much prettier one than she or Angie. "Does Angie know?"

He shook his head.

"But why do you do it?" she burst out and she looked about the room, Angie's small, rather untidy living room, at the radio, the Vogue magazine. "What do you get out of it?" Something came back to her from an article she had read. "Did your mother dress you as a girl when you were little?"

"I don't know," he said. "Maybe. I don't remember. I don't want to be a girl. I just want to dress up as one sometimes."

The first shock of it was past and she began to feel easier with him. It wasn't as if there was anything grotesque about the way he looked. The very last thing he reminded her of was one of those female impersonators. A curious thought came into her head—that it was nicer, somehow more civilized, to be a woman and that if only all men were more like women—That was silly, of course, it couldn't be.

"And it's enough for you just to dress up and be here on your own?"

He was silent for a moment. "Since you ask, what I'd really like would be to go out like this and—" he paused, looking at her— "and be seen by lots of people, that's what I'd like. I've never had the nerve for that."

The bold idea expressed itself without her having to

give it a moment's thought. She wanted to do it. She was beginning to tremble with excitement.

"Let's go out then, you and I. Let's go out now. I'll put my car in your garage and you can get into it so the people next door don't see and then we'll go somewhere. Let's do that, David, shall we?"

She wondered afterwards why she had enjoyed it so much. What had it been, after all, as far as anyone else knew but two girls walking on Hampstead Heath? If Angie had suggested that the two of them do it she would have thought it a poor way of spending the afternoon. But with David—She hadn't even minded that of the two of them he was infinitely the better dressed, taller, better-looking, more graceful. She didn't mind now as he came down the stairs and stood in front of her.

"Where shall we go?"

"Not the Heath this time," he said. "Let's go shopping."

He bought a blouse in one of the big stores. Christine went into the changing room with him when he tried it on. They walked about in Hyde Park. Later on they had dinner and Christine noted that they were the only two women in the restaurant dining together.

"I'm grateful to you," David said. He put his hand over hers on the table.

"I enjoy it," she said. "It's so—crazy. I really love it. You'd better not do that, had you? There's a man over there giving a funny look."

"Women hold hands," he said.

"Only those sort of women. David, we could do this every Friday you don't have to work."

"Why not?" he said.

There was nothing to feel guilty about. She wasn't harming Angie and she wasn't being disloyal to Graham. All she was doing was going on innocent outings with another girl. Graham wasn't interested in her new friend; he didn't even ask her name. Christine came to long for Fridays, especially for the moment when she let herself into Angie's house and saw David coming down the stairs, and for the moment when they stepped out of the car in some public place and the first eyes were turned on him. They went to Holland Park, they went to the zoo, to Kew Gardens. They went to the cinema and a man sitting next to David put his hand on his knee. David loved that, it was a triumph for him, but Christine whispered they must change their seats and they did.

When they parted at the end of an evening he kissed her gently on the lips. He smelt of Aliage or Je Reviens or Opium. During the afternoon they usually went into one of the big stores and sprayed themselves out of the tester bottles.

Angie's mother lived in the north of England. When she had to convalesce after an operation Angie went up there to look after her. She expected to be away two weeks and the second weekend of her absence Graham had to go to Brussels with the sales manager.

"We could go away somewhere for the weekend." David said.

"Graham's sure to phone," Christine said.

"One night then. Just for the Saturday night. You can tell him you're going out with your new girl friend and you're going to be late."

"All right."

It worried her that she had no nice clothes to wear. David had a small but exquisite wardrobe of suits and dresses, shoes and scarves and beautiful underclothes. He kept them in a cupboard in his office to which only he had a key and he secreted items home and back again in his briefcase. Christine hated the idea of going away for the night in her gray flannel skirt and white silk blouse and that velvet jacket while David wore his Zandra Rhodes dress. In a burst of recklessness she spent all of two week's wages on a linen suit.

They went in David's car. He had made the arrangements and Christine had expected they would be going to a motel twenty miles outside London. She hadn't thought it would matter much to David where they went. But he surprised her by his choice of a hotel that was a three-hundred-year-old house on the Suffolk coast.

"If we're going to do it," he said, "we may as well do it in style."

She felt very comfortable with him, very happy. She tried to imagine what it would have felt like going to spend a night in a hotel with a man, a lover. If the person sitting next to her were dressed not in a black-and-white printed silk dress and scarlet jacket but in a man's suit with shirt and tie. If the face it gave her so much pleasure to look at were not powdered and rouged and mascara'd but rough and already showing beard growth. She couldn't imagine it. Or, rather, she could think only how in that case she would have jumped out of the car at the first red traffic lights.

They had single rooms next door to each other. The rooms were very small, but Christine could see that a double might have been awkward for David, who must at some point—though she didn't care to think of this—have to shave and strip down to being what he really was.

He came in and sat on her bed while she unpacked her nightdress and spare pair of shoes.

"This is fun, isn't it?"

She nodded, squinting into the mirror, working on her eyelids with a little brush. David always did his eyes beautifully. She turned round and smiled at him. "Let's go down and have a drink."

The dining room, the bar, the lounge, were all low-ceilinged timbered rooms with carved wood on the walls David said was called linenfold paneling. There were old maps and pictures of men hunting in gilt frames and copper bowls full of roses. Long windows were thrown open onto a terrace. The sun was still high in the sky and it was very warm. While Christine sat on the terrace in the sunshine David went off to get their drinks. When he came back to their table he had a man with him, a thickset paunchy man of about forty who was carrying a tray with four glasses on it.

"This is Ted," David said.

"Delighted to meet you," Ted said. "I've asked my friend to join us. I hope you don't mind."

She had to say she didn't. David looked at her and from his look she could tell he had deliberately picked Ted up.

"But why did you?" she said to him afterward. "Why did you want to? You told me you didn't really like it when that man put his hand on you in the cinema."

"That was so physical. This is just a laugh. You don't suppose I'd let them touch me, do you?"

Ted and Peter had the next table to theirs at dinner. Christine was silent and standoffish but David flirted with them. Ted kept leaning across and whispering to him and David giggled and smiled. You could see he was enjoying himself tremendously. Christine knew they would ask her and David to go out with them after dinner and she began to be afraid. Suppose David got carried away by the excitement of it, the "fun," and went off somewhere with Ted, leaving her and Peter alone together? Peter had a red face and a black mustache and beard and a wart with black hairs growing out of it on his left cheek. She and David were eating steak and the waiter had brought them sharp-pointed steak knives. She hadn't used hers. The steak was very tender. When no one was looking she slipped the steak knife into her bag.

Ted and Peter were still drinking coffee and brandies when David got up quite abruptly and said, "Coming?" to Christine.

"I suppose you've arranged to meet them later?" Christine said as soon as they were out of the dining room.

David looked at her. His scarlet-painted lips parted into a wide smile. He laughed.

"I turned them down."

"Did you *really*?"

"I could tell you hated the idea. Besides, we want to be alone, don't we? I know I want to be alone with you."

She nearly shouted his name so that everyone could hear, the relief was so great. She controlled herself but she was trembling. "Of course I want to be alone with you," she said.

She put her arm in his. It wasn't uncommon, after all, for girls to walk along with linked arms. Men turned to look at David and one of them whistled. She knew it must be David the whistle was directed at because he looked so beautiful with his long golden hair and high-heeled red sandals. They walked along the sea front, along the little low promenade. It was too warm even at eight-thirty to wear a coat. There were a lot of people about but not crowds. The place was too select to attract crowds. They walked to the end of the pier. They had a drink in the Ship Inn and another in the Fishermen's Arms. A man tried to pick David up in the Fishermen's Arms but this time he was cold and distant.

"I'd like to put my arm round you," he said as they were walking back, "but I suppose that wouldn't do, though it is dark."

"Better not," said Christine. She said suddenly, "This has been the best evening of my life."

He looked at her. "You really mean that?"

She nodded. "Absolutely the best."

They came into the hotel. "I'm going to get them to send us up a couple of drinks. To my room. Is that okay?"

She sat on the bed. David went into the bathroom. To do his face, she thought, maybe to shave before he let the man with the drinks see him. There was a knock at the door and a waiter came in with a tray on which were two long glasses of something or other with fruit and leaves floating in it, two pink table napkins, two olives on sticks, and two peppermint creams rapped up in green paper.

Christine tasted one of the drinks. She ate an olive. She opened her handbag and took out a mirror and a lipstick and painted her lips. David came out of the bathroom. He had taken off the golden wig and washed his face. He hadn't shaved. There was a pale stubble showing on his chin and cheeks. His legs and feet were bare and he was wearing a very masculine robe made of navy blue toweling. She tried to hide her disappointment.

"You've changed," she said brightly.

He shrugged. "There are limits."

He raised his glass and she raised her glass and he said: "To us!"

The beginnings of a feeling of panic came over her. Suddenly he was so evidently a man. She edged a little way along the mattress.

"I wish we had the whole weekend."

She nodded nervously. She was aware her body had started a faint trembling. He had noticed it, too. Sometimes before he had noticed how emotion made her tremble.

"Chris," he said.

She sat passive and afraid.

"I'm not really like a woman, Chris. I just play at that sometimes for fun. You know that, don't you?" The hand that touched her smelt of nail-varnish remover. There were hairs on the wrist she had never noticed before. "I'm falling in love with you," he said. "And you feel the same, don't you?"

She couldn't speak. He took her by the shoulders. He brought his mouth up to hers and put his arms round her and began kissing her. His skin felt abrasive and a smell as male as Graham's came off his body. She shook and shuddered. He pushed her down on the bed and his hands began undressing her, his mouth still on hers and his body heavy on top of her.

She felt behind her, put her hand into the open hand-bag, and pulled out the knife. Because she could feel his heart beating steadily against her right breast she knew where to stab and she stabbed again and again. The bright red heart's blood spurted over her clothes and the bed and the two peppermint creams on the tray.

LAWRENCE BLOCK

By the Dawn's Early Light

1984

All this happened a long time ago.

Abe Beame was living in Gracie Mansion, though even he seemed to have trouble believing he was really the mayor of the city of New York. Ali was in his prime, and the Knicks still had a year or so left in Bradley and De-Busschere. I was still drinking in those days, of course, and at the time it seemed to be doing more for me than it was doing to me.

I had already left my wife and kids, my home in Syosset and the N.Y.P.D. I was living in the hotel on West 57th Street where I still live, and I was doing most of my drinking around the corner in Jimmy Armstrong's saloon. Billie was the nighttime bartender. A Filipino youth named Dennis was behind the stick most days.

And Tommy Tillary was one of the regulars.

He was big, probably six-two, full in the chest, big in the belly too. He rarely showed up in a suit but always wore a jacket and tie, usually a navy or burgundy blazer with gray flannel slacks or white duck pants in warmer weather. He had a loud voice that boomed from his barrel chest and a big, clean-shaven face that was innocent around the pouting mouth and knowing around the eyes.

He was somewhere in his late forties and he drank a lot of top-shelf Scotch. Chivas, as I remember it, but it could have been Johnnie Black. Whatever it was, his face was beginning to show it, with patches of permanent flush at the cheekbones and a tracery of broken capillaries across the bridge of the nose.

We were saloon friends. We didn't speak every time we ran into each other, but at the least we always acknowledged each other with a nod or a wave. He told a lot of dialect jokes and told them reasonably well, and I laughed at my share of them. Sometimes I was in a mood to reminisce about my days on the force, and when my stories were funny, his laugh was as loud as anyone's.

Sometimes he showed up alone, sometimes with male friends. About a third of the time he was in the company of a short and curvy blonde named Carolyn. "Carolyn from the Caro-line" was the way he occasionally introduced her, and she did have a faint Southern accent that became more pronounced as the drink got to her.

Then one morning I picked up the *Daily News* and read that burglars had broken into a house on Colonial Road, in the Bay Ridge section of Brooklyn. They had stabbed to death the only occupant present, one Margaret Tillary. Her husband, Thomas J. Tillary, a salesman, was not at home at the time.

I hadn't known Tommy was a salesman or that he'd had a wife. He did wear a wide yellow-gold band on the appropriate finger, and it was clear that he wasn't married to Carolyn from the Caroline, and it now looked as though he was a widower. I felt vaguely sorry for him, vaguely sorry for the wife I'd never even known of, but that was the extent of it. I drank enough back then to avoid feeling any emotion very strongly.

And then, two or three nights later, I walked into Armstrong's and there was Carolyn. She didn't appear to be waiting for him or anyone else, nor did she look as though she'd just breezed in a few minutes ago. She had a stool by herself at the bar and she was drinking something dark from a lowball glass.

I took a seat a few stools down from her. I ordered two double shots of bourbon, drank one, and poured the other into the black coffee Billie brought me. I was sipping the coffee when a voice with a Piedmont softness said, "I forget your name."

I looked up.

"I believe we were introduced," she said, "but I don't recall your name."

"It's Matt," I said, "and you're right, Tommy introduced us. You're Carolyn."

"Carolyn Cheatham. Have you seen him?"

"Tommy? Not since it happened."

"Neither have I. Were you-all at the funeral?"

"No. When was it?"

"This afternoon. Neither was I. There. Whyn't you come sit next to me so's I don't have to shout. Please?"

She was drinking a sweet almond liqueur that she took on the rocks. It tastes like dessert, but it's as strong as whiskey.

"He told me not to come," she said. "To the funeral. He said it was a matter of respect for the dead." She picked up her glass and stared into it. I've never known what people hope to see there, though it's a gesture I've performed often enough myself.

"Respect," she said. "What's he care about respect? I would have just been part of the office crowd; we both work at Tannahill; far as anyone there knows, we're just friends. And all we ever were is friends, you know."

"Whatever you say."

"Oh, *shit*," she said. "I don't mean I wasn't f——ing him, for the Lord's sake. I mean it was just laughs and good times. He was married and he went home to Momma every night and that was jes' fine, because who in her right mind'd want Tommy Tillary around by the dawn's early light? Christ in the foothills, did I spill this or drink it?''

We agreed she was drinking them a little too fast. It was this fancy New York sweet-drink shit, she maintained, not like the bourbon she'd grown up on. You knew where you stood with bourbon.

I told her I was a bourbon drinker myself, and it pleased her to learn this. Alliances have been forged on thinner bonds than that, and ours served to propel us out of Armstrong's, with a stop down the block for a fifth of Maker's Mark—her choice—and a four-block walk to her apartment. There were exposed brick walls, I remember, and candles stuck in straw-wrapped bottles, and several travel posters from Sabena, the Belgian airline.

We did what grownups do when they find themselves alone together. We drank our fair share of the Maker's Mark and went to bed. She made a lot of enthusiastic noises and more than a few skillful moves, and afterward she cried some.

A little later, she dropped off to sleep. I was tired myself, but I put on my clothes and sent myself home. Because who in her right mind'd want Matt Scudder around by the dawn's early light?

Over the next couple of days, I wondered every time I entered Armstrong's if I'd run into her, and each time I was more relieved than disappointed when I didn't. I didn't encounter Tommy, either, and that too was a relief and in no sense disappointing.

Then one morning I picked up the News and read that they'd arrested a pair of young Hispanics from Sunset Park for the Tillary burglary and homicide. The paper ran the usual photo—two skinny kids, their hair unruly, one of them trying to hide his face from the camera, the other smirking defiantly, and each of them handcuffed to a broad-shouldered, grimfaced Irishman in a suit. You didn't need the careful caption to tell the good guys from the bad guys.

Sometime in the middle of the afternoon I went over to Armstrong's for a hamburger and drank a beer with it. The phone behind the bar rang and Dennis put down the glass he was wiping and answered it. "He was here a minute ago," he said, "I'll see if he stepped out." He covered the mouthpiece with his hand and looked quizzically at me. "Are you still here?" he asked. "Or did you slip away while my attention was diverted?"

"Who wants to know?"

"Tommy Tillary."

You never know what a woman will decide to tell a man or how a man will react to it. I didn't want to find out, but I was better off learning over the phone than face to face. I nodded and took the phone from Dennis.

I said, "Matt Scudder, Tommy. I was sorry to hear about your wife."

"Thanks, Matt. Jesus, it feels like it happened a year ago. It was what, a week?"

"At least they got the bastards."

There was a pause. Then he said, "Jesus. You haven't seen a paper, huh?"

"That's where I read about it. Two Spanish kids."

"You didn't happen to see this afternoon's *Post*."

"No. Why, what happened? They turn out to be clean?"

"The two spics. Clean? Shit, they're about as clean as the men's room in the Times Square subway station. The cops hit their place and found stuff from my house everywhere they looked. Jewelry they had descriptions of, a stereo that I gave them the serial number, everything.

Monogrammed shit. I mean, that's how clean they were,
for Christ's sake.''

"So?''

"They admitted the burglary but not the murder.''

"That's common, Tommy.''

"Lemme finish, huh? They admitted the burglary, but
according to them it was a put-up job. According to them,
I hired them to hit my place. They could keep whatever
they got and I'd have everything out and arranged for
them, and in return I got to clean up on the insurance by
overreporting the loss.''

"What did the loss amount to?''

"Shit, I don't know. There were twice as many things
turned up in their apartment as I ever listed when I made
out a report. There's things I missed a few days after I
filed the report and others I didn't know were gone until
the cops found them. You don't notice everything right
away, at least I didn't, and on top of it, how could I think
straight with Peg dead? You know?''

"It hardly sounds like an insurance setup.''

"No, of course it wasn't. How the hell could it be? All
I had was a standard home-owner's policy. It covered
maybe a third of what I lost. According to them, the place
was empty when they hit it. Peg was out.''

"And?''

"And I set them up. They hit the place, they carted
everything away, and I came home with Peg and stabbed
her six, eight times, whatever it was, and left her there so
it'd look like it happened in a burglary.''

"How could the burglars testify that you stabbed your
wife?''

"They couldn't. All they said was they didn't and she
wasn't home when they were there, and that I hired them
to do the burglary. The cops pieced the rest of it together.''

"What did they do, take you downtown?''

"No. They came over to the house, it was early, I don't know what time. It was the first I knew that the spics were arrested, let alone that they were trying to do a job on me. They just wanted to talk, the cops, and at first I talked to them, and then I started to get the drift of what they were trying to put onto me. So I said I wasn't saying anything more without my lawyer present, and I called him, and he left half his breakfast on the table and came over in a hurry, and he wouldn't let me say a word."

"And the cops didn't take you in or book you?"

"No."

"Did they buy your story?"

"No way. I didn't really tell 'em a story, because Kaplan wouldn't let me say anything. They didn't drag me in, because they don't have a case yet, but Kaplan says they're gonna be building one if they can. They told me not to leave town. You believe it? My wife's dead, the *Post* headline says, 'QUIZ HUSBAND IN BURGLARY MURDER,' and what the hell do they think I'm gonna do? Am I going fishing for fucking trout in Montana? 'Don't leave town.' You see this shit on television, you think nobody in real life talks this way. Maybe television's where they get it from."

I wanted for him to tell me what he wanted from me. I didn't have long to wait.

"Why I called," he said, "is Kaplan wants to hire a detective. He figured maybe these guys talked around the neighborhood, maybe they bragged to their friends, maybe there's a way to prove they did the killing. He says the cops won't concentrate on that end if they're too busy nailing the lid shut on me."

I explained that I didn't have any official standing, that I had no license and filed no reports.

"That's OK," he insisted. "I told Kaplan what I want is somebody I can trust, somebody who'll do the job for me. I don't think they're gonna have any kind of a case at all,

Matt, but the longer this drags on, the worse it is for me.
I want it cleared up, I want it in the papers that these
Spanish assholes did it all and I had nothing to do with
anything. You name a fair fee and I'll pay it, me to you,
and it can be cash in your hand if you don't like checks.
What do you say?"

He wanted somebody he could trust. Had Carolyn from
the Caroline told him how trustworthy I was?

What did I say? I said yes.

I met Tommy Tillary and his lawyer in Drew Kaplan's
office on Court Street, a few blocks from Brooklyn's Borough Hall. There was a Syrian restaurant next door and,
at the corner, a grocery store specializing in Middle East-
ern imports stood next to an antique shop overflowing
with stripped-oak furniture and brass lamps and bed-
steads. Kaplan's office ran to wood paneling and leather
chairs and oak file cabinets. His name and the names of
two partners were painted on the frosted-glass door in
old-fashioned gold and black lettering. Kaplan himself
looked conservatively up to date, with a three-piece
striped suit that was better cut than mine. Tommy wore
his burgundy blazer and gray flannel trousers and loafers.
Strain showed at the corners of his blue eyes and around
his mouth. His complexion was off, too.

"All we want you to do," Kaplan said, "is find a key in
one of their pants pockets, Herrera's or Cruz's, and trace
it to a locker in Penn Station, and in the locker there's a
foot-long knife with their prints and her blood on it."

"Is that what it's going to take?"

He smiled. "It wouldn't hurt. No, actually, we're not in
such bad shape. They got some shaky testimony from a
pair of Latins who've been in and out of trouble since
they got weaned to Tropicana. They got what looks to
them like a good motive on Tommy's part."

"Which is?"

I was looking at Tommy when I asked. His eyes slipped away from mine. Kaplan said, "A marital triangle, a case of the shorts and strong money motive. Margaret Tillary inherited a little over a quarter of a million dollars six or eight months ago. An aunt left a million two and it got cut up four ways. What they don't bother to notice is he loved his wife, and how many husbands cheat? What is it they say—ninety percent cheat and ten percent lie?"

"That's good odds."

"One of the killers, Angel Herrera, did some odd jobs at the Tillary house last March or April. Spring cleaning; he hauled stuff out of the basement and attic, a little donkeywork. According to Herrera, that's how Tommy knew him to contact him about the burglary. According to common sense, that's how Herrera and his buddy Cruz knew the house and what was in it and how to gain access."

"The case against Tommy sounds pretty thin."

"It is," Kaplan said. "The thing is, you go to court with something like this and you lose even if you win. For the rest of your life, everybody remembers you stood trial for murdering your wife, never mind that you won an acquittal.

"Besides," he said, "you never know which way a jury's going to jump. Tommy's alibi is he was with another lady at the time of the burglary. The woman's a colleague; they could see it as completely aboveboard, but who says they're going to? What they sometimes do, they decide they don't believe the alibi because it's his girlfriend lying for him, and at the same time they label him a scumbag for screwing around while his wife's getting killed."

"You keep it up," Tommy said, "I'll find myself guilty, the way you make it sound."

"Plus he's hard to get a sympathetic jury for. He's a big, handsome guy, a sharp dresser, and you'd love him in a

gin joint, but how much do you love him in a courtroom?
He's a securities salesman, he's beautiful on the phone,
and that means every clown who ever lost a hundred
dollars on a stock tip or bought magazines over the phone
is going to walk into the courtroom with a hard-on for
him. I'm telling you, I want to stay the hell out of court.
I'll win in court, I know that, or the worst that'll happen
is I'll win on appeal, but who needs it? This is a case that
shouldn't be in the first place, and I'd love to clear it up
before they even go so far as presenting a bill to the grand
jury."

"So from me you want—"

"Whatever you can find, Matt. Whatever discredits
Cruz and Herrera. I don't know what's there to be found,
but you were a cop and now you're private, and you can
get down in the streets and nose around."

I nodded. I could do that. "One thing," I said.
"Wouldn't you be better off with a Spanish-speaking detective? I know enough to buy a beer in a bodega, but I'm
a long way from fluent."

Kaplan shook his head. "A personal relationship's
worth more than a dime's worth of 'Me llamo Matteo y
¿como está usted?' "

"That's the truth," Tommy Tillary said. "Matt, I know
I can count on you."

I wanted to tell him all he could count on was his
fingers. I didn't really see what I could expect to uncover
that wouldn't turn up in a regular police investigation.
But I'd spent enough time carrying a shield to know not to
push away money when somebody wants to give it to
you. I felt comfortable taking a fee. The man was inher-
iting a quarter of a million, plus whatever insurance his
wife had carried. If he was willing to spread some of it
around, I was willing to take it.

*   *   *

So I went to Sunset Park and spent some time in the streets and some more time in the bars. Sunset Park is in Brooklyn, of course, on the borough's western edge, above Bay Ridge and south and west of Green-Wood Cemetery. These days, there's a lot of brownstoning going on there, with young urban professionals renovating the old houses and gentrifying the neighborhood. Back then, the upwardly mobile young had not yet discovered Sunset Park, and the area was a mix of Latins and Scandinavians, most of the former Puerto Ricans, most of the latter Norwegians. The balance was gradually shifting from Europe to the islands, from light to dark, but this was a process that had been going on for ages and there was nothing hurried about it.

I talked to Herrera's landlord and Cruz's former employer and one of his recent girlfriends. I drank beer in bars and the back rooms of bodegas. I went to the local station house, I read the sheets on both of the burglars and drank coffee with the cops and picked up some of the stuff that doesn't get on the yellow sheets.

I found out that Miguelito Cruz had once killed a man in a tavern brawl over a woman. There were no charges pressed; a dozen witnesses reported that the dead man had gone after Cruz first with a broken bottle. Cruz had most likely been carrying the knife, but several witnesses insisted it had been tossed to him by an anonymous benefactor, and there hadn't been enough evidence to make a case of weapons possession, let alone homicide.

I learned that Herrera had three children living with their mother in Puerto Rico. He was divorced, but wouldn't marry his current girlfriend because he regarded himself as still married to his ex-wife in the eyes of God. He sent money to his children when he had any to send.

I learned other things. They didn't seem terribly consequential then and they've faded from memory altogether by now, but I wrote them down in my pocket notebook as I learned them, and every day or so I duly reported my findings to Drew Kaplan. He always seemed pleased with what I told him.

I invariably managed a stop at Armstrong's before I called it a night. One night she was there, Carolyn Cheatham, drinking bourbon this time, her face frozen with stubborn old pain. It took her a blink or two to recognize me. Then tears started to form in the corners of her eyes, and she used the back of one hand to wipe them away.

I didn't approach her until she beckoned. She patted the stool beside hers and I eased myself onto it. I had coffee with bourbon in it and bought a refill for her. She was pretty drunk already, but that's never been enough reason to turn down a drink.

She talked about Tommy. He was being nice to her, she said. Calling up, sending flowers. But he wouldn't see her, because it wouldn't look right, not for a new widower, not for a man who'd been publicly accused of murder.

"He sends flowers with no card enclosed," she said. "He calls me from pay phones. The son of a bitch."

Billie called me aside. "I didn't want to put her out," he said, "a nice woman like that, shit-faced as she is. But I thought I was gonna have to. You'll see she gets home?"

I said I would.

I got her out of there and a cab came along and saved us the walk. At her place, I took the keys from her and unlocked the door. She half sat, half sprawled on the couch. I had to use the bathroom, and when I came back, her eyes were closed and she was snoring lightly.

I got her coat and shoes off, put her to bed, loosened her clothing and covered her with a blanket. I was tired from all that and sat down on the couch for a minute, and I almost dozed off myself. Then I snapped awake and let myself out.

I went back to Sunset Park the next day. I learned that Cruz had been in trouble as a youth. With a gang of neighborhood kids, he used to go into the city and cruise Greenwich Village, looking for homosexuals to beat up. He'd had a dread of homosexuality, probably flowing as it generally does out of a fear of a part of himself, and he stifled that dread by fag bashing.

"He still doesn't like them," a woman told me. She had glossy black hair and opaque eyes, and she was letting me pay for her rum and orange juice. "He's pretty, you know, an' they come on to him, an' he doan' like it."

I called that item in, along with a few others equally earthshaking. I bought myself a steak dinner at The Slate over on Tenth Avenue, then finished up at Armstrong's, not drinking very hard, just coasting along on bourbon and coffee.

Twice, the phone rang for me. Once, it was Tommy Tillary, telling me how much he appreciated what I was doing for him. It seemed to me that all I was doing was taking his money, but he had me believing that my loyalty and invaluable assistance were all he had to cling to.

The second call was from Carolyn. More praise. I was a gentleman, she assured me, and a hell of a fellow all around. And I should forget that she'd been bad-mouthing Tommy. Everything was going to be fine with them.

I took the next day off. I think I went to a movie, and it may have been *The Sting*, with Newman and Redford achieving vengeance through swindling.

The day after that, I did another tour of duty over in Brooklyn. And the day after that, I picked up the *News* first thing in the morning. The headline was nonspecific, something like "KILL SUSPECT HANGS SELF IN CELL," but I knew it was my case before I turned to the story on page three.

Miguelito Cruz had torn his clothing into strips, knotted the strips together, stood his iron bedstead on its side, climbed onto it, looped his homemade rope around an overhead pipe and jumped off the upended bedstead and into the next world.

That evening's six o'clock TV news had the rest of the story. Informed of his friend's death, Angel Herrera had recanted his original story and admitted that he and Cruz had conceived and executed the Tillary burglary on their own. It had been Miguelito who had stabbed the Tillary woman when she walked in on them. He'd picked up a kitchen knife while Herrera watched in horror. Miguelito always had a short temper, Herrera said, but they were friends, even cousins, and they had hatched their story to protect Miguelito. But now that he was dead, Herrera could admit what had really happened.

I was in Armstrong's that night, which was not remarkable. I had it in mind to get drunk, though I could not have told you why, and that *was* remarkable, if not unheard of. I got drunk a lot those days, but I rarely set out with that intention. I just wanted to feel a little better, a little more mellow, and somewhere along the way I'd wind up waxed.

I wasn't drinking particularly hard or fast, but I was working at it, and then somewhere around ten or eleven the door opened and I knew who it was before I turned around. Tommy Tillary, well dressed and freshly barbered, making his first appearance in Jimmy's place since his wife was killed.

"Hey, look who's here!" he called out and grinned that big grin. People rushed over to shake his hand. Billie was behind the stick, and he'd no sooner set one up on the house for our hero than Tommy insisted on buying a round for the bar. It was an expensive gesture—there must have been thirty or forty people in there—but I don't think he cared if there were three hundred or four hundred.

I stayed where I was, letting the others mob him, but he worked his way over to me and got an arm around my shoulders. "This is the man," he announced. "Best effing detective ever wore out a pair of shoes. This man's money," he told Billie, "is no good at all tonight. He can't buy a drink; he can't buy a cup of coffee; if you went and put in pay toilets since I was last here, he can't use his own dime."

"The john's still free," Billie said, "but don't give the boss any ideas."

"Oh, don't tell me he didn't already think of it," Tommy said. "Matt, my boy, I love you. I was in a tight spot, I didn't want to walk out of my house, and you came through for me."

What the hell had I done? I hadn't hanged Miguelito Cruz or coaxed a confession out of Angel Herrera. I hadn't even set eyes on either man. But he was buying the drinks, and I had a thirst, so who was I to argue?

I don't know how long we stayed there. Curiously, my drinking slowed down even as Tommy's picked up speed. Carolyn, I noticed, was not present, nor did her name find its way into the conversation. I wondered if she would walk in—it was, after all, her neighborhood bar, and she was apt to drop in on her own. I wondered what would happen if she did.

I guess there were a lot of things I wondered about, and perhaps that's what put the brakes on my own drinking. I didn't want any gaps in my memory, any gray patches in my awareness.

After a while, Tommy was hustling me out of Armstrong's. "This is celebration time," he told me. "We don't want to sit in one place till we grow roots. We want to bop a little."

He had a car, and I just went along with him without paying too much attention to exactly where we were. We went to a noisy Greek club on the East Side, I think, where the waiters looked like Mob hit men. We went to a couple of trendy singles joints. We wound up somewhere in the Village, in a dark, beery cave.

It was quiet there, and conversation was possible, and I found myself asking him what I'd done that was so praiseworthy. One man had killed himself and another had confessed, and where was my role in either incident?

"The stuff you came up with," he said.

"What stuff? I should have brought back fingernail parings, you could have had someone work voodoo on them."

"About Cruz and the fairies."

"He was up for murder. He didn't kill himself because he was afraid they'd get him for fag bashing when he was a juvenile offender."

Tommy took a sip of Scotch. He said, "Couple days ago, huge black guy comes up to Cruz in the chow line. 'Wait'll you get up to Green Haven,' he tells him. 'Every blood there's gonna have you for a girlfriend. Doctor gonna have to cut you a brand-new asshole, time you get outa there.' "

I didn't say anything.

"Kaplan," he said. "Drew talked to somebody who talked to somebody, and that did it. Cruz took a good look at the idea of playin' drop the soap for half the jigs in captivity, and the next thing you know, the murderous little bastard was dancing on air. And good riddance to him."

I couldn't seem to catch my breath. I worked on it while Tommy went to the bar for another round. I hadn't touched the drink in front of me, but I let him buy for both of us.

When he got back, I said, "Herrera."

"Changed his story. Made a full confession."

"And pinned the killing on Cruz."

"Why not? Cruz wasn't around to complain. Who knows which one of 'em did it, and for that matter, who cares? The thing is, you gave us the lever."

"For Cruz," I said. "To get him to kill himself."

"And for Herrera. Those kids of his in Santurce. Drew spoke to Herrera's lawyer and Herrera's lawyer spoke to Herrera, and the message was, 'Look you're going up for burglary whatever you do, and probably for murder; but if you tell the right story, you'll draw shorter time, and on top of that, that nice Mr. Tillary's gonna let bygones be bygones and every month there's a nice check for your wife and kiddies back home in Puerto Rico.' "

At the bar, a couple of old men were reliving the Louis-Schmeling fight, the second one, where Louis punished the German champion. One of the old fellows was throwing roundhouse punches in the air, demonstrating.

I said, "Who killed your wife?"

"One or the other of them. If I had to bet, I'd say Cruz. He had those little beady eyes; you looked at him up close and you got that he was a killer."

"When did you look at him up close?"

"When they came and cleaned the house, the basement and the attic. Not when they came and cleaned me out; that was the second time."

He smiled, but I kept looking at him until the smile lost its certainty. "That was Herrera who helped around the house," I said. "You never met Cruz."

"Cruz came along, gave him a hand."

"You never mentioned that before."

"Oh, sure I did, Matt. What difference does it make, anyway?"

"Who killed her, Tommy?"

"Hey, let it alone, huh?"

"Answer the question."

"I already answered it."

"You killed her, didn't you?"

"What are you, crazy? Cruz killed her and Herrera swore to it, isn't that enough for you?"

"Tell me you didn't kill her."

"I didn't kill her."

"Tell me again."

"I didn't f——ing kill her. What's the matter with you?"

"I don't believe you."

"Oh, Jesus," he said. He closed his eyes, put his head in his hands. He sighed and looked up and said, "You know, it's a funny thing with me. Over the telephone, I'm the best salesman you could ever imagine. I swear I could sell sand to the Arabs, I could sell ice in the winter, but face to face I'm no good at all. Why do you figure that is?"

"You tell me."

"I don't know. I used to think it was my face, the eyes and the mouth; I don't know. It's easy over the phone. I'm talking to a stranger, I don't know who he is or what he looks like, and he's not lookin' at me, and it's a cinch. Face to face, especially with someone I know, it's a different story." He looked at me. "If we were doin' this over the phone, you'd buy the whole thing."

"It's possible."

"It's effing certain. Word for word, you'd buy the package. Suppose I was to tell you I did kill her, Matt. You couldn't prove anything. Look, the both of us walked in there, the place was a mess from the burglary, we got in an argument, tempers flared, something happened."

"You set up the burglary. You planned the whole thing,

just the way Cruz and Herrera accused you of doing. And now you wriggled out of it."

"And you helped me—don't forget that part of it."

"I won't."

"And I wouldn't have gone away for it anyway, Matt. Not a chance. I'da beat it in court, only this way I don't have to go to court. Look, this is just the booze talkin', and we can forget it in the morning, right? I didn't kill her, you didn't accuse me, we're still buddies, everything's fine. Right?"

Blackouts are never there when you want them. I woke up the next day and remembered all of it, and I found myself wishing I didn't. He'd killed his wife and he was getting away with it. And I'd helped him. I'd taken his money, and in return I'd shown him how to set one man up for suicide and pressure another into making a false confession.

And what was I going to do about it?

I couldn't think of a thing. Any story I carried to the police would be speedily denied by Tommy and his lawyer, and all I had was the thinnest of hearsay evidence, my own client's own words when he and I both had a skinful of booze. I went over it for a few days, looking for ways to shake something loose, and there was nothing. I could maybe interest a newspaper reporter, maybe get Tommy some press coverage that wouldn't make him happy, but why? And to what purpose?

It rankled. But I would just have a couple of drinks, and then it wouldn't rankle so much.

Angel Herrera pleaded guilty to burglary, and in return, the Brooklyn D.A.'s office dropped all homicide charges. He went upstate to serve five to ten.

And then I got a call in the middle of the night. I'd been

sleeping a couple of hours, but the phone woke me and I groped for it. It took me a minute to recognize the voice on the other end.

It was Carolyn Cheatham.

"I had to call you," she said, "on account of you're a bourbon man and a gentleman. I owed it to you to call you."

"What's the matter?"

"He ditched me," she said, "and he got me fired out of Tannahill and Company so he won't have to look at me around the office. Once he didn't need me to back up his story, he let go of me, and do you know he did it over the phone?"

"Carolyn—"

"It's all in the note," she said. "I'm leaving a note."

"Look, don't do anything yet," I said. I was out of bed, fumbling for my clothes. "I'll be right over. We'll talk about it."

"You can't stop me, Matt."

"I won't try to stop you. We'll talk first, and then you can do anything you want."

The phone clicked in my ear.

I threw my clothes on, rushed over there, hoping it would be pills, something that took its time. I broke a small pane of glass in the downstairs door and let myself in, then used an old credit card to slip the bolt of her spring lock.

The room smelled of cordite. She was on the couch she'd passed out on the last time I saw her. The gun was still in her hand, limp at her side, and there was a black-rimmed hole in her temple.

There was a note, too. An empty bottle of Maker's Mark stood on the coffee table, an empty glass beside it. The booze showed in her handwriting and in the sullen phrasing of the suicide note.

I read the note. I stood there for a few minutes, not for very long, and then I got a dish towel from the Pullman kitchen and wiped the bottle and the glass. I took another matching glass, rinsed it out and wiped it, and put it in the drainboard of the sink.

I stuffed the note in my pocket. I took the gun from her fingers, checked routinely for a pulse, then wrapped a sofa pillow around the gun to muffle its report. I fired one round into her chest, another into her open mouth.

I dropped the gun into a pocket and left.

They found the gun in Tommy Tillary's house, stuffed between the cushions of the living-room sofa, clean of prints inside and out. Ballistics got a perfect match. I'd aimed for soft tissue with the round shot into her chest, because bullets can fragment on impact with bone. That was one reason I'd fired the extra shots. The other was to rule out the possibility of suicide.

After the story made the papers, I picked up the phone and called Drew Kaplan. "I don't understand it," I said. "He was free and clear; why the hell did he kill the girl?"

"Ask him yourself," Kaplan said. He did not sound happy. "You want my opinion, he's a lunatic. I honestly didn't think he was. I figured maybe he killed his wife, maybe he didn't. Not my job to try him. But I didn't figure he was a homicidal maniac."

"It's certain he killed the girl?"

"Not much question. The gun's pretty strong evidence. Talk about finding somebody with the smoking pistol in his hand, here it was in Tommy's couch. The idiot."

"Funny he kept it."

"Maybe he had other people he wanted to shoot. Go figure a crazy man. No, the gun's evidence, and there was a phone tip—a man called in the shooting, reported a man running out of there and gave a description that fitted

Tommy pretty well. Even had him wearing that red blazer he wears, tacky thing makes him look like an usher at the Paramount.''

"It sounds tough to square.''

"Well, somebody else'll have to try to do it,'' Kaplan said. "I told him I can't defend him this time. What it amounts to, I wash my hands of him.''

I thought of that when I read that Angel Herrera got out just the other day. He served all ten years because he was as good at getting into trouble inside the walls as he'd been on the outside.

Somebody killed Tommy Tillary with a homemade knife after he'd served two years and three months of a manslaughter stretch. I wondered at the time if that was Herrera getting even, and I don't suppose I'll ever know. Maybe the checks stopped going to Santurce and Herrera took it the wrong way. Or maybe Tommy said the wrong thing to somebody else and said it face to face instead of over the phone.

I don't think I'd do it that way now. I don't drink anymore, and the impulse to play God seems to have evaporated with the booze.

But then, a lot of things have changed. Billie left Armstrong's not long after that, left New York, too; the last I heard, he was off drink himself, living in Sausalito and making candles. I ran into Dennis the other day in a bookstore on lower Fifth Avenue full of odd volumes on yoga and spiritualism and holistic healing. And Armstrong's is scheduled to close the end of next month. The lease is up for renewal, and I suppose the next you know, the old joint'll be another Korean fruit market.

I still light a candle now and then for Carolyn Cheatham and Miguelito Cruz. Not often. Just every once in a while.

JOHN LUTZ

Ride the Lightning

1985

A slanted sheet of rain swept like a scythe across Placid Cove Trailer Park. For an instant, an intricate web of lightning illumined the park. The rows of mobile homes loomed square and still and pale against the night, reminding Nudger of tombs with awnings and TV antennas. He held his umbrella at a sharp angle to the wind as he walked, putting a hand in his pocket to pull out a scrap of paper and double-check the address he was trying to find in the maze of trailers. Finally, at the end of Tranquility Lane, he found Number 307 and knocked on its metal door.

"I'm Nudger," he said when the door opened.

For several seconds the woman in the doorway stood staring out at him, rain blowing in beneath the metal awning to spot her cornflower-colored dress and ruffle her straw blond hair. She was tall but very thin, fragile-looking, and appeared at first glance to be about twelve years old. Second glance revealed her to be in her mid-twenties. She had slight crow's feet at the corners of her luminous blue eyes when she winced as a raindrop struck her face, a knowing cast to her oversized, girlish, full-lipped mouth, and slightly buck teeth. Her looks were hers alone. There was no one who could look much like her, no middle ground with her; men would consider her scrawny and homely, or they would see her as uniquely sensuous. Nudger liked coltish girl-women; he catalogued her as attractive.

"Whoeee!" she said at last, as if seeing for the first time beyond Nudger. "Ain't it raining something terrible?"

"It is," Nudger agreed. "And on me."

Her entire thin body gave a quick, nervous kind of jerk as she smiled apologetically. "I'm Holly Ann Adams, Mr. Nudger. And you are getting wet, all right. Come on in."

She moved aside and Nudger stepped up into the trailer. He expected it to be surprisingly spacious; he'd once lived in a trailer and remembered them as such. This one was cramped and confining. The furniture was cheap and its upholstery was threadbare; a portable black-and-white TV on a tiny table near the Scotch-plaid sofa was blaring shouts of ecstasy emitted by "The Price is Right" contestants. The air was thick with the smell of something greasy that had been fried too long.

Holly Ann cleared a stack of *People* magazines from a vinyl chair and motioned for Nudger to sit down. He folded his umbrella, left it by the door, and sat. Holly Ann started to say something, then jerked her body in that peculiar way of hers, almost a twitch, as if she'd just remembered something not only with her mind but with her blood and muscle, and walked over and switched off the noisy television. In the abrupt silence, the rain seemed to beat on the metal roof with added fury. "Now we can talk," Holly Ann proclaimed, sitting opposite Nudger on the undersized sofa. "You a sure-enough private investigator?"

"I'm that," Nudger said. "Did someone recommend me to you, Miss Adams?"

"Gotcha out of the Yellow Pages. And if you're gonna work for me, it might as well be Holly Ann without the Adams."

"Except on the check," Nudger said.

She grinned a devilish twelve-year-old's grin. "Oh, sure, don't worry none about that. I wrote you out a check already, just gotta fill in the amount. That is, if you agree to take the job. You might not."

"Why not?"

"It has to do with my fiancé, Curtis Colt."

Nudger listened for a few seconds to the rain crashing on the roof. "The Curtis Colt who's going to be executed next week?"

"That's the one. Only he didn't kill that liquor store woman; I know it for a fact. It ain't right he should have to ride the lightning."

"Ride the lightning?"

"That's what convicts call dying in the electric chair, Mr. Nudger. They call that chair lotsa things: Old Sparky . . . The Lord's Frying Pan. But Curtis don't belong sitting in it wired up, and I can prove it."

"It's a little late for that kind of talk," Nudger said. "Or did you testify for Curtis in court?"

"Nope. Couldn't testify. You'll see why. All them lawyers and the judge and jury don't even know about me. Curtis didn't want them to know, so he never told them." She crossed her legs and swung her right calf jauntily. She was smiling as if trying to flirt him into wanting to know more about the job so he could free Curtis Colt by a governor's reprieve at the last minute, as in an old movie.

Nudger looked at her gauntly pretty, country-girl face and said, "Tell me about Curtis Colt, Holly Ann."

"You mean you didn't read about him in the newspapers or see him on the television?"

"I only scan the media for misinformation. Give me the details."

"Well, they say Curtis was inside the liquor store, sticking it up—him and his partner had done three other places that night, all of 'em gas stations, though—when the old man that owned the place came out of a back room and seen his wife there behind the counter with her hands up and Curtis holding the gun on her. So the old man lost his head and ran at Curtis, and Curtis had to shoot him. Then the woman got mad when she seen that and ran at Curtis, and Curtis shot her. She's the one that died. The old man, he'll live, but he can't talk nor think nor even feed himself."

Nudger remembered more about the case now. Curtis Colt had been found guilty of first-degree murder, and because of a debate in the legislature over the merits of cyanide gas versus electricity, the state was breaking out the electric chair to make him its first killer executed by electricity in over a quarter of a century. Those of the back-to-basics school considered that progress.

"They're gonna shoot Curtis full of electricity next Saturday, Mr. Nudger," Holly Ann said plaintively. She sounded like a little girl complaining that the grade on her report card wasn't fair.

"I know," Nudger said. "But I don't see how I can help you. Or, more specifically, help Curtis."

"You know what they say thoughts really are, Mr. Nudger?" Holly Ann said, ignoring his professed helplessness. Her wide blue eyes were vague as she searched for words. "Thoughts ain't really nothing but tiny electrical impulses in the brain. I read that somewheres or other. What I can't help wondering is, when they shoot all that electricity into Curtis, what's it gonna be like to his thinking? How long will it seem like to him before he finally dies? Will there be a big burst of crazy thoughts along with the pain? I know it sounds loony, but I can't help laying awake nights thinking about that, and I feel I just gotta do whatever's left to try and help Curtis."

There was a sort of checkout-line tabloid logic in that, Nudger conceded; if thoughts were actually weak electrical impulses, then high-voltage electrical impulses could become exaggerated, horrible thoughts. Anyway, try to disprove it to Holly Ann.

"They never did catch Curtis's buddy, the driver who sped away and left him in that service station, did they?" Nudger asked.

"Nope. Curtis never told who the driver was, neither, no matter how much he was threatened. Curtis is a stubborn man."

Nudger was getting the idea.

"But you know who was driving the car."

"Yep. And he told me him and Curtis was miles away from that liquor store at the time it was robbed. When he seen the police closing in on Curtis in that gas station where Curtis was buying cigarettes, he hit the accelerator and got out of the parking lot before they could catch him. The police didn't even get the car's license plate number."

Nudger rubbed a hand across his chin, watching Holly Ann swing her leg as if it were a shapely metronome. She was barefoot and wearing no nylon hose. "The jury thought Curtis not only was at the liquor store, but that he shot the old man and woman in cold blood."

"That ain't true, though. Not according to—" she caught herself before uttering the man's name.

"Curtis's friend," Nudger finished.

"That's right. And he ought to know," Holly Ann said righteously, as if that piece of information were the trump card and the argument was over.

"None of this means anything unless the driver comes forward and substantiates that he was with Curtis somewhere other than at the liquor store when it was robbed."

Holly Ann nodded and stopped swinging her leg. "I know. But he won't. He can't. That's where you come in."

"My profession might enjoy a reputation a notch lower

than dognapper," Nudger said, "but I don't hire out to do anything illegal."

"What I want you to do is legal," Holly Ann said in a hurt little voice. Nudger looked past her into the dollhouse kitchen and saw an empty gin bottle. He wondered if she might be slightly drunk. "It's the eyewitness accounts that got Curtis convicted," she went on. "And those people are wrong. I want you to figure out some way to convince them it wasn't Curtis they saw that night."

"Four people, two of them customers in the store, picked Curtis out of a police lineup."

"So what? Ain't eyewitnesses often mistaken?"

Nudger had to admit that they were, though he didn't see how they could be in this case. There were, after all, four of them. And yet, Holly Ann was right; it was amazing how people could sometimes be so certain that the wrong man had committed a crime just five feet in front of them.

"I want you to talk to them witnesses," Holly Ann said. "Find out *why* they think Curtis was the killer. Then show them how they might be wrong and get them to change what they said. We got the truth on our side, Mr. Nudger. At least one witness will change his story when he's made to think about it, because Curtis wasn't where they said he was."

"Curtis has exhausted all his appeals," Nudger said. "Even if all the witnesses changed their stories, it wouldn't necessarily mean he'd get a new trial."

"Maybe not, but I betcha they wouldn't kill him. They couldn't stand the publicity if enough witnesses said they was wrong, it was somebody else killed the old woman. Then, just maybe, eventually, he'd get another trial and get out of prison."

Nudger was awed. Here was foolish optimism that transcended even his own. He had to admire Holly Ann.

The leg started pumping again beneath the cornflower-colored dress. When Nudger lowered his gaze to stare at it, Holly Ann said, "So will you help me, Mr. Nudger?"

"Sure. It sounds easy."

"Why should I worry about it anymore?" Randy Gantner asked Nudger, leaning on his shovel. He didn't mind talking to Nudger; it meant a break from his construction job on the new Interstate 170 cloverleaf. "Colt's been found guilty and he's going to the chair, ain't he?"

The afternoon sun was hammering down on Nudger, warming the back of his neck and making his stomach queasy. He thumbed an antacid tablet off the roll he kept in his shirt pocket and popped one of the white disks into his mouth. With his other hand, he was holding up a photograph of Curtis Colt for Gantner to see. It was a snapshot Holly Ann had given him of the wiry, shirtless Colt leaning on a fence post and holding a beer can high in a mock toast: this one's for Death!

"This is a photograph you never saw in court. I just want you to look at it closely and tell me again if you're sure the man you saw in the liquor store was Colt. Even if it makes no difference in whether he's executed, it will help ease the mind of somebody who loves him."

"I'd be a fool to change my story about what happened now that the trial's over," Gantner said logically.

"You'd be a murderer if you really weren't sure."

Gantner sighed, dragged a dirty red handkerchief from his jeans pocket, and wiped his beefy, perspiring face. He peered at the photo, then shrugged. "It's him, Colt, the guy I seen shoot the man and woman when I was standing in the back aisle of the liquor store. If he'd known me and Sanders was back there, he'd have probably zapped us along with them old folks."

"You're positive it's the same man?"

Gantner spat off to the side and frowned; Nudger was becoming a pest, and the foreman was staring. "I said it to the police and the jury, Nudger; that little twerp Colt did the old lady in. Ask me, he deserves what he's gonna get."

"Did you actually see the shots fired?"

"Nope. Me and Sanders was in the back aisle looking for some reasonable-priced bourbon when we heard the shots, then looked around to see Curtis Colt back away, turn, and run out to the car. Looked like a black or dark green old Ford. Colt fired another shot as it drove away."

"Did you see the driver?"

"Sort of. Skinny dude with curly black hair and a mustache. That's what I told the cops. That's all I seen. That's all I know."

And that was the end of the conversation. The foreman was walking toward them, glaring. *Thunk!* Gantner's shovel sliced deep into the earth, speeding the day when there'd be another place for traffic to get backed up. Nudger thanked him and advised him not to work too hard in the hot sun.

"You wanna help?" Gantner asked, grinning sweatily.

"I'm already doing some digging of my own," Nudger said, walking away before the foreman arrived.

The other witnesses also stood by their identifications. The fourth and last one Nudger talked with, an elderly woman named Iris Langeneckert, who had been walking her dog near the liquor store and had seen Curtis Colt dash out the door and into the getaway car, said something that Gantner had touched on. When she'd described the getaway car driver, like Gantner she said he was a thin man with curly black hair and a beard or mustache, then she had added, "Like Curtis Colt's hair and mustache."

Nudger looked again at the snapshot Holly Ann had given him. Curtis Colt was about five foot nine, skinny, and mean-looking, with a broad bandito mustache and a

mop of curly, greasy black hair. Nudger wondered if it
was possible that the getaway car driver had been Curtis
Colt himself, and his accomplice had killed the shop-
keeper. Even Nudger found that one hard to believe.

He drove to his second-floor office in the near suburb of
Maplewood and sat behind his desk in the blast of cold
air from the window unit, sipping the complimentary paper cup of iced tea he'd brought up from Danny's Donuts
directly below. The sweet smell of the doughnuts was
heavier than usual in the office; Nudger had never quite
gotten used to it and what it did to his sensitive stomach.

When he was cool enough to think clearly again, he
decided he needed more information on the holdup, and
on Curtis Colt, from a more objective source than Holly
Ann Adams. He phoned Lieutenant Jack Hammersmith at
home and was told by Hammersmith's son Jed that Hammersmith had just driven away to go to work on the afternoon shift, so it would be a while before he got to his
office.

Nudger checked his answering machine, proving that
hope did indeed spring eternal in a fool's breast. There
was a terse message from his former wife, Eileen, demanding last month's alimony payment; a solemn-voiced
young man reading an address where Nudger could send
a check to help pay to form a watchdog committee that
would stop the utilities from continually raising their
rates; and a cheerful man informing Nudger that with the
labels from ten packages of a brand-name hot dog he could
get a Cardinals' ballgame ticket at half price. (That meant
eating over eighty hot dogs. Nudger calculated that baseball season would be over by the time he did that.) Everyone seemed to want some of Nudger's money. No one
wanted to pay Nudger any money. Except for Holly Ann
Adams. Nudger decided he'd better step up his efforts on
the Curtis Colt case.

He tilted back his head, downed the last dribble of iced tea, then tried to eat what was left of the crushed ice. But the ice clung stubbornly to the bottom of the cup, taunting him. Nudger's life was like that.

He crumpled up the paper cup and tossed it, ice and all, into the wastebasket. Then he went downstairs where his Volkswagen was parked in the shade behind the building and drove east on Manchester, toward downtown and the Third District station house.

Police Lieutenant Jack Hammersmith was in his Third District office, sleek, obese, and cool-looking behind his wide metal desk. He was pounds and years away from the handsome cop who'd been Nudger's partner a decade ago in a two-man patrol car. Nudger could still see traces of a dashing quality in the flesh-upholstered Hammersmith, but he wondered if that was only because he'd known Hammersmith ten years ago.

"Sit down, Nudge," Hammersmith invited, his lips smiling but his slate gray, cop's eyes unreadable. If eyes were the windows to the soul, his shades were always down.

Nudger sat in one of the straight-backed chairs in front of Hammersmith's desk. "I need some help," he said.

"Sure," Hammersmith said, "you never come see me just to trade recipes or to sit and rock." Hammersmith was partial to irony; it was a good thing, in his line of work.

"I need to know more about Curtis Colt," Nudger said.

Hammersmith got one of his vile greenish cigars out of his shirt pocket and stared intently at it, as if its paper ring label might reveal some secret of life and death. "Colt, eh? The guy who's going to ride the lightning?"

"That's the second time in the past few days I've heard

that expression. The first time was from Colt's fiancée. She thinks he's innocent."

"Fiancées think along those lines. Is she your client?"

Nudger nodded but didn't volunteer Holly Ann's name.

"Gullibility makes the world go round," Hammersmith said. "I was in charge of the Homicide investigation on that one. There's not a chance Colt is innocent, Nudge."

"Four eyewitness I.D.'s is compelling evidence," Nudger admitted. "What about the getaway car driver? His description is a lot like Colt's. Maybe he's the one who did the shooting and Colt was the driver."

"Colt's lawyer hit on that. The jury didn't buy it. Neither do I. The man is guilty, Nudge."

"You know how inaccurate eyewitness accounts are," Nudger persisted.

That seemed to get Hammersmith mad. He lit the cigar. The office immediately fogged up.

Nudger made his tone more amicable. "Mind if I look at the file on the Colt case?"

Hammersmith gazed thoughtfully at Nudger through a dense greenish haze. He inhaled, exhaled; the haze became a cloud. "How come this fiancée didn't turn up at the trial to testify for Colt? She could have at least lied and said he was with her that night."

"Colt apparently didn't want her subjected to taking the stand."

"How noble," Hammersmith said. "What makes this fiancée think her prince charming is innocent?"

"She knows he was somewhere else when the shopkeepers were shot."

"But not with her?"

"Nope."

"Well, that's refreshing."

Maybe it was refreshing enough to make up Hammersmith's mind. He picked up the phone and asked for the

Colt file. Nudger could barely make out what he was saying around the fat cigar, but apparently everyone at the
Third was used to Hammersmith and could interpret
cigarese.

The file didn't reveal much that Nudger didn't know.
Fifteen minutes after the liquor store shooting, officers
from a two-man patrol car, acting on the broadcast description of the gunman, approached Curtis Colt inside a
service station where he was buying a pack of cigarettes
from a vending machine. A car that had been parked near
the end of the dimly lighted lot had sped away as they'd
entered the station office. The officers had gotten only a
glimpse of a dark green old Ford; they hadn't made out
the license plate number but thought it might start with
the letter L.

Colt had surrendered without a struggle, and that night
at the Third District Station the four eyewitnesses had
picked him out of a lineup. Their description of the getaway car matched that of the car the police had seen
speeding from the service station. The loot from the
holdup, and several gas station holdups committed earlier that night, wasn't on Colt, but probably it was in the
car.

"Colt's innocence just jumps out of the file at you,
doesn't it, Nudge?" Hammersmith said. He was grinning
a fat grin around the fat cigar.

"What about the murder weapon?"

"Colt was unarmed when we picked him up."

"Seems odd."

"Not really," Hammersmith said. "He was planning to
pay for the cigarettes. And maybe the gun was still too hot
to touch so he left it in the car. Maybe it's still hot; it got
a lot of use for one night."

Closing the file folder and laying it on a corner of Hammersmith's desk, Nudger stood up. "Thanks, Jack. I'll keep you tapped in if I learn anything interesting."

"Don't bother keeping me informed on this one, Nudge. It's over. I don't see how even a fiancée can doubt Colt's guilt."

Nudger shrugged, trying not to breathe too deeply in the smoke-hazed office. "Maybe it's an emotional thing. She thinks that because thought waves are tiny electrical impulses, Colt might experience time warp and all sorts of grotesque thoughts when all that voltage shoots through him. She has bad dreams."

"I'll bet she does," Hammersmith said. "I'll bet Colt has bad dreams, too. Only he deserves his. And maybe she's right."

"About what?"

"About all that voltage distorting thought and time. Who's to say?"

"Not Curtis Colt," Nudger said. "Not after they throw the switch."

"It's a nice theory, though," Hammersmith said. "I'll remember it. It might be a comforting thing to tell the murder victim's family."

"Sometimes," Nudger said, "you think just like a cop who's seen too much."

"Any of it's too much, Nudge," Hammersmith said with surprising sadness. He let more greenish smoke drift from his nostrils and the corners of his mouth; he looked like a stone Buddha seated behind the desk, one in which incense burned.

Nudger coughed and said goodbye.

"Only two eyewitnesses are needed to convict," Nudger said to Holly Ann the next day in her trailer, "and in this case there are four. None of them is at all in doubt about their identification of Curtis Colt as the killer. I have to be honest; it's time you should face the fact that Colt is guilty and that you're wasting your money on my services."

"All them witnesses know what's going to happen to Curtis," Holly Ann said. "They'd never want to live with the notion they might have made a mistake, killed an innocent man, so they've got themselves convinced that they're positive it was Curtis they saw that night."

"Your observation on human psychology is sound," Nudger said, "but I don't think it will help us. The witnesses were just as certain three months ago at the trial. I took the time to read the court transcript; the jury had no choice but to find Colt guilty, and the evidence hasn't changed."

Holly Ann drew her legs up and clasped her knees to her chest with both arms. Her little-girl posture matched her little-girl faith in her lover's innocence. She believed the white knight must arrive at any moment and snatch Curtis Colt from the electrical jaws of death. She believed hard. Nudger could almost hear his armor clank when he walked.

She wanted him to believe just as hard. "I see you need to be convinced of Curtis's innocence," she said wistfully. There was no doubt he'd forced her into some kind of corner. "If you come here tonight at eight, Mr. Nudger, I'll convince you."

"How?"

"I can't say. You'll understand why tonight."

"Why do we have to wait till tonight?"

"Oh, you'll see."

Nudger looked at the waiflike creature curled in the corner of the sofa. He felt as if they were playing a childhood guessing game while Curtis Colt waited his turn in the electric chair. Nudger had never seen an execution; he'd heard it took longer than most people thought for the condemned to die. His stomach actually twitched.

"Can't we do this now with twenty questions?" he asked.

Holly Ann shook her head. "No, Mr. Nudger."

Nudger sighed and stood up, feeling as if he were about to bump his head on the trailer's low ceiling even though he was barely six feet tall.

"Make sure you're on time tonight, Mr. Nudger," Holly Ann said as he went out the door. "It's important."

At eight on the nose that evening Nudger was sitting at the tiny table in Holly Ann's kitchenette. Across from him was a thin, nervous man in his late twenties or early thirties, dressed in a longsleeved shirt despite the heat, and wearing sunglasses with silver mirror lenses. Holly Ann introduced the man as "Len, but that's not his real name," and said he was Curtis Colt's accomplice and the driver of their getaway car on the night of the murder.

"But me and Curtis was nowhere near the liquor store when them folks got shot," Len said vehemently.

Nudger assumed the sunglasses were so he couldn't effectively identify Len if it came to a showdown in court. Len had lank, dark brown hair that fell to below his shoulders, and when he moved his arm Nudger caught sight of something blue and red on his briefly exposed wrist. A tattoo. Which explained the longsleeved shirt.

"You can understand why Len couldn't come forth and testify for Curtis in court," Holly Ann said.

Nudger said he could understand that. Len would have had to incriminate himself.

"We was way on the other side of town," Len said, "casing another service station, when that liquor store killing went down. Heck, we never held up nothing but service stations. They was our specialty."

Which was true, Nudger had to admit. Colt had done time for armed robbery six years ago after sticking up half a dozen service stations within a week. And all the other holdups he'd been tied to this time around were of service stations. The liquor store was definitely a departure in his M.O., one not noted in court during Curtis Colt's rush to judgment.

"Your hair is in your favor," Nudger said to Len.

"Huh?"

"Your hair didn't grow that long in the three months since the liquor store killing. The witnesses described the getaway car driver as having shorter, curlier hair, like Colt's, and a mustache."

Len shrugged. "I'll be honest with you—it don't help at all. Me and Curtis was kinda the same type. So to confuse any witnesses, in case we got caught, we made each other look even more alike. I'd tuck up my long hair and wear a wig that looked like Curtis's hair. My mustache was real, like Curtis's. I shaved it off a month ago. We did look alike at a glance; sorta like brothers."

Nudger bought that explanation; it wasn't uncommon for a team of holdup men to play tricks to confuse witnesses and the police. Too many lawyers had gotten in the game; the robbers, like the cops, were taking the advice of their attorneys and thinking about a potential trial even before the crime was committed.

"Is there any way, then, to prove you were across town at the time of the murder?" Nudger asked, looking at the two small Nudgers staring back at him from the mirror lenses.

"There's just my word," Len said, rather haughtily.

Nudger didn't bother telling him what that was worth. Why antagonize him?

"I just want you to believe Curtis is innocent," Len said with desperation. "Because he is! And so am I!"

And Nudger understood why Len was here, taking the risk. If Colt was guilty of murder, Len was guilty of being an accessory to the crime. Once Curtis Colt had ridden the lightning, Len would have hanging over him the possibility of an almost certain life sentence, and perhaps even his own ride on the lightning, if he were ever caught. It wasn't necessary to actually squeeze the trigger to be convicted of murder.

"I need for you to try extra hard to prove Curtis is innocent," Len said. His thin lips quivered; he was near tears.

"Are you giving Holly Ann the money to pay me?" Nudger asked.

"Some of it, yeah. From what Curtis and me stole. And I gave Curtis's share to Holly Ann, too. Me and her are fifty-fifty on this."

Dirty money, Nudger thought. Dirty job. Still, if Curtis Colt happened to be innocent, trying against the clock to prove it was a job that needed to be done.

"Okay. I'll stay on the case."

"Thanks," Len said. His narrow hand moved impulsively across the table and squeezed Nudger's arm in gratitude. Len had the look of an addict; Nudger wondered if the longsleeved shirt was to hide needle tracks as well as the tattoo.

Len stood up. "Stay here with Holly Ann for ten minutes while I make myself scarce. I gotta know I wasn't followed. You understand it ain't that I don't trust you; a man in my position has gotta be sure, is all."

"I understand. Go."

Len gave a spooked smile and went out the door. Nudger heard his running footfalls on the gravel outside the trailer. Nudger was forty-three years old and ten pounds overweight; lean and speedy Len needed a ten-minute head start like Sinatra needed singing lessons.

"Is Len a user?" Nudger asked Holly Ann.

"Sometimes. But my Curtis never touched no dope."

"You know I have to tell the police about this conversation, don't you?"

Holly Ann nodded. "That's why we arranged it this way. They won't be any closer to Len than before."

"They might want to talk to you, Holly Ann."

She shrugged. "It don't matter. I don't know where Len is, nor even his real name nor how to get in touch with him. He'll find out all he needs to know about Curtis by reading the papers."

"You have a deceptively devious mind," Nudger told her, "considering that you look like Barbie Doll's country kid cousin."

Holly Ann smiled, surprised and pleased. "Do you find me attractive, Mr. Nudger?"

"Yes. And painfully young."

For just a moment Nudger almost thought of Curtis Colt as a lucky man. Then he looked at his watch, saw that his ten minutes were about up, and said goodbye. If Barbie had a kid cousin, Ken probably had one somewhere, too. And time was something you couldn't deny. Ask Curtis Colt.

"It doesn't wash with me," Hammersmith said from behind his desk, puffing angrily on his cigar. Angrily because it did wash a little bit; he didn't like the possibility, however remote, of sending an innocent man to his death. That was every good homicide cop's nightmare. "This Len character is just trying to keep himself in the clear on a murder charge."

"You could read it that way," Nudger admitted.

"It would help if you gave us a better description of Len," Hammersmith said gruffly, as if Nudger were to blame for Curtis Colt's accomplice still walking around free.

"I gave you what I could," Nudger said. "Len didn't

give me much to pass on. He's streetwise and scared and knows what's at stake."

Hammersmith nodded, his fit of pique past. But the glint of weary frustration remained in his eyes.

"Are you going to question Holly Ann?" Nudger said.

"Sure, but it won't do any good. She's probably telling the truth. Len would figure we'd talk to her; he wouldn't tell her how to find him."

"You could stake out her trailer."

"Do you think Holly Ann and Len might be lovers?"

"No."

Hammersmith shook his head. "Then they'll probably never see each other again. Watching her trailer would be a waste of manpower."

Nudger knew Hammersmith was right. He stood up to go.

"What are you going to do now?" Hammersmith asked.

"I'll talk to the witnesses again. I'll read the court transcript again. And I'd like to talk to Curtis Colt."

"They don't allow visitors on Death Row, Nudge, only temporary boarders."

"This case is an exception," Nudger said. "Will you try to arrange it?"

Hammersmith chewed thoughtfully on his cigar. Since he'd been the officer in charge of the murder investigation, he'd been the one who'd nailed Curtis Colt. That carried an obligation.

"I'll phone you soon," he said, "let you know."

Nudger thanked Hammersmith and walked down the hall into the clear, breathable air of the booking area.

That day he managed to talk again to all four eyewitnesses. Two of them got mad at Nudger for badgering them. They all stuck to their stories. Nudger reported this to Holly Ann at the Right-Steer Steakhouse, where she worked as a waitress. Several customers that afternoon got tears with their baked potatoes.

Hammersmith phoned Nudger that evening.

"I managed to get permission for you to talk to Colt," he said, "but don't get excited. Colt won't talk to you. He won't talk to anyone, not even a clergyman. He'll change his mind about the clergyman, but not about you."

"Did you tell him I was working for Holly Ann?"

"I had that information conveyed to him. He wasn't impressed. He's one of the stoic ones on Death Row."

Nudger's stomach kicked up, growled something that sounded like a hopeless obscenity. If even Curtis Colt wouldn't cooperate, how could he be helped? Absently Nudger peeled back the aluminum foil on a roll of antacid tablets and slipped two chalky white disks into his mouth. Hammersmith knew about his nervous stomach and must have heard him chomping the tablets. "Take it easy, Nudge. This isn't your fault."

"Then why do I feel like it is?"

"Because you feel too much of everything. That's why you had to quit the department."

"We've got another day before the execution," Nudger said. "I'm going to go through it all again. I'm going to talk to each of those witnesses even if they try to run when they see me coming. Maybe somebody will say something that will let in some light."

"There's no light out there, Nudge. You're wasting your time. Give up on this one and move on."

"Not yet," Nudger said. "There's something elusive here that I can't quite grab."

"And never will," Hammersmith said. "Forget it, Nudge. Live your life and let Curtis Colt lose his."

Hammersmith was right. Nothing Nudger did helped Curtis Colt in the slightest. At eight o'clock Saturday morning, while Nudger was preparing breakfast in his apartment, Colt was put to death in the electric chair. He'd offered no last words before two thousand volts had turned him from something into nothing.

Nudger heard the news of Colt's death on his kitchen radio. He went ahead and ate his eggs, but he skipped the toast.

That afternoon he consoled a numbed and frequently sobbing Holly Ann and apologized for being powerless to stop her true love's execution. She was polite, trying to be brave. She preferred to suffer alone. Her boss at the Right-Steer gave her the rest of the day off, and Nudger drove her home.

Nudger slept a total of four hours during the next two nights. On Monday, he felt compelled to attend Curtis Colt's funeral. There were about a dozen people clustered around the grave, including the state-appointed clergyman and pallbearers. Nudger stood off to one side during the brief service. Holly Ann, looking like a child playing dress-up in black, stood well off to the other side. They didn't exchange words, only glances.

As the coffin was lowered into the earth, Nudger watched Holly Ann walk to where a taxi was waiting by a weathered stone angel. The cab wound its way slowly along the snaking narrow cemetery road to tall iron gates and the busy street. Holly Ann never looked back.

That night Nudger realized what was bothering him, and for the first time since Curtis Colt's death, he slept well.

In the morning he began watching Holly Ann's trailer.

At seven-thirty she emerged, dressed in her yellow waitress uniform, and got into another taxi. Nudger followed in his battered Volkswagen Beetle as the cab drove her the four miles to her job at the Right-Steer Steakhouse. She didn't look around as she paid the driver and walked inside through the molded plastic Old-West-saloon swinging doors.

At six that evening another cab drove her home, making a brief stop at a grocery store.

It went that way for the rest of the week, trailer to work to trailer. Holly Ann had no visitors other than the plain brown paper bag she took home every night.

The temperature got up to around ninety-five and the humidity rose right along with it. It was one of St. Louis's legendary summer heat waves. Sitting melting in the Volkswagen, Nudger wondered if what he was doing was really worthwhile. Curtis Colt was, after all, dead, and had never been his client. Still, there were responsibilities that went beyond the job. Or perhaps they were actually the essence of the job.

The next Monday, after Holly Ann had left for work, Nudger used his Visa card to slip the flimsy lock on her trailer door, and let himself in.

It took him over an hour to find what he was searching for. It had been well hidden, in a cardboard box inside the access panel to the bathroom plumbing. After looking at the box's contents—almost seven hundred dollars in loot from Curtis Colt's brief life of crime, and another object Nudger wasn't surprised to see—Nudger resealed the box and replaced the access panel.

He continued to watch and follow Holly Ann, more confident now.

Two weeks after the funeral, when she left work one evening, she didn't go home.

Instead her taxi turned the opposite way and drove east on Watson Road. Nudger followed the cab along a series of side streets in South St. Louis, then part way down a dead-end alley to a large garage, above the door of which was lettered "Clifford's Auto Body."

Nudger backed out quickly onto the street, then parked the Volkswagen near the mouth of the alley. A few minutes later the cab drove by without a passenger. Within ten minutes, Holly Ann drove past in a shiny red Ford. Its license plate number began with an L.

When Nudger reached Placid Cove Trailer Park, he saw the Ford nosed in next to Holly Ann's trailer.

On the way to the trailer door, he paused and scratched the Ford's hood with a key. Even in the lowering evening light he could see that beneath the new red paint the car's color was dark green.

Holly Ann answered the door right away when he knocked. She tried a smile when she saw it was him, but she couldn't quite manage her facial muscles, as if they'd become rigid and uncoordinated. She appeared ten years older. The little-girl look had deserted her; now she was an emaciated, grief-eroded woman, a country Barbie doll whose features some evil child had lined with dark crayon. The shaded crescents beneath her eyes completely took away their innocence. She was holding a glass that had once been a jelly jar. In it were two fingers of a clear liquid. Behind her on the table was a crumpled brown paper bag and a half-empty bottle of gin.

"I figured it out," Nudger told her.

Now she did smile, but it was fleeting, a sickly bluish shadow crossing her taut features. "You're like a dog with a rag, Mr. Nudger. You surely don't know when to let go." She stepped back and he followed her into the trailer. It was warm in there; something was wrong with the air conditioner. "Hot as hell, ain't it," Holly Ann commented. Nudger thought that was apropos.

He sat down across from her at the tiny Formica table, just as he and Len had sat facing each other two weeks ago. She offered him a drink. He declined. She downed the contents of the jelly jar glass and poured herself another, clumsily striking the neck of the bottle on the glass. It made a sharp, flinty sound, as if sparks might fly.

"Now, what's this you've got figured out, Mr. Nudger?" She didn't want to, but she had to hear it. Had to share it.

"It's almost four miles to the Right-Steer Steakhouse," Nudger told her. "The waitresses there make little more than minimum wage, so cab fare to and from work has to eat a big hole in your salary. But then you seem to go everywhere by cab."

"My car's been in the shop."

"I figured it might be, after I found the money and the wig."

She bowed her head slightly and took a sip of gin. "Wig?"

"In the cardboard box inside the bathroom wall."

"You been snooping, Mr. Nudger." There was more resignation than outrage in her voice.

"You're sort of skinny, but not a short girl," Nudger went on. "With a dark curly wig and a fake mustache, sitting in a car, you'd resemble Curtis Colt enough to fool a dozen eyewitnesses who just caught a glimpse of you. It was a smart precaution for the two of you to take."

Holly Ann looked astounded.

"Are you saying I was driving the getaway car at the liquor store holdup?"

"Maybe. Then maybe you hired someone to play Len and convince me he was Colt's accomplice and that they were far away from the murder scene when the trigger was pulled. After I found the wig, I talked to some of your neighbors, who told me that until recently you'd driven a green Ford sedan."

Holly Ann ran her tongue along the edges of her protruding teeth.

"So Curtis and Len used my car for the holdups."

"I doubt if Len ever met Curtis. He's somebody you

paid in stolen money or drugs to sit there where you're sitting now and lie to me."

"If I was driving that getaway car, Mr. Nudger, and knew Curtis was guilty, why would I have hired a private investigator to try to find a hole in the eyewitnesses' stories?"

"That's what bothered me at first," Nudger said, "until I realized you weren't interested in clearing Curtis. What you were really worried about was Curtis Colt talking in prison. You didn't want those witnesses' stories changed, you wanted them verified. And you wanted the police to learn about not-his-right-name Len."

Holly Ann raised her head to look directly at him with eyes that begged and dreaded. She asked simply, "Why would I want that?"

"Because you were Curtis Colt's accomplice in all of his robberies. And when you hit the liquor store, he stayed in the car to drive. You fired the shot that killed the old woman. He was the one who fired the wild shot from the speeding car. Colt kept quiet about it because he loved you. He never talked, not to the police, not to his lawyer, not even to a priest. Now that he's dead you can trust him forever, but I have a feeling you could have anyway. He loved you more than you loved him, and you'll have to live knowing he didn't deserve to die."

She looked down into her glass as if for answers and didn't say anything for a long time. Nudger felt a bead of perspiration trickle crazily down the back of his neck. Then she said, "I didn't want to shoot that old man, but he didn't leave me no choice. Then the old woman came at me." She looked up at Nudger and smiled ever so slightly. It was a smile Nudger hadn't seen on her before, one he didn't like. "God help me, Mr. Nudger, I can't quit thinking about shooting that old woman."

"You murdered her," Nudger said, "and you murdered

Curtis Colt by keeping silent and letting him die for you.''

"You can't prove nothing," Holly Ann said, still with her ancient-eyed, eerie smile that had nothing to do with amusement.

"You're right," Nudger told her, "I can't. But I don't think legally proving it is necessary, Holly Ann. You said it: thoughts are actually tiny electrical impulses in the brain. Curtis Colt rode the lightning all at once. With you, it will take years, but the destination is the same. I think you'll come to agree that his way was easier."

She sat very still. She didn't answer. Wasn't going to.

Nudger stood up and wiped his damp forehead with the back of his hand. He felt sticky, dirty, confined by the low ceiling and near walls of the tiny, stifling trailer. He had to get out of there to escape the sensation of being trapped.

He didn't say goodbye to Holly Ann when he walked out. She didn't say goodbye to him. The last sound Nudger heard as he left the trailer was the clink of the bottle on the glass.

ROBERT SAMPSON

Rain in Pinton County

1986

Fat raindrops rapped circles across puddles the color of rusty iron. Ed Ralston, special assistant to the sheriff, said, " 'Scuse me," and pushed through the rain-soaked farmers staring toward the house. Ducking under the yellow plastic strip—CRIME SCENE, KEEP OUT—that bordered the road, he followed the driveway up past a brown sedan, mud-splashed and marked "Sheriff's Patrol."

Behind him, a voice drawled, "He's her brother."

The house, painted dark green and white, sat fifty feet back from the country road. That road arced behind him across farmland to hills fringed darkly with pine. Black cattle peppered a distant field. The air was cold.

In the rear parking lot, a second patrol car sat beside a square white van with "Pinton County Emergency Squad" painted across the state outline of Alabama. On the shallow porch, a deputy in a black slicker watched rain beat into the yard.

Ralston said, "Punk day, Johnny. Fleming get here yet?"

The deputy shook his head. "They're still calling for him. Broucel's handling things inside." And, as the door opened, "I'm sure as hell sorry, Ed."

"Thanks."

He entered a narrow kitchen, went through it to a dark hallway that smelled faintly of dog, turned left into the front room. There a handful of men watched the photographers put away their gear.

When he entered the room, their voices hesitated and softened, as if a volume control had been touched. Men stepped forward, hands out, voices low: "Sorry. Sorry. Ed, I'm real sorry."

He crossed the familiar room, keeping to a wide plastic strip laid across the beige carpet. He shook hands with a little, narrow-faced man who looked as if he had missed a lot of meals. "Morning, Nick."

"Sorry as hell about this, Ed," Nick Broucel said.

Ralston nodded. His glasses had fogged, and he began rubbing them with a piece of tissue that left white particles on the glass. Without the glasses, his eyes seemed too narrow, too widely separated for his long face. His dark hair was already receding. Scowling at the flecks on his glasses, he said, "Well, I guess I better look at her."

A gray blanket covered a figure stretched out by the fireplace. Ralston twitched back a corner, exposing a woman's calm face. Her hair was pale blond, her face long, her lipstick bright pink and smudged. On the bloodless skin, patches of eye and cheek makeup glared like plastic decals.

He looked down into the face without feeling anything. There was no connection between the painted thing under the blanket and his sister, Sue Ralston, who lived in his mind, undisciplined, sharp-tongued, merry.

He stripped back the blanket. She was elaborately dressed in an expensive blue outfit, earrings and necklace, heels; nails glittered on hands crossed under her breasts. "Well, now," he said at last. "It's Sue. What happened?"

Nick said, "She went over backward. Hit her head on

the corner of the fireplace. Pure bad luck. Somebody moved her away. Smoothed her clothes. Folded her hands. Somebody surprised, I'd say."

"Somebody shoved her and she fell?"

"Could be."

"Or she just slipped."

"Could be."

Rain nibbled at the windows. The investigative work had started now, and the room squirmed with men standing, bending, looking, methodically searching for any scrap of fact to account for that stillness under the gray blanket.

Ralston asked, "Why the full crew? How'd we hear about this?"

"Anonymous call. Male. Logged at 5:32 this morning. Gave route and box number. Said the bodies were here."

"Bodies? More than one?"

"Not so far." Broucel looked sour and ill at ease. "This is Fleming's job, not mine. I'm just marking time here. I don't know where the hell he's got to. Where's the sheriff?"

Ralston said carefully, "He's taking a couple of days' vacation." He slowly scanned the room. Money had been freshly spent here, money not much controlled by taste. New blue brocade chairs bulked too large for the room. The couch seethed with flowered cushions. The lamps were fat glass creations with distorted shades. Tissues smeared with lipstick scattered a leather-topped coffee table.

"And there's something else," Broucel said.

He gestured toward the shelves flanking the fireplace. Cassettes of country music littered the bottom shelves. On upper shelves clustered carved wooden animals, ceramic pots, weed vases. Centered on the top shelf was the photograph of a grinning young man. It was inscribed "To Sue, With Ever More Love, Tommy."

"You recognize that kid?" Broucel asked.

"Isn't that Tommy Richardson? His daddy owns the south half of the county."

"That's the one."

"Daddy's going to enforce the dry laws, jail the bootleggers, clean up the sheriff's department—come elections. That's a mike, isn't it?"

"Yes, sir, that's a mike."

A fat wooden horse had tumbled from the second shelf. Its fall had exposed the black button of a microphone, the line vanishing back behind the shelves.

In a slow, reflective voice, Ralston said, "Sue never had a damn bit of sense."

"Let's go down in the basement," Broucel told him.

Steep wooden stairs took them to a cool room running the length of the house. Windows along the east foundation emitted pallid light. Behind the gas furnace, a small chair and table crowded against the wall and black cables snaked out of the ceiling to connect a silver-gray amplifier and cassette tape recorder. On the table, three cassette cases lay open and empty, like the transparent egg cases of insects.

Broucel said, "We found three mikes. About any place you cough upstairs, down it goes on tape."

Ralston gestured irritably at the equipment. "I don't understand this. She didn't think this way. She couldn't turn on the TV. Why this?"

Broucel fingered his mouth, said in a hesitant voice, "I sort of hoped you could help me out on that."

"I can't. I don't know. We didn't speak but once a year."

"Your own sister?"

"My own damnfool sister. She had no sense. But she had more sense than this."

"Somebody put this rig in. She had to know about it."

"Must have," Ralston agreed. "Must have. But what do I know? I'm no investigator. I'm a spoiled newspaper man. My job's explaining what the sheriff thought he said."

Feet hammered down the stairway. A deputy in a dripping slicker thumped into the basement, excitement patching his face red. He yelped, "Nick, we found Fleming."

Broucel snapped, "Where the hell's he . . ."

"He's in his car, quarter of a mile down the road. Tucked in behind the brush. Rittenhoff saw it. Fleming's shot right through the head."

Broucel sucked in his breath. He became a little more thin, a little more gray. "Dead?"

"Dead, yeah. He's getting stiff."

"Oh, my God," Broucel said. His mouth twitched. He put two fingers over his lips, as his eyes jerked around to Ralston.

Who said, with hard satisfaction, "I guess we're going to have to interrupt the sheriff's vacation."

He drove his blue Honda fast across twelve miles of back-country road. A thick gray sky, seamed with deeper gray and black, wallowed overhead. Thunder complained behind the pines.

He felt anger turn in him, an orange-red ball hot behind his ribs. Not anger about Sue. That part remained cold, sealed, separate. It's Piggott's doing, he thought. Piggott, Piggott, Piggott the beer runner and liquor trucker, the gambler, briber, the sheriff's poker-playing buddy. Now blackmailer. What else? And Sue's very particular good friend, thank you.

Whatever Piggott suggested, she would, bright-eyed, laughing, follow. No thought. No foresight. Do what you want today, ha ha. More fun again tomorrow.

When he last visited her, they had quarreled about Piggott.

"He's lots of fun," she said loudly. Her voice always rose with her temper. "He's interesting. He's different all the time. You never know with him."

"You always know. He'll always go for the crooked buck. He handles beer for six dry counties. He owns better than two thousand shot houses. He's broke heads all over the state. Even a blond lunatic knows better than to climb the sty to kiss the pig."

It ended in a shouting match. She told Piggott the next day, with quotations, and Piggott told Ralston and the sheriff the day after.

"A full-time liar and a postage-stamp Capone." Piggott pushed back in his leather chair and yelled with laughter. "I swear, Ed, I didn't know I was that good."

"Hardly good," Ralston said.

The sheriff's eyes, like frosted glass, glared silence.

Ralston said, "Look, Piggott, Sue's just a nice, empty-headed kid. She sees the fun, but she don't smell the dirt. She's got no sense of self-protection. She's different."

Piggott swabbed his laughing mouth with a handkerchief and straightened in his old leather chair. Amusement warmed his face. "I know she's different. I'm going to marry her, Ed."

The Honda reeled on the road. He jerked the wheel straight. It was not quite nine o'clock in the morning and cold, and the road twisted as complexly as his thoughts.

Two miles from the highway the fields smoothed out, bordered by white fencing that might have been transplanted from a Kentucky horse farm. When the fence reared to an elaborate entrance, he turned right along a crushed-gravel road gray with rain. A square, big house loomed sternly white behind evergreen and magnolia. In the parking lot, two Continentals and a dark green BMW sat like all the money in the world. Rain sprinkled his glasses. As he walked across the road to a porch set with frigid white ornamental-iron chairs, the front door swung open to meet him. A slight man with very light blue eyes and a chin like a knife point waved him in.

"Out early, Ed."

Ralston nodded. "I need the sheriff bad, Elmer."

"He just got to bed."

"Tough. Tell him it's official and urgent."

The man behind Elmer snorted and showed his teeth. "Official and urgent," he said, arrogantly contemptuous. He was thick-shouldered, heavy-bodied, round-faced, and scowled at Ralston with raw dislike.

Elmer said, "I can't promise. The game lasted all night. You and Buddy mind waiting here?"

He stepped quietly away down a high white hallway lined with mirrors and horse paintings. The hall, running the length of the house, was intercepted halfway by a broad staircase. Beyond lounged a man with a news-paper, his presence signifying that Piggott was in.

A sharp blow jarred his arm. He turned to see Buddy's cocked fist.

"We got time for a couple of rounds, Champ."

Ralston said, "Crap off."

Buddy, hunched over shuffling feet, punched again. "Ain't he bad this morning." Malice rose from him like visible fumes. "The sheriff's little champ's real bad. Cou-ple of rounds do you good. You lucked out, that last time."

"You got a glass jaw," Ralston said.

Elmer appeared on the stairway to the second floor. He jerked his hand, called, "Come on up."

Ralston walked around Buddy, not looking at him.

Buddy, clenching his hands, said distinctly, "You and me's going to have a little talk, sometime."

The second floor was carpeted, dim, silent, expensive, and smelled sourly of cigars. Elmer pointed to a carved wooden door, said, "In there," wheeled back down the hall.

Ralston pushed open the door and looked at Tom Huber, sheriff of Pinton County, sitting on an unmade bed. The sheriff wore a white cotton undershirt, tight over the hairy width of his chest, and vivid green and yellow undershorts. Hangover sallowed his face. He was a solid, hard-muscled old roughneck, with a hawk-nosed look of competence that had been worth eighty thousand votes in the last four elections.

He said, "Talk to me slow, son, I'm still drunk."

Easing the door shut, Ralston said, "Last night, Fleming was shot dead. In his own car. In the country. With his own gun, couple of inches from the right temple. Gun in car. Wiped off. Far as we know, he wasn't on duty. You need to show up out there. Broucel's in charge, and he's got the white shakes."

"Fleming shot?" A slow grin spread the sheriff's mouth. "So that grease-faced little potlicker went and got himself killed. That's not worth getting a man out of bed for. Let Broucel fumble it."

"Fleming was your chief deputy," Ralston said sharply. "You have to make a show. The media's going to crawl all over this. You got to talk to the TV—sheriff swears vengeance. Hell, we got an election coming."

"There's that." The sheriff touched his eyes and shuddered. "Lord a'mighty, I didn't hardly get to sleep. Cards went my way all night."

In a neutral tone, Ralston said, "You don't ever lose, playing at Piggott's."

"That's why I play at Piggott's." He got up carefully. "God, what a head. Well, now, that's one less candidate for the high office of Pinton County Sheriff. Ain't it a shame about poor old Lloyd Fleming?"

He moved heavily into the bathroom to slop water on his head and guzzle from the faucet. Ralston drifted around the bedroom, face somber, peering about curiously, fingering the telephone, light fixtures, pictures.

The sheriff emerged, toweling his head. "I'm scrambling along, Ed. Don't prance around like a mare in heat."

Ralston said, "I need to tell you a little more. But I'll save it. Too many bugs here."

"I counted one," Huber said pleasantly.

"Two, anyhow." He knelt to reach under the airspace of a dresser and jerked. His fingers emerged holding a microphone button and line. It seemed a twin of the one on Sue's shelf. "These may be dummies to fake you off an open phone tap."

The sheriff sighed. "It's hard for an old fellow like me to bend over to squint in every hole. You know, you got to like Piggott. He don't trust nobody."

They returned unescorted to the first floor. "I best make my good-byes," the sheriff said. "Not fit for a guest to leave without he thanks his host for all those blessings."

Ralston followed him to the rear of the white hall. The watcher there, a burly youngster with a face like half a ham, stared at them eagerly. The sheriff asked, "Piggott up?"

"Oh, Lordy, sure," the youngster said. "He don't hardly ever sleep."

He clubbed the door with his fist, opened it, saying, "Mr. Piggott, it's the sheriff."

A cheerful voice bawled, "You tell him to bring himself right in here."

It was a narrow, bright room stretched long under a hammered-tin ceiling. The walls were crowded with filing cabinets and messy bookshelves, stuffed with as many papers and magazines as books. A worn carpet, the color of pecan shells, led to an ancient wooden table flanked by straight-backed chairs. Behind the table, Piggott lolled in an old leather chair.

He bounced up as they entered. He burst around the table, vibrating with enthusiasm, grinning and loud. He had curly black hair over a smooth face, deeply sunburned, and he looked intelligent and deeply pleased to see them. "Didn't expect you up till noon, Tom." He smiled brilliantly. "Lordy, you're tough."

He pounded nervously on the sheriff's shoulders, then seized Ed's arm. "Now you come over here and look at this picture. You'll like this."

He extended a large color photograph. Sue Ralston beamed from it. She stood close to Piggott, arms clutching each other, heads together, delighted with themselves.

Through rigid lips Ralston said, "Nice photo." He felt nauseated.

Piggott burst into his rolling laughter. "That's our engagement photo, Ed. Listen, don't look so sour." His arm slipped around Ralston's shoulders. "It's okay. I'll make a great husband. I grow on you."

Ralston swallowed, standing stiff within the embrace. "Piggott . . ."

" 'S all right, Ed. I know." He smacked Ralston's shoulder amiably. "It's a funny world. Who wants a postage-stamp Capone for a brother-in-law?"

He emitted a howl of joy, throwing back his head, opening the deep hollow of his mouth. "Even us booze merchants fall in love, Ed. We even get married. Ain't it a crime?"

Ralston forced, "Congratulations, then," from his

closed throat. It was now imperative to tell them about Sue. But he could not. He listened to Piggott and the sheriff bantering. He could not.

Piggott had set it up, sometime, for some purpose. And she was dead because of it. Somehow. Set a trap and what dies in it is your own responsibility.

"Fleming!" Piggott was saying. "I can't believe it. Who's Moneybucks Richardson going to run for sheriff now?"

Laughter. The sheriff edged toward the door.

The need to tell them about Sue, the urgency of it, tore at him. At the door, he blundered to a halt, said, "Piggott . . ." Terrible pressure locked his throat. He said, instead, "Piggott—what about that ancy-fancy recording stuff in Sue's basement?"

Fleeting hardness in Piggott's face softened to laughter. He flung out joyous arms. "Wasn't that something. We told some friends we were engaged. Then I went out to the car and let them warn her about me. Then we played the cassettes back to them. Funny! Hell, they'll never speak to me again. Hey, you got to hear those tapes. And they're my good friends."

Joy wrinkled his big face. He bellowed with laughter like a furnace. "I mean, funny."

They sat in the sheriff's car behind Piggott's house. Rain rattled on the hood and glass.

Ed asked, "What are they doing with Tommy Richardson?"

"Son, you probably don't want to know anything about that."

"I got to. It's important." Their eyes met, held, strained, force against force. "Yes," Ralston said. "I mean it's important. It's important to me."

The sheriff shrugged. " 'Tain't but a trifle. They're just

roping the boy a little. Just a little business insurance."

"Business insurance?"

"Why sure. Here's a nice respectable boy gaming around with beer runners. Well, shoot, people game and people have a drink now and then. Least I've known them to do it in Pinton County. Don't expect they'll change. No harm in it, less they get mean. The mean ones is what sheriffing is about. But you can't never tell when sin's going to get a bad name. So maybe old Richardson goes and gets a hard-on against sin. Then they got something for him to listen to while he gets calm. Or maybe not. You can't ever know."

"That's all?"

"All there is. Nothing a'tall."

"Merciful God," Ralston said. "Is that all?"

He got out into the rain. He stood staring blankly, hunching up his shoulders, rain smearing his glasses, distorting the world so that it appeared twisted and in strange focus. He circled the car and tapped the sheriff's window, and rain ran in his hair, wet his forehead, ran from his chin.

The sheriff's window rolled down.

Ralston said, "Sheriff, Sue's dead. At home. Fell and hit her head. I couldn't tell Piggott."

He turned away and walked toward the front parking lot. The cement driveway danced with silver splashes.

Behind him, a car door slammed and heavy footsteps hurried back toward the house.

The Honda streaked toward Pintonville. He had, perhaps, a ten-, even fifteen-minute start on them. More if Piggott delayed. The road flew at him, glistening like the back of a wet serpent. Soon they too would think of questions to ask Tommy Richardson.

If it had been Tommy who was with Sue last night.

If he had read the evidence correctly.

If Sue had got herself up, polished and shining, to daz-zle the son of Old Man Richardson, the fun and indiscre-tion funneling into the cassette's hollow maw.

If the boy had found the mike. If his suspicions blazed. . . .

But Fleming. He could not understand Fleming's pres-ence.

The Honda slid on the shining asphalt, and the back end fought to twist around. He corrected the wheel, iron-wristed, jabbed the accelerator.

First, talk to Tommy Richardson. Before Piggott.

The car leaped. The rain came down.

"I'm Tommy Richardson," the boy said in a low voice, affirming that being Tommy Richardson was futile and burdensome. His head drooped, his shoulders slumped, his body was lax with self-abasement.

"I'm Sue Ralston's brother Ed. I'm with the sheriff's department. I'd like to talk with you."

"I guess so." He pushed open the screen door separat-ing them, exposing his consumed face. He was unshaven, uncombed, unwashed. He smelled of sweat and ciga-rettes, and despair had drawn his young face and glazed his eyes. "Dad says you guys are incompetent, but you got here quick enough."

He looked without hope past Ralston's shoulder at the rain sheeting viciously into the apartment complex. Light-ning snapped and glared, blanching the pastel fronts of the apartments and rattling them with thunder. "Come in. You're getting soaked."

Ralston stepped into the front room, saturated trousers slopping against his legs. Tension bent his tall frame.

Stereo equipment, lines of LPs, neat rows of paperbacks packed the cream-colored walls. A table lamp spilled light across the card table holding a typewriter and a litter of typed pages, heavily corrected.

"I've been up all night," Richardson said. He gestured toward the typewriter. "Writing out my incredible . . . stupidity."

He turned away, reaching for a typed page. As he did so, Ralston saw, behind the boy's left ear, a vivid pink smudge of lipstick.

The room convulsed around him, as if the walls had clenched like a fist.

"Mr. Ralston?"

He became aware that Tommy was holding out type-written pages to him, eyes anxious. "This explains it."

"Sit down," Ralston said.

"Thank you. Yes, I will." The boy collapsed loosely on a tan davenport, long legs sprawled, head back, eyes closed, hands turned palms uppermost, the sacrifice at the altar. On the wall behind, two fencing foils crossed above the emblem of the university team.

Tommy added, without emphasis, "I thought really serious things were more formal. You expect personal tragedy to have dignity and form. But it doesn't. It's only caused by trivialities—stupid mistakes, misjudgments. Nothing of weight. All accident." He might have been whispering prayers before sleep.

Ralston, set-faced, read:

CONFESSION
of
Thomas Raleigh Richardson

I am a murderer.

Last night, I murdered two people that I cared for.

One I loved and loved deeply. The other was my friend.

But it was wholly by capricious and accidental chance,

which now seems inescapable, that I murdered both of them. That it was essentially accidental does not excuse me.

The balance of the paragraph was crossed out. There were four pages, scarred by revision, ending with his full signature.

Ralston took out his pen and laid the pages in Tommy's lap. "Sign your usual signature diagonally across each page." He watched, immobile, as the boy wrote. Then he folded the sheets and thrust them into his breast pocket.

"Now tell me what happened," he said.

"I loved her. We were planning to get engaged. At first I thought she was a criminal with Piggott. But she was sensitive and warm. You're her brother. You know. She didn't know about Piggott, what he did. We fell in love. We were going to get engaged after I graduated."

"How did you get involved with Piggott?" Ralston asked. The tremor shaking his legs and body was not reflected in his voice.

"It was Fleming. Dad had a Citizen's Committee for Law and Order meeting at the house. Fleming came. He said that the sheriff and the bootleggers were cooperating. But he needed more evidence. He said that Piggott would try to blackmail me to make it seem like I was participating in his business. He called it a business. Dad didn't like it, but he agreed that I would let them try to blackmail me."

"So then Fleming introduced you to Sue."

"I met her at his house. Twice. He said that she knew Piggott. Then I went to her house, and Piggott was there a couple of times. He doesn't look like a criminal, but he laughs too much. It makes you distrustful."

"Why was Fleming there last night?" He glanced at his watch, and anxiety crawled in him.

"I told him I loved her. That we were almost engaged.
Fleming wouldn't believe me. I told him to wait outside,
last night, I could prove it easily. He thought that if I were
right, she could help us.

"I walked down to his car. This was after the accident.
There was lightning on the horizon, like a bad movie. I
told him they'd been recording everything I said. He
laughed and said he knew it. I asked to see his gun. I
didn't tell him about Sue. When I shot, there was all this
light. I thought lightning had struck by us. Then it smelled
like blood and toilets. I wiped off the gun. I wrote it all
down. You just have to read it."

Ralston asked gently, "I don't understand. Why did you
shoot Fleming?"

"He would have known right off I killed her. He said
she was working for Piggott."

His head shook blindly, and he jerked forward in his
seat.

"He would have been sorry for me. I couldn't have
faced him if he had known. Isn't that a dumb reason? It
doesn't even make sense. But she told me she wouldn't
have given the cassettes to Piggott. She told me. She loved
me. We were almost engaged.

"You and I," he said, "would have been brothers-in-
law."

He lifted his head.

"Are you corrupt, Mr. Ralston?"

"Not always," Ed said at last. He glanced again at his
watch, and his heart pulsed. "Will you come with me and
make a formal statement?"

"I wrote it down."

"We still need a statement."

"Okay."

He rose slowly, a sleepwalker awake in his dream. He
looked slowly around the room. "This is real, isn't it? I

keep thinking that I'm going to wake up, but I am awake."

Ralston said, "You better hurry. I think Piggott knows you were there last night. He knows Sue . . . had an accident. He'll want to ask you about it."

"I pushed her away from me and she fell."

"He doesn't know that."

"It's just that simple. I pushed her away and she fell."

"We have to get moving."

He followed the boy into the bedroom, watched him find a coat, pick up wallet, keys, money from the dresser.

"Not that." He took a fat pocketknife from Tommy's fingers.

"Dad gave me that."

"You'll get it back. Better give me the cassettes, too."

"Sure."

They left the apartment. Driving rain lashed their faces. As they came into the parking lot, a black sedan jerked to a stop before them. Its doors opened, like an insect spreading its wings, and Buddy and Elmer bobbed out.

Ralston whispered urgently, "You left the house early. Nothing happened."

"But that's a lie," Tommy said.

The two men splashed toward them. Buddy's mouth was opened. He stopped before Ralston, hunching in the rain, hands jammed into his pockets. "Goin' somewhere, Champ?"

Elmer said, "Hello, Tommy. I think we met once at Sue's. Mr. Piggott would appreciate it if you could stop by and see him."

Tommy nodded gravely. "I'd like to see him. I have a lot to say."

Elmer looked respectfully at Ralston. "Mind if we borrow him, Ed?"

Ralston looked at Buddy's weighted pocket. He said, "I was just going that way, myself. Might as well join you."

*   *   *

They sat in the rear seat of the rain-whipped car. Elmer drove. Buddy, in the front seat, sat turned, looking at them.

Tommy lay back on the brown leather upholstery, his unshaven face wan in the pale light. His eyes were closed. His lips twitched and jerked with internal dialogue.

When they had driven for a quarter of an hour, he said unexpectedly, "Mr. Ralston?"

"Yes?"

"It feels—it's rather complicated to describe. It's as if I had been walking along someplace high and it fell apart under my feet. I feel as if I am in the act of falling. I'm suspended. I haven't started to fall yet. But I will. I don't understand how I feel. Is that guilt?"

"It's lack of sleep."

"I think it is the perception of guilt."

"Get some sleep if you can. Keep quiet and get some sleep."

Buddy said sharply, "Nobody asked you, Ralston. Let the kid talk. What'd you do, kid?"

Tommy's unkempt head threshed right and left.

Ralston jerked hands from pockets as he said, "Tommy, keep quiet," in a savage voice.

"Can it, Ralston," Buddy said.

"Screw you."

Buddy's arm flashed across the seat. He hit Ralston on the side of the head with a revolver. Ralston grunted and, trying to turn, was struck twice more.

He let himself fall loosely into Tommy's lap. To his surprise, he felt himself rising very swiftly up a shimmering incline. As he rose, he thrust the knife he had taken from his pocket into Tommy's hand. Light turned about him in an expanding spiral, and his speed became infinite.

                    *   *   *

He awoke almost at once. His nose and cheek were pressed against Tommy's coat. Elmer was snarling at Buddy with soft violence. Tommy was saying, "Mr. Ralston, Mr. Ralston," his voice horrified. The blows, Ralston decided, had not been hard. He reasoned methodically that the angle for striking was wrong, and therefore insufficient leverage existed for a forceful blow. This conclusion amused him. Tommy's coat faded away.

When it returned, he heard Tommy saying: "You're bleeding."

"Let it bleed," he muttered.

He levered himself erect. His stomach pitched with the movement of the automobile and, when he moved his head, pain flared, stabbed hot channels down his neck. He closed his eyes and laid his head back against the seat and bled on Piggott's upholstery until the car stopped. He felt triumphant, in an obscure way.

The door opened. Ralston worked his legs from the car, gingerly hauled himself out. Rain flew against his face. Pain hammered his skull, and nausea still worked in him. He stood swaying, both hands clamped on the car door until his footing steadied.

Buddy stood smirking by the open door.

Ralston hit him on the side of the jaw. The effort threw white fire through his head. He fell to his knees. Buddy tumbled back against the side of the car, striking his head on the fender. He lay in the rain, eyes blinking.

Ralston staggered up, got his hand in Buddy's pocket, removed a heavy .38 with a walnut handle, a beautiful weapon. He stood swaying as Elmer glided around the side of the car.

Looking down at Buddy, Elmer said, "He never got past the third round, any time."

"Let him lay," Ralston said, with effort.

"Gotta take him in," Elmer said. He and Tommy hoisted Buddy between them, hauled him loose-legged, foul-mouthed, into the white hall. They flopped him into a chair, walked toward Piggott's office. The ham-faced youngster bumbled up from his chair, stared round-eyed at them.

"Mr. Piggott's busy," he said.

"Go back to sleep," Ralston said, and pushed the door open.

Piggott was working at his table, shuffling papers with two other men. He looked sharply up as Ralston came in, then began to chuckle. "Ed, it must have been a strenuous morning." He glanced at the two men. "Boys, let's chase this around again in half an hour, okay?"

They left silently, not looking around, their arms full of paper.

Tommy, at the table now, looking down on Piggott, asked, "Mr. Piggott, why did you feel it necessary to involve Sue?" His voice was formal and mildly curious. "I mean—I should say, in your efforts to entrap me."

Glee illuminated Piggott's face. "Lordy, Tommy, there wasn't a thing personal. You're a real nice boy. Sue just completely enjoyed it."

Amusement shook his shoulders. He added, "Now, don't you take it too hard. Women just fool men all the time. It's their way."

Tommy said in a clipped voice, shoving hands into his pockets, "I blamed her at first. I made a serious mistake. I should have realized that you were responsible. I was most certainly warned. But she would never have turned those cassettes over to you. She loved me, and she wouldn't have countenanced blackmail."

Incredulous delight lifted Piggott's shoulders. "Tommy, my friend, you are one of a kind. You really are."

"She loved me. We were going to get engaged."

Piggott's laughter poured into Tommy's face, a stream of sound. "Son, she did a real job on you. Not that she didn't like you. She thought you were grand. You just look here."

He tossed the engagement photograph across the table.

He said, "I was marrying her next month, Tommy. You were just a mite late."

"I love her," Tommy said, looking at the photograph. His voice began breaking up. "You never did."

The hall door came open hard, and Buddy came into the room, taking neat little steps. In his plaster face the eyes were terrible things. He called, "You, Ralston." A silver pistol jetted from his clasped hands.

Laughter stiffened on Piggott's face. In an unfamiliar voice, the texture of metal, he said, "Buddy, did I call . . ."

"I love her," Tommy said again.

He executed a fencer's flowing movement, an arc of graceful force that glided up the leg to the curved body to the extended right arm. His knife blade glinted as it entered Piggott's throat. His shoulders heaved with effort as he slashed right.

Incoherent noise tore from Piggott and a sudden scarlet jetting. He fell back in his chair, his expression amazed. His feet beat the floor. The chair toppled over with a heavy noise.

Gunfire, sudden, violent, repetitious, battered the room.

Tommy was slammed face forward onto the table. Papers cascaded, and a single yellow pencil spun across the pecan carpet.

The gunfire continued.

Pieces jumped out of the tabletop as Tommy's legs collapsed. He sprawled across the table, right arm extended, body jerking.

Buddy darted forward, the revolver bright in his brown hand, concentration wrinkling his face. He fired into Tommy's back.

Ralston shot him in the side of the head. Buddy fell over sideways and his gun, bounding across the floor, thudded against a gray filing cabinet.

Ralston whirled, knelt, looked down his gunsights into the enormous hollow hole of the .45 in Elmer's hand.

Confused shouting in the hallway.

Elmer said, white-lipped, "There's not five-cents profit for more shooting, Ed."

"No."

"We'd best put the guns up."

"All right."

The thumping of feet behind the table had stopped.

Men poured into the room.

Ralston sucked air, roared, "I'm Ed Ralston of the sheriff's department. This is police business, and I want this room cleared." He paced savagely toward them, face rigid, eyes gleaming, the horror in him intolerably bright.

Their faces glared anger, fear, shock. His voice beat at them. Elmer pushed at them, a confusion of voices and shoving bodies.

After one lifetime or two, the room emptied. Ralston shoved the gun away, said, "I'll call the sheriff."

"You might want to give us maybe half an hour. Some of the boys might want to fade. Give them a chance to get packed."

"Fifteen minutes. It'll have to be fifteen minutes."

Elmer nodded. "See you around, Ed."

The door closed and he was alone with the dead.

The strength leaked out of his body. He dropped into a chair and began to shake. His head blazed with pain. He could not control the shaking, which continued on and on.

Outside, engines began to roar, and he heard automobiles begin to go.

At last he wavered up on fragile legs, took a tissue from his pocket, and approached the table. Splinter-rimmed holes pocked the wood. He removed Tommy's wallet, took thirty of the sixty-two dollars. When he replaced the wallet, the body shifted and he thought that it would slip from the table to press its torn back against him. He wrenched back, white-faced. The body did not move again.

Piggott's wallet contained nearly six thousand dollars. Ralston removed four thousand in fifties and hundreds, counting them out slowly. He returned the wallet to a pocket the blood had not touched.

"They can both help bury her," he said.

His voice sounded stiff and high.

"We're all dead together," he said. He began to laugh.

When he heard himself, he became suddenly silent. Hard rain whipped the windows.

At last, his hand reached for the telephone.

Psychologists specializing in ethology know of the soft monkey experiment. A mother orangutan, whose baby has died, given a plush toy doll, will nurture it as if it were alive, as if it were her own. Nurture and protect and savage any creature that menaces the surrogate. Given a wire image, or a ceramic doll, the mother will ignore it. She must have the soft monkey. It sustains her.

HARLAN ELLISON

Soft Monkey

1987

A̲t twenty-five minutes past midnight on 51st Street, the wind-chill factor was so sharp it could carve you a new asshole.

Annie lay huddled in the tiny space formed by the wedge of a locked revolving door that was open to the street when the document copying service had closed for the night. She had pulled the shopping cart from the Food Emporium at First Avenue near 57th into the mouth of the revolving door, had carefully tipped it onto its side, making certain her goods were jammed tightly in the cart, making certain nothing spilled into her sleeping space. She had pulled out half a dozen cardboard flats—broken-down sections of big Kotex cartons from the Food Emporium, the half dozen she had not sold to the junkman that afternoon—and she had fronted the shopping cart with two of them, making it appear the doorway was blocked by the management. She had wedged the others around the edges of the space, cutting the wind, and placed the two rotting sofa pillows behind and under her.

She had settled down, bundled in her three topcoats, the thick woolen merchant marine stocking cap rolled down to cover her ears, almost to the bridge of her broken nose. It wasn't bad in the doorway, quite cozy, really. The wind shrieked past and occasionally touched her, but mostly was deflected. She lay huddled in the tiny space, pulled out the filthy remnants of a stuffed baby doll, cradled it under her chin, and closed her eyes.

She slipped into a wary sleep, half in reverie and yet alert to the sounds of the street. She tried to dream of the child again. Alan. In the waking dream she held him as she held the baby doll, close under her chin, her eyes closed, feeling the warmth of his body. That was important: his body was warm, his little brown hand against her cheek, his warm, warm breath drifting up with the dear smell of baby.

Was that just today or some other day? Annie swayed in reverie, kissing the broken face of the baby doll. It was nice in the doorway; it was warm.

The normal street sounds lulled her for another moment, and then were shattered as two cars careened around the corner off Park Avenue, racing toward Madison. Even asleep, Annie sensed when the street wasn't right. It was a sixth sense she had learned to trust after the first time she had been mugged for her shoes and the small change in her snap-purse. Now she came fully awake as the sounds of trouble rushed toward her doorway. She hid the baby doll inside her coat.

The stretch limo sideswiped the Caddy as they came abreast of the closed repro center. The Brougham ran up over the curb and hit the light stanchion full in the grille. The door on the passenger side fell open and a man scrabbled across the front seat, dropped to all fours on the sidewalk, and tried to crawl away. The stretch limo, angled in toward the curb, slammed to a stop in front of the Brougham, and three doors opened before the tires stopped rolling.

They grabbed him as he tried to stand, and forced him back to his knees. One of the limo's occupants wore a fine navy blue cashmere overcoat; he pulled it open and reached to his hip. His hand came out holding a revolver. With a smooth stroke he laid it across the kneeling man's forehead, opening him to the bone.

Annie saw it all. With poisonous clarity, back in the V of the revolving door, cuddled in darkness, she saw it all. Saw a second man kick out and break the kneeling victim's nose. The sound of it cut against the night's sudden silence. Saw the third man look toward the stretch limo as a black glass window slid down and a hand emerged from the backseat. The electric hum of opening. Saw the third man go to the stretch and take from the extended hand a metal can. A siren screamed down Park Avenue, and kept going. Saw him return to the group and heard him say, "Hold the motherf——er. Pull his head back!" Saw the other two wrench the victim's head back, gleaming white and pumping red from the broken nose, clear in the sulfurous light from the stanchion overhead. The man's shoes scraped and scraped the sidewalk. Saw the third man reach into an outer coat pocket and pull out a pint of scotch. Saw him unscrew the cap and begin to pour booze into the face of the victim. "Hold his mouth open!" Saw the man in the cashmere topcoat spike his thumb and index fingers into the hinges of the victim's jaws, forcing his mouth open. The sound of gagging, the glow of spittle. Saw the scotch spilling down the man's front. Saw the third man toss the pint bottle into the gutter where it shattered, and saw him thumb press the center of the plastic cap of the metal can, and saw him make the cringing, crying, wailing victim drink the Drano. Annie saw and heard it all.

The cashmere topcoat forced the victim's mouth closed, massaged his throat, made him swallow the Drano. The dying took a lot longer than expected. And it was a lot noisier.

The victim's mouth was glowing a strange blue in the calcium light from overhead. He tried spitting, and a gobbet hit the navy blue cashmere sleeve. Had the natty dresser from the stretch limo been a dunky slob uncaring of what *GQ* commanded, what happened next would not have gone down.

Cashmere cursed, swiped at the slimed sleeve, let go of the victim; the man with the glowing blue mouth and the gut being boiled away wrenched free of the other two, and threw himself forward. Straight toward the locked revolving door blocked by Annie's shopping cart and cardboard flats.

He came at her in fumbling, hurtling steps, arms wide and eyes rolling, throwing spittle like a racehorse; Annie realized he'd fall across the cart and smash her flat in another two steps.

She stood up, backing to the side of the V. She stood up: into the tunnel of light from the Caddy's headlights.

"The nigger saw it all!" yelled the cashmere.

"F——in' bag lady!" yelled the one with the can of Drano.

"He's still moving!" yelled the third man, reaching inside his topcoat and coming out of his armpit with a blued steel thing that seemed to extrude to a length more aptly suited to Paul Bunyan's armpit.

Foaming at the mouth, hands clawing at his throat, the

driver of the Brougham came at Annie as if he were spring-loaded.

He hit the shopping cart with his thighs just as the man with the long armpit squeezed off his first shot. The sound of the .45 magnum tore a chunk out of 51st Street, blew through the running man like a crowd roar, took off his face and spattered bone and blood across the panes of the revolving door. It sparkled in the tunnel of light from the Caddy's headlights.

And somehow he kept coming. He hit the cart, rose as if trying to get a first down against a solid defense line, and came apart as the shooter hit him with a second round.

There wasn't enough solid matter to stop the bullet and it exploded through the revolving door, shattering it open as the body crashed through and hit Annie.

She was thrown backward, through the broken glass, and onto the floor of the document copying center. And through it all, Annie heard a fourth voice, clearly a fourth voice, screaming from the stretch limo, "Get the old lady! Get her, she saw everything!"

Men in topcoats rushed through the tunnel of light.

Annie rolled over, and her hand touched something soft. It was the ruined baby doll. It had been knocked loose from her bundled clothing. *Are you cold, Alan?*

She scooped up the doll and crawled away, into the shadows of the reproduction center. Behind her, crashing through the frame of the revolving door, she heard men coming. And the sound of a burglar alarm. Soon police would be here.

All she could think about was that they would throw away her goods. They would waste her good cardboard, they would take back her shopping cart, they would toss her pillows and the hankies and the green cardigan into some trash can; and she would be empty on the street

again. As she had been when they made her move out of
the room at 101st and First Avenue. After they took Alan
from her. . . .

A blast of sound, as the shot shattered a glass-framed
citation on the wall near her. They had fanned out inside
the office space, letting the headlight illumination shine
through. Clutching the baby doll, she hustled down a
hallway toward the rear of the copy center. Doors on both
sides, all of them closed and locked. Annie could hear
them coming.

A pair of metal doors stood open on the right. It was
dark in there. She slipped inside, and in an instant her
eyes had grown acclimated. There were computers here,
big crackle-gray-finish machines that lined three walls.
Nowhere to hide.

She rushed around the room, looking for a closet, a
cubbyhole, anything. Then she stumbled over something
and sprawled across the cold floor. Her face hung over
into emptiness, and the very faintest of cool breezes
struck her cheeks. The floor was composed of large re-
movable squares. One of them had been lifted and replaced, but not flush. It had not been locked down; an
edge had been left ajar; she had kicked it open.

She reached down. There was a crawl space under the
floor.

Pulling the metal-rimmed vinyl plate, she slid into the
empty square. Lying face up, she pulled the square over
the aperture, and nudged it gently till it dropped onto its
tracks. It sat flush. She could see nothing where, a moment before, there had been the faintest scintilla of fil-
tered light from the hallway. Annie lay very quietly,
emptying her mind as she did when she slept in the doorways; making herself invisible. A mound of rags. A pile of
refuse. Gone. Only the warmth of the baby doll in that
empty place with her.

She heard the men crashing down the corridor, trying doors. *I wrapped you in blankets, Alan. You must be warm.* They came into the computer room. The room was empty, they could see that.

"She *has* to be here, dammit!"

"There's gotta be a way out we didn't see."

"Maybe she locked herself in one of those rooms. Should we try? Break 'em open?"

"Don't be a bigger asshole than usual. Can't you hear that alarm? We gotta get out of here!"

"He'll break our balls."

"Like hell. Would he do anything else than we've done? He's sittin' on the street in front of what's left of Beaddie. You think he's happy about it?"

There was a new sound to match the alarm. The honking of a horn from the street. It went on and on, hysterically.

"We'll find her."

Then the sound of footsteps. Then running.

Annie lay empty and silent, holding the doll.

It was warm, as warm as she had been all November. She slept there through the night.

The next day, in the last Automat in New York with the wonderful little windows through which one could get food by insertion of a coin, Annie learned of the two deaths.

Not the death of the man in the revolving door; the deaths of two black women. Beaddie, who had vomited up most of his internal organs, boiled like Maine lobsters, was all over the front of the *Post* that Annie now wore as insulation against the biting November wind. The two women had been found in midtown alleys, their faces blown off by heavy-caliber ordnance. Annie had known one of them; her name had been Sooky and Annie got the word from a good Thunderbird worshipper who stopped by her table and gave her the skinny as she carefully ate her fish cakes and tea.

She knew who they had been seeking. And she knew why they had killed Sooky and the other street person; to white men who ride in stretch limos, all old nigger bag ladies look the same. She took a slow bite of fish cake and stared out at 42nd Street, watching the world swirl past; what was she going to do about this?

They would kill and kill till there was no safe place left to sleep in midtown. She knew it. This was mob business, the *Post* inside her coats said so. And it wouldn't make any difference trying to warn the women. Where would they go? Where would they *want* to go? Not even she, knowing what it was all about . . . not even she would leave the area: this was where she roamed, this was her territorial imperative. And they would find her soon enough.

She nodded to the croaker who had given her the word, and after he'd hobbled away to get a cup of coffee from the spigot on the wall, she hurriedly finished her fish cake and slipped out of the Automat as easily as she had the document copying center this morning.

Being careful to keep out of sight, she returned to 51st Street. The area had been roped off, with sawhorses and green tape that said POLICE INVESTIGATION—KEEP OFF. But there were crowds. The streets were jammed, not only with office workers coming and going, but with loiterers who were fascinated by the scene. It took very little to gather a crowd in New York. The falling of a cornice could produce a *minyan*.

Annie could not believe her luck. She realized the police were unaware of a witness: when the men had charged the doorway, they had thrown aside her cart and goods, had spilled them back onto the sidewalk to gain entrance; and the cops had thought it was all refuse, as one with the huge brown plastic bags of trash at the curb. Her cart and the good sofa pillows, the cardboard flats and her sweaters . . . all of it was in the area. Some in trash cans, some amid the piles of bagged rubbish, some just lying in the gutter.

That meant she didn't need to worry about being sought from two directions. One way was bad enough.

And all the aluminum cans she had salvaged to sell, they were still in the big Bloomingdale's bag right against the wall of the building. There would be money for dinner.

She was edging out of the doorway to collect her goods when she saw the one in navy blue cashmere who had held Beaddie while they fed him Drano. He was standing three stores away, on Annie's side, watching the police lines, watching the copy center, watching the crowd. Watching for her. Picking at an ingrown hair on his chin.

She stepped back into the doorway. Behind her a voice said, "C'mon, lady, get the hell outta here, this's a place uhbizness." Then she felt a sharp poke in her spine.

She looked behind her, terrified. The owner of the haberdashery, a man wearing a bizarrely cut gray pinstripe worsted with lapels that matched his ears, and a passion flame silk hankie spilling out of his breast pocket like a crimson afflatus, was jabbing her in the back with a wooden coat hanger. "Move it on, get moving," he said, in a tone that would have gotten his face slapped had he used it on a customer.

Annie said nothing. She *never* spoke to anyone on the street. Silence on the street. *We'll go, Alan; we're okay by ourselves. Don't cry, my baby.*

She stepped out of the doorway, trying to edge away. She heard a sharp, piercing whistle. The man in the cashmere topcoat had seen her; he was whistling and signalling up 51st Street to someone. As Annie hurried away, looking over her shoulder, she saw a dark blue Oldsmobile that had been doubled-parked pull forward. The cashmere topcoat was shoving through the pedestrians, coming for her like the number 5 uptown Lexington express.

Annie moved quickly, without thinking about it. Being poked in the back, and someone speaking directly to her . . . that was frightening: it meant coming out to respond to another human being. But moving down her streets, moving quickly, and being part of the flow, that was comfortable. She knew how to do that. It was just the way she was.

Instinctively, Annie made herself larger, more expansive, her raggedy arms away from her body, the dirty overcoats billowing, her gait more erratic: opening the way for her flight. Fastidious shoppers and suited businessmen shied away, gave a start as the dirty old black bag lady bore down on them, turned sidewise praying she would not brush a recently Martinized shoulder. The Red Sea parted, miraculously permitting flight, then closed over instantly to impede navy blue cashmere. But the Olds came on quickly.

Annie turned left onto Madison, heading downtown. There was construction around 48th. There were good alleys on 46th. She knew a basement entrance just three doors off Madison on 47th. But the Olds came on quickly.

Behind her, the light changed. The Olds tried to rush the intersection, but this was Madison. Crowds were already crossing. The Olds stopped, the driver's window rolled down and a face peered out. Eyes tracked Annie's progress.

Then it began to rain.

Like black mushrooms sprouting instantly from concrete, Totes blossomed on the sidewalk. The speed of the flowing river of pedestrians increased, and in an instant Annie was gone. Cashmere rounded the corner, looked at the Olds, a frantic arm motioned to the left, and the man pulled up his collar and elbowed his way through the crowd, rushing down Madison.

Low places in the sidewalk had already filled with water. His wing-tip cordovans were quickly soaked.

He saw her turn into the alley behind the novelty sales shop (NOTHING OVER $1.10!!!); he *saw* her; turned right and ducked in fast; *saw* her, even through the rain and the crowd and half a block between them; *saw* it!

So where was she?

The alley was empty.

It was a short space, all brick, only deep enough for a big Dempsey dumpster and a couple of dozen trash cans; the usual mounds of rubbish in the corners; no fire escape ladders low enough for an old bag lady to grab; no loading docks, no doorways that looked even remotely accessible, everything cemented over or faced with sheet steel; no basement entrances with concrete steps leading down; no manholes in the middle of the passage; no open windows or even broken windows at jumping height; no stacks of crates to hide behind.

The alley was empty.

Saw her come in here. *Knew* she had come in here, and couldn't get out. He'd been watching closely as he ran to the mouth of the alley. She was in here somewhere. Not too hard figuring out where. He took out the .38 Police Positive he liked to carry because he lived with the delusion that if he had to dump it, if it were used in the commission of a sort of kind of felony he couldn't get snowed on, and if it were traced, it would trace back to the cop in Teaneck, New Jersey, from whom it had been lifted as he lay drunk in the back room of a Polish social club three years earlier.

He swore he would take his time with her, this filthy old porch monkey. His navy blue cashmere already smelled like soaked dog. And the rain was not about to let up; it now came sheeting down, traveling in a curtain through the alley.

He moved deeper into the darkness, kicking the piles of trash, making sure the refuse bins were full. She was in here somewhere. Not too hard figuring out where.

Warm. Annie felt warm. With the ruined baby doll under her chin, and her eyes closed, it was almost like the apartment at 101st and First Avenue, when the Human Resources lady came and tried to tell her strange things about Alan. Annie had not understood what the woman meant when she kept repeating *soft monkey, soft monkey*, a thing some scientist knew. It had made no sense to Annie, and she had continued rocking the baby.

Annie remained very still where she had hidden. Basking in the warmth. *Is it nice, Alan? Are we toasty; yes, we are. Will we be very still and the lady from the City will go away? Yes, we will.* She heard the crash of a garbage can being kicked over. *No one will find us. Shh, my baby.*

There was a pile of wooden slats that had been leaned against a wall. As he approached, the gun leveled, he realized they obscured a doorway. She was back in there, he knew it. Had to be. Not too hard figuring that out. It was the only place she could have hidden.

He moved in quickly, slammed the boards aside, and threw down on the dark opening. It was empty. Steel-plate door, locked.

Rain ran down his face, plastering his hair to his fore-head. He could smell his coat, and his shoes, oh god, don't ask. He turned and looked. All that remained was the huge dumpster.

He approached it carefully, and noticed: the lid was still dry near the back side closest to the wall. The lid had been open just a short time ago. Someone had just lowered it.

He pocketed the gun, dragged two crates from the heap thrown down beside the Dempsey, and crawled up onto them. Now he stood above the dumpster, balancing on the crates with his knees at the level of the lid. With both hands bracing him, he leaned over to get his fingertips under the heavy lid. He flung the lid open, yanked out the gun, and leaned over. The dumpster was nearly full. Rain had turned the muck and garbage into a swimming porridge. He leaned over precariously to see what floated there in the murk. He leaned in to see. *Effin' porch monk—*

As a pair of redolent, dripping arms came up out of the muck, grasped his navy blue cashmere lapels, and dragged him headfirst into the metal bin. He went down, into the slime, the gun going off, the shot spanging off the raised metal lid. The coat filled with garbage and water.

Annie felt him struggling beneath her. She held him down, her feet on his neck and back, pressing him face first deeper into the goo that filled the bin. She could hear him breathing garbage and fetid water. He thrashed, a big man, struggling to get out from under. She slipped, and braced herself against the side of the dumpster, regained her footing, and drove him deeper. A hand clawed out of the refuse, dripping lettuce and black slime. The hand was empty. The gun lay at the bottom of the bin. The thrashing intensified, his feet hitting the metal side of the container. Annie rose up and dropped her feet heavily on the back of his neck. He went flat beneath her, trying to swim up, unable to find purchase.

He grabbed her foot as an explosion of breath from down below forced a bubble of air to break on the surface. Annie stomped as hard as she could. Something snapped beneath her shoe, but she heard nothing.

It went on for a long time, for a time longer than Annie could think about. The rain filled the bin to overflowing. Movement under her feet lessened, then there was hysterical movement for an instant, then it was calm. She stood there for an even longer time, trembling and trying to remember other, warmer times.

Finally, she closed herself off, buttoned up tightly, climbed out dripping and went away from there, thinking of Alan, thinking of a time after this was done. After that long time standing there, no movement, no movement at all in the bog beneath her waist. She did not close the lid.

When she emerged from the alley, after hiding in the shadows and watching, the Oldsmobile was nowhere in sight. The foot traffic parted for her. The smell, the dripping filth, the frightened face, the ruined thing she held close to her.

She stumbled out onto the sidewalk, lost for a moment, then turned the right way and shuffled off.

The rain continued its march across the city.

No one tried to stop her as she gathered together her goods on 51st Street. The police thought she was a scavenger, the gawkers tried to avoid being brushed by her, the owner of the document copying center was relieved to see the filth cleaned up. Annie rescued everything she could, and hobbled away, hoping to be able to sell her aluminum for a place to dry out. It was not true that she was dirty; she had always been fastidious, even in the street. A certain level of dishevelment was acceptable, but this was unclean.

And the blasted baby doll needed to be dried and brushed clean. There was a woman on East 60th near Second Avenue; a vegetarian who spoke with an accent, a white lady who sometimes let Annie sleep in the basement. She would ask her for a favor.

It was not a very big favor, but the white woman was not home, and that night Annie slept in the construction of the new Zeckendorf Towers where S. Klein-On-The-Square used to be, down on 14th and Broadway.

The men from the stretch limo didn't find her again for almost a week.

She was salvaging newspapers from a wire basket on Madison near 44th when he grabbed her from behind. It was the one who had poured the liquor into Beaddie, and then made him drink the Drano. He threw an arm around her, pulled her around to face him, and she reacted instantly, the way she did when the kids tried to take her snap-purse.

She butted him full in the face with the top of her head, and drove him backward with both filthy hands. He stumbled into the street, and a cab swerved at the last instant to avoid running him down. He stood in the street, shaking his head, as Annie careened down 44th, looking for a place to hide. She was sorry she had left her cart again. This time, she knew, her goods weren't going to be there.

It was the day before Thanksgiving.

Four more black women had been found dead in midtown doorways.

Annie ran, the only way she knew how, into stores that had exits on other streets. Somewhere behind her, though she could not figure it out properly, there was trouble coming for her and the baby. It was so cold in the apartment. It was always so cold. The landlord cut off the heat, he always did it in early November, till the snow came. And she sat with the child, rocking him, trying to comfort him, trying to keep him warm. And when they came from Human Resources, from the city, to evict her, they found her still holding the child. When they took it away from her, so still and blue, Annie ran from them, into the streets; and she ran, she knew how to run, to keep running so she could live out here where they couldn't reach her and Alan. But she knew there was trouble behind her.

Now she came to an open place. She knew this. It was a new building they had put up, a new skyscraper, where there used to be shops that had good throwaway things in the cans and sometimes on the loading docks. It said Citicorp Mall and she ran inside. It was the day before Thanksgiving and there were many decorations. Annie rushed through into the central atrium, and looked around. There were escalators, and she dashed for one, climbing to a second storey, and then a third. She kept moving. They would arrest her or throw her out if she slowed down.

At the railing, looking over, she saw the man in the court below. He didn't see her. He was standing, looking around.

Stories of mothers who lift wrecked cars off their children are legion.

When the police arrived, eyewitnesses swore it had been a stout, old black woman who had lifted the heavy potted tree in its terra-cotta urn, who had manhandled it up onto the railing and slid it along till she was standing above the poor dead man, and who had dropped it three storeys to crush his skull. They swore it was true, but beyond a vague description of old, and black, and dissolute looking, they could not be of assistance. Annie was gone.

*   *   *

On the front page of the *Post* she wore as lining in her
right shoe, was a photo of four men who had been ar-
raigned for the senseless murders of more than a dozen
bag ladies over a period of several months. Annie did not
read the article.

It was close to Christmas, and the weather had turned
bitter, too bitter to believe. She lay propped in the doorway alcove of the post office on 43rd and Lexington. Her
rug was drawn around her, the stocking cap pulled down
to the bridge of her nose, the goods in the string bags
around and under her. Snow was just beginning to come
down.

A man in a Burberry and an elegant woman in a mink
approached from 42nd Street, on their way to dinner.
They were staying at the New York Helmsley. They were
from Connecticut, in for three days to catch the shows
and to celebrate their eleventh wedding anniversary.

As they came abreast of her, the man stopped and stared
down into the doorway. "Oh, Christ, that's awful," he
said to his wife. "On a night like this, Christ, that's just
awful."

"Dennis, *please!*" the woman said.

"I can't just pass her by," he said. He pulled off a kid
glove and reached into his pocket for his money clip.

"Dennis, they don't like to be bothered," the woman
said, trying to pull him away. "They're very self-
sufficient. Don't you remember that piece in the *Times?*"

"It's damned near Christmas, Lori," he said, taking a
twenty-dollar bill from the folded sheaf held by its clip.
"It'll get her a bed for the night, at least. They can't make
it out here by themselves. God knows, it's little enough to
do." He pulled free of his wife's grasp and walked to the
alcove.

He looked down at the woman swathed in the rug, and

he could not see her face. Small puffs of breath were all that told him she was alive. "Ma'am," he said, leaning forward. "Ma'am, please take this." He held out the twenty.

Annie did not move. She never spoke on the street.

"Ma'am, please, let me do this. Go somewhere warm for the night, won't you . . . please?"

He stood for another minute, seeking to rouse her, at least for a *Go away* that would free him, but the old woman did not move. Finally, he placed the twenty on what he presumed to be her lap, there in that shapeless mass, and allowed himself to be dragged away by his wife.

Three hours later, having completed a lovely dinner, and having decided it would be romantic to walk back to the Helmsley through the six inches of snow that had fallen, they passed the post office and saw the old woman had not moved. Nor had she taken the twenty dollars. He could not bring himself to look beneath the wrappings to see if she had frozen to death, and he had no intention of taking back the money. They walked on.

In her warm place, Annie held Alan close up under her chin, stroking him and feeling his tiny black fingers warm at her throat and cheeks. *It's all right, baby, it's all right. We're safe. Shh, my baby. No one can hurt you.*

BILL CRENSHAW

Flicks

1988

He knew it wasn't a question of if his beeper would go off.

This time Devin Corley was home, his apartment, had just opened a beer, turned on the TV, stretched out on the couch. He phoned in. Dispatcher said Majestic Theater, across town. He started the VCR, took a last pull at the beer, gave the cat fresh water, got a quick shower. Then he left. Speed was not of the essence.

He knew what he'd find. A body; Ray Tasco, his partner, taking statements, popping his gum, looking amused and surprised at once; Maggie Epps with her wedge face and her black forensic kit, diagramming the scene, scooping nameless little forensic glops into baggies; Joe Franks in a safari shirt, slung with cameras, smiling like always, always smiling, always angry. He'd give Corley grief about being away from his desk again, or being late. Corley had been away from his desk a lot. He was always late.

At the Majestic there were two uniforms in the men's john. The room was done in men's room tile, blue and white, smelled of urine, wet tobacco, stale drains, pine. Trash can on side, brown paper towels spilling out, balled up, dark with water, some with red smears. Floor around sinks wet, scattered splashes and small pools. Hints of blood in wet footprints running back and forth across the tile. In near stall somebody retching. The uniform watching the somebody was pointedly not looking at him.

"What we got?" Corley asked the uniforms.

"Got a slashing, lieutenant," said the older uniform, twenty-six maybe, Lopez maybe. Corley glanced down at the nametag. Lopez. The younger uniform looked green at the gills. Corley didn't know him, knew he wouldn't be green long, not this kind of green. Lots of greens in Homicide, green like Greengills, green like a two-day corpse, green like Corley, like old copper.

"In here?" Corley asked.

Lopez snapped his head back. "In the first theater."

Corley moved to the stall. Lopez moved beside him. Greengills went to the sink and splashed water on his face.

"Who we got?" said Corley.

"Pickpocket, he says. Says he just lifted the guy's wallet. Says he didn't know he was dead."

The pickpocket turned around, face pasty, hair matted. "I didn't know, man," he said, whiney, rocking. "Jesus, I didn't know. That was blood, oh God, that was blood, man, and I didn't even feel it. My hands . . ." He grabbed for the john again. Corley turned away.

"Any of that blood his?" he asked.

"Don't think so."

The wallet was on the stainless-steel shelf over the sinks. It was smeared with bloody fingerprints. Corley took out a silver pen and flipped the wallet open. "Find it in the trash can?"

"Yessir," said the younger uniform, wiping the water from his face, looking at Corley in the mirror.

"Money still in it? Credit cards?"

"Yessir."

The driver's license showed a fifty-five-year-old business type, droopy eyes, saggy chin, looking above the camera, trying to decide if he should smile for this official picture. Bussey, Tyrone, Otis. Toccoa Falls, Georgia.

The pickpocket told Corley that he'd like seen this chubby dude asleep at the end of his row, which he'd seen him before with a big wad of cash in his wallet at the candy counter and seen him put the wallet inside his coat and not in his pants. Near the end of the flick when he got to the guy he kind of tripped and caught himself on the guy's seat and said sorry, excuse me, while lifting his wallet real neat, and he dropped the wallet into his popcorn box and headed right for the john to ditch the wallet and just stroll out with the plastic and the cash, but in the john his hands were bloody and the guy's wallet and his shoes, and then he heard screaming in the lobby and he ditched the wallet and tried to wash the blood off but there was too much, the more he looked, the more he saw, and somebody came in and went out, so he tried to hide. He didn't know what was happening, but he knew it was real bad.

There was a spritzing noise and thin, piney mist settled into the stall and spotted Corley's glasses. Corley tore off a little square of toilet paper and smeared the spots around on the lenses. He had the pickpocket arrested on robbery and on suspicion of murder, but he knew he wasn't the killer.

"Victim here alone?" asked Corley.

"As far as we know," said Lopez.

"Convention, maybe. Is Tasco here? Do you know Sergeant Tasco?"

Joe Franks leaned into the restroom, cameras swinging at his neck. "Hey, Corley, you in on this or not? The meat wagon's waiting. Come show me what you want."

Corley smiled. "You know what I want."

"Yeah, show me anyway so if you don't get it all, you don't blame me. Where've you been?"

"You shoot in here?"

"Yeah, I shot in here." He sounded impatient.

"You get the footprints?"

"Yeah, I got the footprints."

"Get the towels and the sink?"

"Yeah, the towels, the sink, and the stall, and the punk, and I even got a close-up of his puke, okay?"

"See, Joe," said Corley, smiling again, "you know exactly what I want."

"I hate working with you, Corley," said Franks as Corley pushed past him.

In the theater Maggie Epps was sitting on the aisle across from the body, sketchpad on her knees. "Glad you could make it, Devin," she said.

Corley fished for a snappy comeback, couldn't hook anything he hadn't said a hundred times before, said hello.

Franks showed Corley the angles he had shot. Corley asked for a couple more. The flashes illuminated the body like lightning, burned distorted images into Corley's retina.

Tasco came in, talking to somebody, squinting over his notebook. "Ray, you got the manager there?" Corley called.

"I'm the owner," the man said.

"Think you could give us some more light?"

"This is as bright as it gets, officer. This is a movie theater."

Corley turned back around. Franks snorted.

Mr. T. O. Bussey sat on the aisle in the high-backed chair, sagging left, head forward, eyes opened. Blood covered everything from his tie on down, had run under the seats toward the screen. People had tracked it back toward the lobby, footprints growing fainter up the aisle.

"You shoot that?" asked Corley.

Franks nodded. "Probably thought they were walking through cola."

Corley bent over Mr. Bussey. He put a hand on the forehead and raised the head an inch or two so that he could see the wound. "You see this?"

"Yeah. Want a shot?"

"Can I lift his head, Maggie?"

"Just watch where you plant your big feet," she said.

Corley stood behind Mr. Bussey, put his hands above the ears, and raised the head face forward, chin up. He turned his eyes away from the flashes.

"What did he get?" said Corley.

"Everything," said Maggie. "Jugular, carotid, trachea, carotid, jugular. Something real sharp. This guy never made a sound, never felt a thing. Maybe a hand on his hair jerking his head back. Nothing after that."

"From behind?" Corley lowered the head back to where he had found it.

"Left to right, curving up. You got your man in the john?"

"Don't think so. Too much blood on his shoes. He walked out in front, not behind."

"So what have you got?"

"Headache."

Maggie smiled. "It's going to get worse."

Corley smiled back. "It always does."

Corley made Greengills help bag the body. He could say that he was helping the kid get used to it, that it didn't get any better, that as bodies went this one wasn't bad, but he wasn't sure he had done it as a favor. He was afraid he'd done it to be mean.

They spent half an hour looking for the weapon. Corley didn't expect to find anything. They didn't.

He had a videotape unit brought over and sent Lopez

and Greengills into the other theaters to block the parking lot exits and send the audiences through the lobby.

The owner pulled him aside and protested. Corley told him that the killer might be in another theater. The owner said something about losing the last *Deathdancer* audience and not needing any publicity hurting ticket sales and being as much a victim as that poor man. "I own nine screens in this town," he said, dragging his hand over his jaw. "I'm not responsible for this. Let's keep the profile low, okay?" There was nothing Corley could say, so he said nothing, and the owner bristled and said he had friends in this town. "I'll speak to your superior about this, Officer . . . ?"

"Corley," he said, walking away. "That's l-e-y."

The other movies ended and the audiences pushed into the lobby. Corley had them videotaped as they bunched and swayed toward the street. Two more uniforms arrived and he started them searching the other theaters for the weapon.

He left Tasco in charge and went to the station and hung around the darkroom while Franks did his printing and bitched about wasting his talent on corpses and about Corley's always wanting more shots and more prints than anybody else. Corley didn't bother to tell Franks again that it was his own fault, that Franks was the one who always waxed eloquent over his third beer and said that the camera always lied, that the image distorted as much as it revealed, that photographs were fictions. He had convinced Corley, so Corley always wanted more and more pictures, each to balance others, to offer new angles, so that reality became a sort of compromise, an average. Corley didn't say any of that again. He made the right noises at the right times, like he did when Franks said how he was going to quit as soon as he finished putting his portfolio together, as soon as he got a show somewhere.

Maybe Franks really was working on a project. Maybe he should be a real photographer. Corley didn't know. He knew Franks about as well as he could, down to a certain level, no further. He imagined that Franks knew him in about the same way. It wasn't the kind of thing they talked about.

Corley lifted a dripping print out of the fixer. "Why'd you become a cop anyway?" he said.

Franks took the print from him and put it back. It was hard to read Franks's eyes in the red light. "You're asking that like you thought there were real answers," Franks said.

Corley took the prints to his desk and did what paperwork he could. He worked until the sky got gray. By the time he stopped for doughnuts on the way home, the first edition of the *News* was in the stands. It didn't have the murder.

He thought sometimes there were real answers instead of just the same patterns and ways to deal with patterns and levels beyond which you couldn't go. He thought sometimes that there was a way to get to the next level. He thought sometimes he'd quit, do insurance fraud, something. He thought maybe he hated his job, but he didn't know that either. He had thought there was something essential about working Homicide, essential in the sense of dealing with the essences of things, a job that butted as close to the raw edge of reality as he was likely to get, and how would he do insurance after that? But whatever kind of essence he was seeing, it was mute, images beyond articulation. None of it made any sense, and he was bone-marrow tired.

The landing at his apartment was dim, and as he slid his key into the second lock, he could see the peephole darken in the apartment next door. Half past five in the morning and Gianelli was already up and prowling. Corley stood an extra second in the rectangle of light from his apartment so that Gianelli could see who he was, whoever the hell Gianelli was besides a name on a mailbox downstairs, an eye at the peephole, the sounds of pacing footsteps, of a TV. Corley's cat sniffed at the flecks of dried blood on his shoes.

Corley tossed the paper and Franks's pictures on the desk, opened a can of smelly catfood, had a couple of doughnuts and some milk. Then he rewound the tape in the VCR and stretched out on the couch to watch the program that the call to the theater had interrupted. It was a cop show. At the station they laughed at cop shows. Things made sense in cop shows. He fell asleep before the first commercial.

Corley woke up with the cat in his face again. He got a hand under its middle and flicked it away, watched it twist in the air, land on all fours, sit and stretch, lick its paws. It wasn't even his cat. The apartment had come with the cat and a wall of corky tile covered with pictures of the previous occupant. The super hadn't bothered to take them down. "Throw 'em away if you want," he'd said. "What do I care?" She was pale and blonde. An actress who never made it, maybe. A model. A photographer. Corley wondered what kind of person would leave a cat and a wall covered with her own image. He still had the pictures in a box somewhere. He used the cork as a dart board, to pin up grocery lists and phone numbers. After eight months he was getting used to the cat, except when it tried to lie in his face, which it always did when he fell asleep on the couch. One of these times he was going to toss it out of the window, down to the street. Four floors down, it didn't matter if it landed on its feet or not.

He looked at his watch. Only nine-thirty, but he knew he wouldn't get back to sleep. He might as well go in.

He stopped for doughnuts and coffee and the second edition. Big headline. HORROR FLICK HORROR. *Blood flowed on the screen and in the aisles last night at the Majestic Theater.* . . . Great copy, he thought, great murder for the papers. Stupid murder in a stupid place. Not robbery. Not a hit, not on some salesman from upstate Georgia. Tasco would say somebody boozed, whacked, dusted. Corley didn't think so. This one was weird. There was something going on here, something interesting, a new level, maybe, something new. He sat for a long time thinking.

It was going on eleven by the time he dropped the paper on his desk.

"My kids love those things," said Tasco.

"What things?"

Tasco pointed to the headline. "Horror flicks."

Corley looked at the paper. The story was covered in green felt tip pen with questions about the case, with ideas, with an almost unrecognizable sketch of the scene. Corley didn't remember doodling.

There was a tapping of knuckle on glass. Captain Hupmann motioned them into his office.

"Finally," said Tasco.

"How long you been waiting?" said Corley.

"Too long."

"Sorry." He knew the captain had been waiting on him, had made Tasco wait on him, too.

"Just go easy, okay?" Tasco said.

The captain shut the door and turned to Corley. "So where are we on this one?"

Tasco looked at Corley. Corley shrugged.

The captain started to snap something but Tasco flipped open his notebook. "Family notified," he said. "Victim in town for sales convention, goes to the same

convention every year, never takes wife. Concession girl
remembers him because he talked funny, had an accent
she meant, and he made her put extra butter on his popcorn twice and called her ma'am. Nobody else remembers
him. Staying at the Plaza, single room, no roommate. They
don't take roll at the meetings, so we don't know if he's
been to any or if he's been seeing the sights." Tasco looked
up, popping his gum, then looked at Corley.

"I think we've got a nut," said Corley. "Random. Maybe
a one-shot, maybe a serial."

The captain raised his eyebrows in mock surprise. "Are
we taking an interest in our work again?"

Corley shifted his weight.

"A nut," said the captain. "Ray?"

Tasco shrugged. "Seems reasonable, but we're not married to it. Might be a user flipped out by the flick."

The captain turned back to Corley. "Why did he pick
Bussey?"

Corley could picture Bussey at the convention, anonymous in the city and the crowd, free to cuss and stay out
late if he wanted, hit the bars and the ladies, drink too
much and smoke big cigars. But Mr. Bussey hadn't gone
that far. He'd just gone to a movie he wouldn't be caught
dead in at home.

"He sat in the wrong place," said Corley. "He was on
the aisle. Quick exit."

"What quick exit? This is a theater, for chrissake. This
is public. You don't do a random in public." The captain drew his lips together. "Where do you want to go
with this?" he asked finally, looking more at Tasco than
Corley.

Corley looked at Tasco before answering. He hadn't told
Tasco anything. "We want to talk to the pickpocket again,
the employees again. We've got some names from the
audience, the paper had some more. We want them to see

the tapes, see if they recognize somebody coming out of the other theaters. Ray wants to do more with Mr. Bussey's movements, see if there's some connection we don't know about."

"Okay," said the captain. "You've both got plenty of other work, but you can keep this one warm for a couple of days. Check the gangs. Maybe something there, initiation ritual, something. If it's some kind of hit, or if it's a user, it won't go far."

"I think it's a serial," said Corley.

"You mean you hope it's a serial," said the captain. "Otherwise you're not going to get him. That it?"

"Yessir," said Tasco.

"Oh, and Corley," the captain said as Corley was halfway through the door, "welcome back. Back to stay?"

They followed up with the employees and what members of the audience they could find, asked if they'd known anybody else in the theater, seen anything unusual, remembered someone walking around near the end of the movie. They showed them pictures of the pickpocket and Mr. Bussey's driver's license, the tapes of the other audiences, asked if anybody looked familiar.

Corley tried to make himself ask the questions as if they were new, as if he'd never even thought of them before. Same questions, same answers, and if you didn't listen because it all seemed the same, you missed something. Tasco always asked the questions right and was somehow not dulled by the routine, by the everlasting sameness. Tasco hunkered down and did his job, would see the waste and the stupidity of it all, say, "Jeez, why do they do that, we got to get the SOB that did this, aren't people horrible." Tasco's saving grace was that he didn't think about it. Corley didn't mean that in a mean way. It was a quality he envied, maybe even admired. Welcome back,

back to stay? Sometimes he wondered why he didn't just walk away from it all.

They got Maggie to draw a seating chart and they put little pins in the squares, red for Mr. Bussey, yellow for the people they questioned, blue in seats that yellows remembered being occupied. The media played the story and boosted ratings and circulation, and more people from the audience came forward, and others who claimed to have been there but who Tasco said were probably on Mars at the time. The number of pins increased, but that was all.

"They sat all around him," said Corley, "and they didn't see anything."

"So who in this city ever sees anything?"

"Yeah, well, they should have seen something. Maybe they were watching the movie. Maybe we should see it."

They used their shields to get into the seven o'clock show. The ticket girl told them that the crowd was down, especially in *Deathdancer*. Tasco bought a big tub of popcorn and two Cokes, and they sat in the middle, about halfway to the screen.

The horror flicks that had scared Corley as a kid played with the dark, the uncertain, the unknown, where you might not even see the killer clearly, where you were never sure if the clicking in the night outside was the antenna wire slapping in the wind or the sound of the giant crabs moving. One thing might be another, and there was no way to tell, and you never really knew if you were safe.

But this wasn't the same. Here the only unknowns were when the next kid was going to get it and how gross it would be. A series of bright red brutalities, each more bizarre than the last, more grotesque, more unreal. Corley couldn't take it seriously. But maybe the audience could.

Unless they were cops, or medics, maybe this was what it was like. Corley started watching them.

They were mostly under forty, sat in couples or groups, boys close to the screen or all the way to the wall and the corners, girls in the middle, turning their heads away and looking sideways; dates close, touching, copping feels; marrieds a married distance apart. They all talked and laughed too loud. On the screen the killer stalked the victim and the audience got quiet and focused on the movie. Corley could feel muscles stiffen, tension build as the sequence drew the moment out, the moment you knew would come, was coming, came, and they screamed at the killing, and after the killing sank back spent, then started laughing nervously, talking, wisecracking at the screen, at each other. Corley watched three boys sneak up behind a row of girls and grab at their throats, the girls shrieking, leaping, the boys collapsing in laughter. A girl chanted, "Esther wet her panties," and the whole audience broke up. On the screen, the killer started stalking his next victim and the cycle began again.

"What do you think?" asked Corley, lighting a cigarette as soon as they hit the lobby. People in line for the next show stared at their faces as if trying to see if they would be scared or bored or disgusted. Corley thought they all looked hopeful somehow.

Tasco shrugged, placid as ever. "It was a horror flick."

"Was it any good?"

"Who can tell? You'll have to ask my kids."

The summer wind was warm and filled with exhaust fumes.

"You wanta come up for a beer or something?" Corley asked.

Tasco looked at his watch. "Nah, better get back. Evelyn. See you tomorrow."

Corley thought about rephrasing it, asking if he wanted

to stop in for a beer somewhere, but Tasco had already made his excuse. Used to be they'd have a beer once or twice a week before Tasco started his thirty-minute drive back to Evelyn and the kids and the postage-stamp yard he was so proud of, but that was before Corley had moved across town, out of his decent apartment, with the court-yard and the pool, into what he lived in now. Tasco had been to the new place once only. He'd looked around and popped his gum and looked surprised and amused and inhaled his beer and left. Corley was relieved that Tasco hadn't asked him why he'd moved. He asked himself the same thing.

After he fed the cat, Corley put on the tape of the au-dience leaving the other screens. At first they ignored the camera, looked away, pretended not to see it, nudged a companion, pointed discreetly. Some made faces and more people saw it, and more made faces or shot birds or mouthed "Hi, Mom" or walked straight at the camera so that their faces filled the pictures, stuck hands or popcorn boxes in front of the lens, waved, mugged, danced, pre-tended to strip, to moon the camera, to kiss Corley through the TV screen.

They had taped three audiences. They acted about the same.

Before he went to bed, Corley posted the newspaper articles and Franks's pictures on the cork wall, with a shot of Mr. Bussey in the center.

The heat woke him. He lay sweating, disoriented, fingers knotted in sheets. The night-light threw a yellow oval on the wall opposite, gave the room a focus, showed him right where he was. He hated the panic that came from not being sure. He took three or four deep, slow breaths.

He hadn't always had the night-light. He hadn't always strapped an extra gun to his leg or carried two speedloaders in his coat pockets every time he went out. He hadn't always spent so much time in his apartment, in front of the TV, asleep in front of the TV, in bed. He tried not to think about it. He tried not to think.

It was too early to be up, too late to go back to sleep, too hot to stay in the apartment. He could make coffee and go to the roof before the sun hit the tar, could catch the breeze off the river, let the cat stalk pigeons.

While the coffee dripped he sat on the couch and looked at the pictures on the wall. In the central picture Mr. Bussey sat with head up and eyes open like he was watching the movie, the wound like a big smile. Death in black and white. Not like the deaths in the movie. Real was more . . . something. Casual. Anticlimactic. Prosaic. Unaccompanied by soundtrack. Maybe Bussey wasn't really dead. Maybe it was just special effects. In the picture his hands held Mr. Bussey's head just above the ears. He wiped his palms on his shorts.

Mr. Gianelli's peephole darkened as Corley shut his door and the cat slid up the stairs. He was halfway to the landing when the door opened the width of the chain and Gianelli's face pressed into the crack, cheeks bulging around the wood. Over his shoulder a room was lit by a television's multicolored glow.

"I know what you're doing, young man," Gianelli called in a rasping voice.

"Sorry if I woke you," Corley said, kept climbing, smiled. Maybe thirty-eight seemed young to Gianelli.

"You leave my antenna alone," Gianelli said. "The one on the chimney. I been seventeen years in this building. I got rights. You hear me, young man? Next time my picture goes I'm calling a cop." He slammed his door and it echoed in the stairwell like a gunshot.

Corley beat Tasco to work.

"Whoa," said Franks on his way to the coffee pot. "On time and everything. You must have figured it out."

"Figured what out?" said Corley.

Franks smiled. "That you won't get fired for being late. You want out, you got to quit."

"So who wants out?"

"Who doesn't?"

Tasco had never said anything about Corley's being late. When Tasco came in, he didn't say anything about Corley's being early.

Another homicide came in and they spent the morning and most of the afternoon down by the river and the warehouses, Tasco and Corley and Maggie and Joe and the smells of creosote and fish and gasoline. Some punk had taken a twelve-gauge to the gut, sawed-off, Maggie said, because of the spread and the powder burns, another drug hit as the new champions of free enterprise tried to corner the market. It wasn't going to get solved unless somebody rolled over. A crowd gathered at the yellow police line ribbons. Lopez and Greengills came in for crowd control. The paramedics bitched about hauling corpses. Greengills didn't seem to be bothered by the body.

It was late when they got back to the station.

"I'm going to the movie," said Corley. "I'm going to take our pickpocket. Want to come?"

"What for?"

"Like you said, maybe something in the movie freaked this guy. Maybe we can find something."

"I don't think we're going to get anywhere on this one."

"So you want to come, or not?" Tasco said no.

The pickpocket didn't want to go either. "My treat," Corley told him, not smiling.

Corley sat in Mr. Bussey's seat and told the pickpocket to reconstruct exactly what he had done, when he had done it. He got popcorn and grape soda like Bussey, put the empties into the next seat like Bussey, concentrated on the movie, tried not to see the pickpocket in the corner of his eye, tired to ignore the feeling that his back was to the door, tried to control his breathing. He hated this, hated the dark, the people around him, the long empty aisle on his left, he felt full of energy demanding use, fought to sit still. Finally on the screen the killer reached for the last survivor and the background music shrieked, and Corley slumped left and lowered his head and sat, and on the screen the girl fought off the killer, and they rescued her just in time, and they killed the killer and comforted the girl, and they discovered that the killer wasn't dead and had escaped, and then Corley felt the pickpocket fall across him, heard his "Sorry," felt the wallet slide out of his coat only because he was waiting for it. He sat slumped over while the audience filed out, giggling or groaning or silent. He sat until a nervous usher shook him and asked him to wake up.

He found the pickpocket throwing up in the men's room.

We're just going to leave this open for a while," said the captain. "Put the river thing on warm."

Tasco nodded, popping his gum. Corley said nothing.

"Problem, Devin?"

"I'd like to stay on this awhile."

"Got something to sell? New leads? Anything?"

Corley shook his head. "Not really."

"Okay, then."

They went back to their desks.

"Learn anything last night?" asked Tasco.

Corley shrugged, remembering the dark, palpable and pressing; the icy air pushing on his lungs as he sat and waited, the effort to exhale; trying to concentrate on the movie, on what might have snapped somebody; and after, trying to help the pickpocket out of the stall, embarrassed for him now, and sorry, and the pickpocket twisting his elbow out of Corley's grip and tearing in half the twenty that Corley had stuffed into his shirt pocket, bloody money maybe, something, he wouldn't have it. "Not much," he said. "Bussey must have gotten it in that last sequence, like we thought."

"Funny, isn't it, all that stuff up there on the screen, and out in the audience some dude flicks out a blade and that's that."

"Yeah," said Corley. "That's that."

Corley found himself at a movie again that night, a horror flick near the university. He sat on the aisle, last row, back to the wall. The movie looked the same as the other, felt the same, same rhythms, same victims, same bright gore. The audience was younger, more the age of the characters on the screen, and louder, maybe, but still much the same as the others, shouting at the screen, groaning, cracking jokes, laughing in the wrong places, trying to scare each other, strange responses, inappropriate somehow. They had come for the audience as much as the movie. They had come to be in a group.

He found himself the next night in another movie, on the aisle, last row, back to the wall, fingering the speed-loader in his pocket, trying to remember why he was wasting his time there.

Near the end of the show, he saw a silhouette down front rise and edge toward the aisle, stop, and his guts iced as he saw it reach out its left hand and pull back someone's head, heard a scream, saw it slash across the throat with its right hand and turn and run up the aisle for the exit, coming right for him, too perfect. He braced, tightening his grips on the armrests, fought to sit, sit, as the silhouette ran toward him, then he stuck out a leg and the man went down hard and Corley was on him with his knee in the back and his gun behind the right ear. He yelled for an ambulance, ordered the man to open his fist. The man was slow. Corley brought a gun butt down on the back of his hand. The fingers opened, and something bright rolled onto the carpet. Corley stared at it for a few seconds before he saw it was a tube of lipstick.

"It's only a game, man," said a voice above him, quavering. Corley looked up. The owner of the voice was pointing with a shaking finger to the bright red lipstick slash along his throat. "Only a game."

Corley cuffed them to each other and took them in. He was not gentle with them.

The papers had fun with the story. "OFF-DUTY DETECTIVE NABS LIPSTICK SLASHER," said one headline. Corley posted the stories on the corkboard.

They gave him a hard time when he got to work, asked if he'd been wounded, if the stain would come out, warned him about the chapstick chopper. He didn't let it get to him.

What got to him was how much fun the slasher and his victim had. He tried to tell Tasco about it. He'd almost lost it, he said. He'd been shaking with rage, wanted to push them around, run them in hard, give them a dose of the fear of God, but it didn't sink in. They just kept replaying it all the way into the station.

"You really didn't know for sure, did you?" the slasher had asked.

"Thought I was gone," said the victim. "For a second there I thought this was it." He laid his head back on the seat, his face suddenly blue fading to black as the unit passed under a street light. "Oh, wow," he said.

"Shut up," Corley had snarled. "Just shut the hell up." They had gone silent, then looked at each other and giggled.

"Drugs," said Tasco.

"They weren't looped. It was like they were, but they weren't. This guy, the victim—for all he knew it was the killer. He was scared shitless, Ray, and he loved it."

Tasco shrugged. "It's a cheap high. Love that rush, maybe. Or maybe it's like they're in the flick. Makes 'em movie stars. Everybody wants to be a movie star. Put a Walkman on your head and your *life's* an effing movie."

"I just wish I knew what the hell was going on." Corley rocked back in his chair. "I'm going to a movie tonight. Want to come?"

Tasco stared at Corley for a second or two. "This on your own time?"

"You want to come, or not?"

"The river's on warm, remember? We're not going to get this one. It was a one-shot." He paused a second. "You okay?"

Corley rocked forward. "What the hell is that supposed to mean?"

"It's not supposed to mean anything. I only wanted . . ."

"All I did was ask if you wanted to go to a flick."

"Keep your voice down. Jesus. For six months you've been a walking burnout. I've been like partnered with a zombie . . ."

"I do my job, nobody can say I don't do my job."

". . . now suddenly you're doing overtime. I'm your partner. I just want to know if you're okay, that's all."

"I'm fine," Corley snapped.

"Okay, great. I'm just asking."

Corley got up and crossed the squad room and refilled his coffee cup and sat back down. He took a sip, burned his tongue. "Yeah, well," he said, "thanks for asking. You want to come?"

Tasco shook his head. "It's going to be a long day without that."

It was a long day, but Corley made the nine o'clock at the Majestic. The ticket girl let him in on his shield again, said the numbers were up, really up. The lobby was crowded, people two deep at the candy counter, clumped around video games, whooping over electronic explosions as someone blasted something on the screen. There were no seats left at the back or on the aisle, and Corley had to sit between two people. He kept his elbows off the armrests. During the movie the audience seemed more tense, everybody wide-eyed and alert, but he caught himself with knotted muscles more than once and thought the tension maybe was in him.

The lipstick game spread like bad news, and every night Corley ran in one or two slashers for questioning, and for anger, because it wasn't a game when he saw a head snap back or heard a scream, wasn't a game when the man moving down his row or running up the aisle might have a razor tucked in his fist. The games got elaborate, became contests with teams, slashers and victims alternating roles and tallying points in the lobby between shows. Sometimes someone would slash a stranger, and Corley broke up the fights at first, but later didn't bother, didn't waste time to risk injury for a pair of idiots. He went to movies every night that week, and every night he saw more people than the night before, and felt more alert and tense, and left more exhausted. His ulcer flared like sulfur; he was smoking again.

On Friday night near the end of the movie his beeper went off and half the audience screamed and jumped and clutched in their seats, then sank back as a wave of relief swept over them and they gave themselves to laughter and curses and groans and chatter, ignoring the movie.

Corley phoned in from the lobby. They had found a

body after the last show at the Astro. He had been slashed.

Corley was strangely pleased.

"Could be some frigging copycat," said Tasco the next day, yawning.

Corley wasn't sleepy. "No way," he said. "Exactly the same."

"The paper had the details."

"It's the same guy, Ray."

"Okay, okay," said Tasco, palms up. "Same guy."

The routine began again, interviews, hunting up the audience, blue and yellow pins, lack of a good witness. Tasco asked where they'd sat, what they'd seen, who they'd known. Corley asked them why they'd gone, whether they'd liked it, if they went to horror flicks often, if they'd played the assassin games. They didn't know how to answer him. He made them uncomfortable, sometimes angry, and they addressed their answers to Tasco, who looked amused and popped his gum and wrote it all down.

Corley posted the new pictures on the corkboard, and the articles and the editorials, and the movie ads. Various groups blasted the lipstick game, called for theaters to quit showing horror movies, called for theaters to close completely. Corley's theater owner wrote a guest editorial calling on readers not to be made prisoners by one maniac, not to give in to the creatures of the night. The Moviola ads promised armed guards; the Majestic dared people to come to the late show. The corkboard was covered by the end of the week, a vast montage filling the wall behind the blank television.

Tasco went with him to the movies now. There were lines at every ticket window, longer lines every night. The Moviola's security guards roamed the lobby and aisles; the Majestic installed airport metal detectors at the door; the Astro frisked its patrons, who laughed nervously, or cracked wise like Cagney or Bogart, and the guards made a big production when they found tubes of lipstick, asked if they had a license, were told it was for protection only or that they were collectors or with the FBI. They were all having a great time. The ticket girl said they gave her the creeps.

"That's two of us," Corley said.

Corley and Tasco sat on opposite sides of the theater, on the aisle, backs to the wall, linked with lapel mikes and earphones. Fewer and fewer played the lipstick game, but the audiences seemed electric and intense; Corley felt sharp and coiled, felt he could see everything, felt he was waiting for something.

After the movies, when he came home drained and sagged down on the couch, Corley found himself staring at the wall, at the picture of T. O. Bussey looking out at him from the aisle seat, his hands holding up the head, and he felt like he didn't know anything at all.

Corley turned off his electric razor and turned up the radio. An early morning DJ was interviewing a psychiatrist about the slasher. Corley knew he'd give the standard whacko profile, a quiet, polite, boy-next-door type who repressed sex and hated Daddy, and that everybody who knew him would be surprised and say what a nice guy he was and how they could hardly believe it. He got his notebook to write it down so he could quote it to Tasco.

"Said he was 'quiet, withdrawn, suffers repressed sexuality and sexual expression, experiences intense emotional build-up and achieves orgasm at climax of movie and murder, cycle of build-up and release, release of life, fluids, satisfaction.' " He flipped the notebook shut.

"Jeez, I hate that," said Tasco. "I hate the hell out of that. That doesn't mean squat. That's just words. Who is he, gets paid to say crap like that? He doesn't know anything."

"I want to talk to this guy," said Corley. "I just want to sit down and talk to him, you know? I just want to buy him a drink or something and ask him what the hell is going on."

"You mean the shrink?" Tasco was squinting.

"Our guy," said Corley. "The slasher."

Tasco didn't say anything.

"He knows something," said Corley.

Tasco looked angry again. "He doesn't know anything. What are you talking about?"

Corley tried to say what he meant, couldn't find it, couldn't make it concrete. Why was it so important to get this guy, see him, find out what he looked like, why he did it, not why, exactly, but how, maybe, how in the sense of giving people a chance to maybe have their throats cut, and having them line up like it was a raffle? What would that tell him about what was driving him off the street, what kept drawing him back down, why he was carrying an extra piece, what kept him in that lousy apartment in the middle of all of this tar and pavement when he could just walk away? What did he want?

"He knows something about people," Corley said finally.

Tasco waved his hand like he was fanning flies. "What could he know? He's just a sicko. . . ."

"Come on, Ray, we've seen sickos. They don't slash in public, not like this."

Anger was in both voices now.

"Maybe they do. Maybe he just wanted to see if he could. Ever think of that? Maybe it's the thrill of offing somebody in front of a live audience. Maybe that's all."

"Yeah, that's all, and all those people out there know

he's out there, too, and they can't stay away. Why can't they stay away, Tasco?"

"We can't just keep going to movies, Devin. We got lives, you know."

"We're not going to get him unless we get him in the act."

"That's just stupid. That won't happen. That's a stupid thing to say."

"Watch it, sergeant."

"Oh, kiss it, Corley. Jesus."

They were silent again, avoiding each other's eyes.

"I just want to bust this guy," said Corley.

"Yeah, well," said Tasco, looking out of the window, "what I want is to go home, see my wife and kids, maybe watch a ball game." He looked back to Corley. "So, we going out again tonight or what?"

They went again that night and the next night and the next. They always sat on the aisle at opposite ends of the last row so that they could cover both rear exits. Tasco would sit through only one show; Corley sat through both. He felt better when Tasco was at the other end, when he could hear him clear his throat, or mutter something to himself, or even snore when he nodded off as he sometimes did, which amazed Corley. Corley stayed braced in his seat.

When Tasco left, Corley felt naked on the aisle, so he'd move in one seat and drape a raincoat across the aisle seat so it looked occupied, so no one would sit there. The nine o'clock show was usually a sell-out, the audience filling every seat and pressing in on him, a single vague mass in the dark at a horror flick, hiding a man with a razor, maybe even inviting him, desiring him, seeking him. After five nights, Corley was ragged and jumpy.

"I'm going to sit in the projection booth," he told Tasco. "Better view."

Tasco shrugged. "End of the week and that's it, okay?"
"We'll see."

"That's got to be it, Devin."

The booth gave Corley a broader view, and gave him
distance, height, a thick glass wall. At first he felt con-
spicuous whenever a pale face lifted his way as the audience waited for the movie to start. The manager showed
him how to override the automatics and turn up the house
lights, otherwise hands off. The projector looked like a
giant tommy gun sighted on the screen through a little
rectangle outlined on the glass in masking tape. He had
expected something more sophisticated.

Tasco was just out of sight below him, left aisle, last
row, back to the wall. Through his earphone, Corley could
hear the audience from Tasco's lapel mike, a general mur-
mur, a burst of high-pitched laughter, the crying of a baby
who shouldn't even be there. Corley wiped his glasses on
his tie. Hundreds of people out there, could be any one of
them, and what the hell were the rest of them doing out
there, and what the hell was he doing up here?

The lights dimmed and the projector lit up, commer-
cials, previews, the main feature. A little out-of-focus
movie danced in the rectangle on the glass, blobs of color
and movement bleeding out onto the masking tape; the
soundtrack was thin and tinny from the booth speaker
and just half a beat behind in the earphone, disconcert-
ing. Beyond the glass, on exhibition, the audience stirred
and rippled; beyond them the huge and distorted images
filled the screen. He watched, and when someone stood
and moved toward the aisle, he warned Tasco and felt
adrenaline heat arms and legs and the figure reached the
aisle and turned and walked toward the restroom or
candy counter, and Corley tried to relax again. It was
easier to relax up here, above it all.

The movie dragged on. Corley found by staring at a

central point in the audience and unfocusing his eyes, he could see all movement instantly, and everybody was moving, scratching ears and noses and scalps, lifting hands to mouths to cover coughs or to feed, rocking, putting arms around dates, leaning forward, leaning back, covering eyes with fingers. Again he saw the patterns emerge around the on-screen killings, movements ebbing as the killing neared, freezing at the death itself, melting after, and flowing across the audience again, strong and choppy, then quieter and smooth. He had to concentrate, breathe slowly and carefully, to keep himself from narrowing his vision, focusing on one person. He didn't see the movie.

A flicker in the corner of his eye, flick of light on steel. He swung eyes right, locked on movement, saw the head pulled back, the blade flicker again, realized it was happening, that he hadn't seen the killer move down the row because he was sitting right behind his victim, it was happening now, all the way across the theater from Tasco. He radioed Tasco as he turned for the stairs and punched the lights, heard Tasco yell for the man to stop, knew they were too late for the victim, but they had him now, they had him now, they had him now. He took the stairs three at a time, slipped, skidded down, arms flailing, wrenched his shoulder as he tried to break the fall, then on his feet and bursting through the door behind the concession stand, drawing his pistol as he ran, putting out his left arm and vaulting over the counter, popcorn and patron flying. He stopped in front of the double doors, pistol leveled, waiting for the maniac to run into his arms.

Nobody came. Corley crouched, frozen, pistol extended in two hands, and in his left ear the theater, voices and screams and music, and Tasco maybe, Tasco shouting something, and still nobody came. He moved forward, gun still extended, and jerked open a door with his left hand.

Lights still brightening, movie running, and the screams and shouts and music in the earphone echoed, echoed in his right ear and for an instant he lost where he was. Then he heard Tasco calling him in his earphone and saw him trying to hammer his way into a knot of people below the screen, the rest of the audience in their seats, watching the movie or those down front attacking the slasher.

Corley ran down the stairs, yelling for Tasco. The earphone went dead and Tasco was gone. Corley reached the mass, started pulling people out of his way, stepping on them, pushing. Some pushed back and turned on him, and he knocked one down and another man grabbed him, and he hit the man in the face, and backed toward the wall, gun leveled. The man changed his mind, backed away. Corley called Tasco, heard nothing through the earphone. He tried to elbow his way in the crowd, started clubbing with both hands around the pistol, fighting the urge to just start pulling the trigger and have done with hit. A huge man turned and started to swing; Corley watched the fist come around in slow motion, easily deflected the blow, put a knee in the solar plexus, watched the man fall like a great tree, cuffed him across the jaw as he went down, felt that he could count the pores in the potato nose. They were right beneath the speakers, the music pounding his bones. He reached for the next one in his way.

He heard a shot, saw Tasco cornered by four or five, his gun pointed toward the ceiling but lowering. The next one wouldn't be a warning shot and those guys knew it and they weren't backing off. Corley tried to shout above the music, raised his pistol and fired toward the ceiling, fired again, heard Tasco's gun answer, fired a third time, and the crowd started breaking at the edges, some hurt, some bloody. Corley tried to hold them back, grabbed at one who twisted away, and they pushed past, ignoring him, laughing or shouting, and the others were leaving their seats now, mixing with them, and some in their seats were applauding and cheering.

There were people lying all around them, some groaning, some bleeding. The slasher's victim sprawled across an aisle seat, throat opened to the stars painted on the ceiling. "Help me, Jesus," someone was saying over and over. "Jesus, help me." He heard someone calling his name, saying something. It was Tasco.

"I couldn't stop them," Tasco was saying. Corley looked down. They had used the slasher's blade, and whatever else was handy. The slasher's features were unrecognizable, the head almost severed from the body. A sudden fury flashed through Corley, and he kicked the person lying nearest to him. "Couldn't stop them," Tasco repeated, his voice trembling.

"Is this him, do you think?" asked Corley.

Tasco didn't say anything.

"Maybe Maggie can tell us," said Corley. "Maybe the M.E." He could hear the desperation in his voice.

"It could be anybody," said Tasco.

When he used the phone in the ticket office to call it all in, he heard people demanding a refund because they hadn't gotten to see the end of the movie.

Corley didn't get home until late the next afternoon. He'd made it through the last eighteen hours by thinking about the crummy little apartment high above the street, with the couch and the double locks and the television. He heard the cat yowling before he even put the key in the first lock.

He fed the cat and opened a beer, and turned on his television, but the pictures were wrong, fuzzy, filled with snow. He tried to fix the image, but nothing worked, and he grew angry. Finally he checked the roof and found his antenna bent over.

"Gianelli," he shouted, pounding, standing to one side of the door, seeing an image of Gianelli spinning in slow motion toward pavement four floors down. "Come out of there, Gianelli." No answer. He spread the name out, kicking on the door once for each syllable. "*Gi—a—nel—li!*"

"You go away now," came a voice from inside. "You go away. I'm calling the cops."

"I *am* a cop," Corley shouted, dragging out his shield and holding it to the peephole.

"You go away now," Gianelli said after a moment of silence.

Corley gave the door one last kick.

He tried to salvage the antenna, but Gianelli had done a job on it, twisting the crosspieces, cutting the wires into a dozen pieces.

Before he went to sleep, he took down the pictures and clippings about Mr. Bussey, and he dug around until he found the pictures of the previous occupant, and he pinned them all up. He crossed the room and sat on the couch to look at them. They were all black and white, blonde and pale eyes, and he wondered if she had walked away from whatever brought her here. He thought she was very beautiful. But who could tell from pictures?

He locked the doors and put on the night-light.

About the Contributors

LAWRENCE BLOCK is the author of numerous novels with such memorable repeating characters as Matthew Scudder, Chip Harrison, Bernie Rhodenbarr, and Evan Tanner. With humor and suspense, Mr. Block holds the reader until the final page is turned.

BILL CRENSHAW is a short-story writer of the eighties. "Flicks" is his first work to be honored with the Mystery Writers of America's Edgar award, and his is a voice that the nineties will honor again and again. Mr. Crenshaw lives in South Carolina.

HARLAN ELLISON has won many awards, especially in the field of science fiction and fantasy. This hasn't stopped him from winning for his mystery stories as well! "Soft Monkey" earned him his second award from the Mystery Writers of America.

FREDERICK FORSYTH won an Edgar in 1971 with his celebrated thriller The Day of the Jackal, and again in 1982 for "There Are No Snakes in Ireland." His "Used in Evidence" was nominated in 1979. Other Forsyth best-sellers have been The Odessa File, The Devil's Alternative, The Fourth Protocol, and The Negotiator.

CLARK HOWARD has been writing for thirty years, full time for fifteen. He is a five-time Edgar nominee, and a one-time Edgar winner for his short story "Horn Man." The winner of numerous other awards and a recent nominee for a writing honor, Mr. Howard is also the author of eighteen novels.

JOHN LUTZ is an award-winning author who has written dozens of suspense novels and short stories. He is "an expert—he'll have you glued to the book page" (Denver *Post*). Mr. Lutz lives in St. Louis, Missouri.

GEOFFREY NORMAN is a freelance magazine writer. He lives in Vermont with his wife and two children. In addition to his short story "Armed and Dangerous," Mr. Norman has a mystery novel, *Sweetwater Ranch*, coming soon from Atlantic Monthly Press.

RUTH RENDELL won her first short-story Edgar in 1974 for "The Fallen Curtain." She is well loved in the mystery field and has written many psychological novels of the human condition. She lives in England—one of the many overseas friends of the Mystery Writers of America. Among her many novels are *An Unkindness of Ravens*, *A Guilty Thing Surprised*, *One Across, Two Down*, and *Wolf to Slaughter*.

JACK RITCHIE wrote literally hundreds of short crime fiction stories. Packed with not a wasted word, they read like full-length novels. For more than thirty years he wove sparkling tales that were crisp, clear, straight and that cut like a razor.

ROBERT SAMPSON was born in Ohio and has been writing for thirty years. He has published a number of short stories and has written seven nonfiction books, of which five are from the Yesterday's Faces series. Mr. Sampson lives in Alabama.

DONALD E. WESTLAKE is a winner of the Edgar award for his novel *God Save the Mark*. He was born in Brooklyn and raised in Albany, New York. Mr. Westlake has approximately thirty novels published under his own name since 1960, in addition to twenty novels under the pseudonym Richard Stark and five under the name Tucker Coe. Among his novels are *The Hot Rock, Too Much, Jimmy the Kid*, and *Trust Me on This*; his screenplays include *Cops and Robbers, Hot Stuff*, and *The Stepfather*.

EDGAR AWARDS
Winners and
Nominees—Fiction

Grand Master

1988	Hillary Waugh
1987	Phyllis A. Whitney
1986	Michael Gilbert
1985	Ed McBain (Evan Hunter)
1984	Dorothy Salisbury Davis
1983	John le Carré
1982	Margaret Millar
1981	Julian Symons
1980	Stanley Ellin
1979	W.R. Burnett
1978	Aaron Marc Stein
1977	Daphne du Maurier, Dorothy B. Hughes, Ngaio Marsh
1976	Graham Greene
1975	Eric Ambler
1973	Ross Macdonald
1972	Judson Philips
1971	John D. MacDonald
1970	Mignon G. Eberhart
1969	James M. Cain
1968	John Creasey
1966	Baynard Kendrick
1965	Georges Simenon
1963	George Harmon Coxe
1962	John Dickson Carr
1961	Erle Stanley Gardner
1960	Ellery Queen
1958	Rex Stout
1957	Vincent Starrett
1954	Agatha Christie

Best Novel

1988 A COLD RED SUNRISE by Stuart M. Kaminsky (Scribner). Also: A THIEF OF TIME by Tony Hillerman (Harper & Row), JOEY'S CASE by K.C. Constantine (Mysterious Press), IN THE LAKE OF THE MOON by David L. Linsey (Atheneum), SACRIFICIAL GROUND by Thomas H. Cook (Putnam).

1987 OLD BONES by Aaron Elkins (Mysterious Press). Also: THE CORPSE IN OOZAK'S POND by Charlotte MacLeod (Mysterious Press), NURSERY CRIMES by B.M. Gill (Scribner), ROUGH CIDER by Peter Lovesey (Mysterious Press), A TROUBLE OF FOOLS by Linda Barnes (St. Martin's Press).

1986 A DARK-ADAPTED EYE by Barbara Vine (Bantam). Also: THE BLIND RUN by Brian Freemantle (Bantam), COME MORNING by Joe Gores (Mysterious Press), THE STRAIGHT MAN by Roger L. Simon (Villard), A TASTE FOR DEATH by P.D. James (Knopf).

1985 THE SUSPECT by L.R. Wright (Viking Penguin). Also: CITY OF GLASS:

THE NEW YORK TRIL-OGY, PART I by Paul Auster (Sun & Moon Press), A SHOCK TO THE SYSTEM by Simon Brett (Scribner), THE TREE OF HANDS by Ruth Rendell (Pantheon), AN UNKIND-NESS OF RAVENS by Ruth Rendell (Pantheon).

1984 BRIARPATCH by Ross Thomas (Simon & Schuster). Also: THE BLACK SERAPHIM by Michael Gilbert (Harper & Row), CHESSPLAYER by William Pearson (Viking Penguin/The Viking Press), EMILY DICKIN-SON IS DEAD by Jane Langton (St. Martin's/A Joan Kahn Book), THE TWELFTH JUROR by B.M. Gill (Scribner).

1983 LA BRAVA by Elmore Leonard (Arbor House). Also: THE LITTLE DRUMMER GIRL by John le Carré (Knopf), THE NAME OF THE ROSE by Umberto Eco, translated by William Weaver (A Helen & Kurt Wolff Book/ Harcourt Brace Jovanovich), THE PAPERS OF TONY VEITCH by William McIlvanney (Pantheon), TEXAS STA-TION by Christopher Leach (A Helen & Kurt Wolff Book/Harcourt Brace Jovanovich).

1982 BILLINGSGATE SHOAL by Rick Boyer (Houghton Mifflin). Also: THE CAP-TAIN by Seymour Shubin (Stein & Day), EIGHT MILLION WAYS TO DIE by Lawrence Block (Ar-bor House), KAHAWA by Donald E. Westlake (Vi-king), SPLIT IMAGES by Elmore Leonard (Arbor House).

1981 PEREGRINE by William Bayer (Congdon & Lat-tes). Also: THE AMA-TEUR by Robert Littell (Simon & Schuster), BOGMAIL by Patrick McGinley (Ticknor & Fields), DEATH IN A COLD CLIMATE by Rob-ert Barnard (Scribner), DUPE by Liza Cody (Scribner), THE OTHER SIDE OF SILENCE by Ted Allebeury (Scribner).

1980 WHIP HAND by Dick Francis (Harper & Row). Also: DEATH OF A LIT-ERARY WIDOW by Rob-ert Barnard (Scribner), DEATH DROP by B.M. Gill (Scribner), SPY'S WIFE by Reginald Hill (Pantheon), MAN ON FIRE by A.J. Quinell (Morrow).

1979 THE RHEINGOLD ROUTE by Arthur Maling (Harper & Row). Also: DEATH OF A MYSTERY WRITER by Robert Bar-nard (Scribner), FIRE IN THE BARLEY by Frank Parrish (Dodd, Mead), MAKE DEATH LOVE ME by Ruth Rendell (Double-day), A COAT OF VAR-NISH by C.P. Snow (Scribner).

1978 THE EYE OF THE NEE-DLE by Ken Follett (Ar-bor House). Also: THE SNAKE by John Godey

(Putnam), LISTENING WOMAN by Tony Hillerman (Harper & Row), A SLEEPING LIFE by Ruth Rendell (Doubleday), THE SHALLOW GRAVE by Jack S. Scott (Harper & Row).

1977 CATCH ME: KILL ME by William Hallahan (Bobbs-Merrill). Also: LAIDLAW by William McIlvanney (Pantheon), NIGHTWING by Martin Cruz Smith (Norton).

1976 PROMISED LAND by Robert Parker (Houghton Mifflin). Also: A MADNESS OF THE HEART by Richard Neeley (Crowell), THE MAIN by Trevanian (Harcourt Brace Jovanovich), THE CAVANAUGH QUEST by Thomas Gifford (Putnam).

1975 HOPSCOTCH by Brian Garfield (M. Evans). Also: THE GARGOYLE CONSPIRACY by Marvin Albert (Doubleday), THE MONEY HARVEST by Ross Thomas (William Morrow), HARRY'S GAME by Gerald Seymour (Random House), OPERATION ALCESTIC by Maggie Rennert (Prentice-Hall).

1974 PETER'S PENCE by Jon Cleary (Morrow). Also: GOOD-BYE AND AMEN by Francis Clifford (Harcourt Brace Jovanovich), THE LESTER AFFAIR by Andrew Garve (Harper & Row), THE MAN WHO LOVED ZOOS by Malcolm Bosse (Putnam), THE SILVER BEARS by Paul E. Erdman (Scribner).

1973 DANCE HALL OF THE DEAD by Tony Hillerman (Harper & Row). Also: AMIGO, AMIGO by Francis Clifford (Coward, McCann & Geoghegan), DEAR LAURA by Jean Stubbs (Stein & Day), THE RAINBIRD PATTERN by Victor Canning (William Morrow), AN UNSUITABLE JOB FOR A WOMAN by P.D. James (Scribner).

1972 THE LINGALA CODE by Warren Kiefer (Random House). Also: CANTO FOR A GYPSY by Martin Smith (Putnam), FIVE PIECES OF JADE by John Ball (Little, Brown), THE SHOOTING GALLERY by Hugh C. Rae (Coward, McCann & Geoghegan), TIED UP IN TINSEL by Ngaio Marsh (Little, Brown).

1971 THE DAY OF THE JACKAL by Frederick Forsyth (Viking). Also: SHROUD FOR A NIGHTINGALE by P.D. James (Scribner), THE FLY ON THE WALL by Tony Hillerman (Harper & Row), WHO KILLED ENOCH POWELL? by Arthur Wise (Harper & Row), SIR, YOU BASTARD by G.F. Newman (Simon & Schuster).

1970 THE LAUGHING POLICEMAN by Maj Sjowall and Per Wahloo (Pantheon). Also: THE

HOUND AND THE FOX AND THE HARPER by Shaun Herron (Random House), BEYOND THIS POINT ARE MONSTERS by Margaret Millar (Random House), MANY DEADLY RETURNS by Patricia Moyes (Holt, Rinehart & Winston), THE HOT ROCK by Donald E. Westlake (Simon & Schuster).

1969 FORFEIT by Dick Francis (Harper & Row). Also: THE OLD ENGLISH PEEP SHOW by Peter Dickinson (Harper & Row), MIRO by Shaun Herron (Random House), BLIND MAN WITH A PISTOL by Chester Himes (William Morrow), WHEN IN GREECE by Emma Latham (Simon & Schuster), WHERE THE DARK STREETS GO by Dorothy Salisbury Davis (Scribner).

1968 A CASE OF NEED by Jeffery Hudson (World). Also: PICTURE MISS SEETON by Heron Carvic (Harper & Row), THE GLASS-SPIDER ANTS' NEST by Peter Dickinson (Harper & Row), BLOOD SPORT by Dick Francis (Harper & Row), GOD SPEED THE NIGHT by Dorothy Salisbury Davis and Jerome Ross (Scribner), THE VALENTINE ESTATE by Stanley Ellin (Random House).

1967 GOD SAVE THE MARK by Donald E. Westlake (Random House). Also:

FLYING FINISH by Dick Francis (Harper & Row), THE GIFT SHOP by Charlotte Armstrong (Coward-McCann), A PARADE OF COCKEYED CREATURES by George Baxt (Random House), LEMON IN THE BASKET by Charlotte Armstrong (Coward-Mc-Cann), ROSEMARY'S BABY by Ira Levin (Random House).

1966 KING OF THE RAINY COUNTRY by Nicolas Freeling (Harper & Row). Also: ODDS AGAINST by Dick Francis (Harper & Row), KILLER DOLPHIN by Ngaio Marsh (Little, Brown), THE BUSY BODY by Donald E. Westlake (Random House).

1965 THE QUILLER MEMORANDUM by Adam Hall (Simon & Schuster). Also: THE FAR SIDE OF THE DOLLAR by Ross Macdonald (Knopf), THE PALE BETRAYER by Dorothy Salisbury Davis (Scribner), AIRS ABOVE THE GROUND by Mary Stewart (Morrow), THE PERFECT MURDER by H.R.F. Keating (Dutton), FUNERAL IN BERLIN by Len Deighton (Putnam).

1964 THE SPY WHO CAME IN FROM THE COLD by John le Carré (Coward-McCann). Also: THE NIGHT OF THE GENERALS by Hans Hellmut Kirst (Harper & Row), THE FIEND by Margaret Millar (Random House),

THIS ROUGH MAGIC by Mary Stewart (Morrow).

1963 THE LIGHT OF DAY by Eric Ambler (Knopf). Also: THE MAKE-BELIEVE MAN by Elizabeth Fenwick (Harper & Row), GRIEVE FOR THE PAST by Stanton Forbes (Crime Club), THE EXPENDABLE MAN by Dorothy B. Hughes (Random House), THE PLAYER ON THE OTHER SIDE by Ellery Queen (Random House).

1962 DEATH OF THE JOYFUL WOMAN by Ellis Peters (Crime Club). Also: THE ZEBRA-STRIPED HEARSE by Ross Macdonald (Knopf), SEANCE by Mark McShane (Crime Club), THE EVIL WISH by Jean Potts (Scribner), KNAVE OF HEARTS by Dell Shannon (Morrow), THE BALLAD OF THE RUNNING MAN by Shelly Smith (Harper & Row).

1961 GIDEON'S FIRE by J.J. Marric (Harper). Also: NIGHTMARE by Anne Blaisdell (Knopf), THE GREEN STONE by Suzanne Blanc (Harper), NIGHT OF WENCESLES by Lionel Davidson (Harper), THE WYCHERLY WOMAN by Ross Macdonald (Knopf).

1960 PROGRESS OF A CRIME by Julian Symons (Harper). Also: THE TRACES OF BRILIHART by Herbert Brean (Harper), THE DEVIL'S OWN by Peter Curtis (Doubleday), WATCHER IN THE SHADOWS by Geoffrey Household (Little, Brown).

1959 THE HOURS BEFORE DAWN by Celia Fremlin (Lippincott). Also: THE LIST OF ADRIAN MESSENGER by Philip MacDonald (Crime Club).

1958 THE EIGHTH CIRCLE by Stanley Ellin (Random House). Also: A GENTLEMAN CALLED by Dorothy Salisbury Davis (Scribner), THE MADHOUSE IN WASHINGTON SQUARE by David Alexander (Lippincott), WOMAN IN THE WOODS by Lee Blackstock (Crime Club).

1957 ROOM TO SWING by Ed Lacy (Harper). Also: THE LONGEST SECOND by Bill Ballinger (Harper), THE NIGHT OF THE GOOD CHILDREN by Marjorie Carleton (Morrow), THE BUSHMAN WHO CAME BACK by Arthur Upfield (Crime Club).

1956 A DRAM OF POISON by Charlotte Armstrong (Coward-McCann). Also: THE MAN WHO DIDN'T FLY by Margot Bennett (Harper).

1955 BEAST IN VIEW by Margaret Millar (Random House). Also: THE CASE OF THE TALKING BUG by The Gordons (Crime Club), THE TALENTED MR. RIPLEY by Patricia

Highsmith (Coward-McCann).

1954 THE LONG GOODBYE by Raymond Chandler (Houghton Mifflin).

1953 BEAT NOT THE BONES by Charlotte Jay (Harper).

Best First Novel

1988 CAROLINA SKELETONS by David Stout (Mysterious Press). Also: A GREAT DELIVERANCE by Elizabeth George (Bantam), JULIAN SOLO by Shelley Reuben (Dodd, Mead), MURDER ONCE DONE by Mary Lou Bennett (Perseverance Press), THE MURDER OF FRAU SCHÜTZ by J. Madison Davis (Walker).

1987 DEATH AMONG STRANGERS by Deidre S. Laiken (Macmillan). Also: DETECTIVE by Parnell Hall (Donald I. Fine), HEAT LIGHTNING by John Lantigua (Putnam), LOVER MAN by Dallas Murphy (Scribner), THE SPOILER by Domenic Stansberry (Atlantic Monthly).

1986 NO ONE RIDES FOR FREE by Larry Beinhart (Morrow). Also: DEAD AIR by Mike Lupica (Villard), FLOATER by Joseph Koenig (Mysterious Press), LOST by Gary Devon (Knopf), RICEBURNER by Richard Hyer (Scribner).

1985 WHEN THE BOUGH BREAKS by Jonathan Kellerman (Atheneum). Also: THE ADVENTURE OF THE ECTOPLASMIC MAN by Daniel Stashower (Morrow), THE GLORY HOLE MURDERS by Tony Fennelly (Carroll & Graf), SLEEPING DOG by Dick Lochte (Arbor House).

1984 STRIKE THREE, YOU'RE DEAD by R.D. Rosen (Walker). Also: A CREATIVE KIND OF KILLER by Jack Early (Franklin Watts), FOUL SHOT by Doug Hornig (Scribner), SOMEONE ELSE'S GRAVE by Alison Smith (St. Martin's/A Joan Kahn Book), SWEET, SAVAGE DEATH by Orania Papazoglou (Doubleday Crime Club).

1983 THE BAY PSALM BOOK MURDER by Will Harriss (Walker). Also: CAROLINE MINUSCULE by Andrew Taylor (Dodd, Mead), DEAD MAN'S THOUGHTS by Carolyn Wheat (St. Martin's), THE GOLD SOLUTION by Herbert Resnicow (St. Martin's/A Joan Kahn Book), RED DIAMOND, PRIVATE EYE by Mark Schorr (St. Martin's).

1982 THE BUTCHER'S BOY by Thomas Perry (Scribner). Also: BY FREQUENT ANGUISH by S.F.X. Dean (Walker), IN THE HEAT OF THE SUMMER by John Katzenbach (Atheneum), TWO IF BY SEA by Ernest Savage (Scribner), UNHOLY

COMMUNION by Richard Hughes (Doubleday).

1981 CHIEFS by Stuart Woods (Norton). Also: THE BLACK GLOVE by Geoffrey Miller (Viking), GIANT KILLER by Vernon Tom Hyman (Marek), MURDER AT THE RED OCTOBER by Anthony Olcott (Academy Chicago), NOT A THROUGH STREET by Ernest Larsen (Random House).

1980 THE WATCHER by Kay Nolte Smith (Coward, McCann & Geoghegan). Also: WINDS OF THE OLD DAYS by Betsy Aswald (Dial), THE REMBRANDT PANEL by Oliver Banks (Little, Brown), DOUBLE NEGATIVE by David Carkeet (Dial), THE OTHER ANN FLETCHER by Susanne Jaffe (NAL).

1979 THE LASKO TANGENT by Richard North Patterson (Norton). Also: NIGHT TRAINS by Peter Heath Fine (Lippincott), FOLLOW THE LEADER by John Logue (Crown).

1978 KILLED IN THE RATINGS by William L. DeAndrea (Harcourt Brace Jovanovich). Also: THE SCOURGE by Thomas L. Dunne (Coward, McCann & Geoghegan), FALLING ANGEL by William Hjortsberg (Harcourt Brace Jovanovich), BLOOD SECRETS by Craig Jones (Harper & Row), THE MEMORY OF EVA RYKER by Donald A. Stanwood (Coward, McCann & Geoghegan).

1977 A FRENCH FINISH by Robert Ross (Putnam). Also: DEWEY DECIMATED by Charles A. Goodrun (Crown), THE FAN by Bob Randall (Random House).

1976 THE THOMAS BERRYMAN NUMBER by James Patterson (Little, Brown). Also: STRAIGHT by Steven Knickmeyer (Random House), YOUR DAY IN THE BARREL by Alan Furst (Atheneum), FINAL PROOF by Marie R. Reno (Harper & Row), THE BIG PAY-OFF by Janice Law (Houghton Mifflin).

1975 THE ALVAREZ JOURNAL by Rex Burns (Harper & Row). Also: THE DEVALINO CAPER by A.J. Russell (Random House), HARMATTAN by Thomas Klop (Bobbs-Merrill), WALTZ ACROSS TEXAS by Max Crawford (Farrar, Straus & Giroux), PAPERBACK THRILLER by Lynn Meyer (Random House).

1974 FLETCH by Gregory Mcdonald (Bobbs-Merrill). Also: THE JONES MAN by Vern E. Smith (Henry Regnery), THE KREUTZMAN FORMULA by Virgil Scott & Dominic Koski (Simon & Schuster), SATURDAY GAMES by Brown Meggs (Random House), TARGET PRACTICE by Nicholas Meyer (Harcourt Brace Jovanovich).

1973 THE BILLION DOLLAR SURE THING by Paul E. Erdman (Scribner). Also: KICKED TO DEATH BY A CAMEL by Clarence Jackson (Harper & Row), MAN ON A STRING by Michael Wolfe (Harper & Row), MANY HAPPY RETURNS by Justin Scott (David McKay), SOMEONE'S DEATH by Charles Larson (Lippincott).

1972 SQUAW POINT by R.H. Shimer (Harper & Row). Also: BOX 100 by Frank Leonard (Harper & Row), THE DEAD OF WINTER by William H. Hallahan (Bobbs-Merrill), THE HEART OF THE DOG by Thomas A. Roberts (Random House), A PERSON SHOULDN'T DIE LIKE THAT by Arthur Goldstein (Random House).

1971 FINDING MAUBEE by A.H.Z. Carr (Putnam). Also: GYPSY IN AMBER by Martin Smith (Putnam), ASK THE RIGHT QUESTION by Michael Z. Lewin (Putnam), TO SPITE HER FACE by Hildegarde Dolson (Lippincott), THE STALKER by Bill Pronzini (Random House).

1970 THE ANDERSON TAPES by Lawrence Sanders (Putnam). Also: INCIDENT AT 125TH STREET by J.E. Brown (Doubleday), TAKING GARY FELDMAN by Stanley Cohen (Putnam), THE BLESSING WAY by Tony Hillerman (Harper & Row), THE NAKED FACE by Sidney Sheldon (Morrow).

1969 A TIME FOR PREDATORS by Joe Gores (Random House). Also: YOU'LL LIKE MY MOTHER by Naomi Hintze (Putnam), QUICKSAND by Myrick Land (Harper & Row).

1968 SILVER STREET by E. Richard Johnson (Harper & Row), and (double winner) THE BAIT by Dorothy Uhnak (Simon & Schuster). Also: THE DINOSAUR by Lawrence Kamarck (Random House).

1967 ACT OF FEAR by Michael Collins (Dodd, Mead). Also: MORTISSIMO by P.E.H. Dunston (Random House), THE KILLING SEASON by John Redgate (Trident), THE TIGERS ARE HUNGRY by Charles Early (Morrow), HELL GATE by James Dawson (McKay).

1966 THE COLD WAR SWAP by Ross Thomas (Morrow). Also: A KIND OF TREASON by Robert S. Elegant (Holt, Rinehart & Winston), FANCY'S KNELL by Babs Deal (Doubleday), THE PEDESTAL by George Lanning (Harper & Row).

1965 IN THE HEAT OF THE NIGHT by John Ball (Harper & Row). Also: BEFORE THE BALL WAS OVER by Alexandra Roudybush (Crime Club),

THE EXPENDABLE SPY by Jack D. Hun (Dutton), THE FRENCH DOLL by Vincent McConner (Hill & Wang).

1964 FRIDAY THE RABBI SLEPT LATE by Harry Kemelman (Crown). Also: THE GRAVE-MAKER'S HOUSE by Rubin Weber (Harper & Row), IN THE LAST ANALYSIS by Amanda Cross (Macmillan).

1963 THE FLORENTINE FINISH by Cornelius Hirschberg (Harper & Row). Also: THE PROWLER by Francis Rickett (Simon & Schuster), THE NEON HAYSTACK by James M. Ullman (Simon & Schuster), THE FIFTH WOMAN by M. Fagyas (Crime Club).

1962 THE FUGITIVE by Robert L. Fish (Simon & Schuster). Also: COUNTERWEIGHT by Daniel Broun (Holt, Rinehart & Winston), THE CHASE by Richard Unekis (Walker).

1961 THE GREEN STONE by Suzanne Blanc (Harper). Also: FELONY TANK by Malcolm Braley (Gold Medal), CLOSE HIS EYES by Olivian Dwight (Harper), THE CIPHER by Alex Gordon (Simon & Schuster), NIGHT OF THE KILL by Breni James (Simon & Schuster), SHOCK TREATMENT by Winfred Van Atta (Crime Club).

1960 THE MAN IN THE CAGE by John Holbrook Vance (Random House). Also: THE MERCENARIES by Donald E. Westlake (Random House), CASE PENDING by Dell Shannon (Harper), KILLING AT BIG TREE by David McCarthy (Doubleday), THE MARRIAGE CAGE by William Johnston (Lyle Stuart).

1959 THE GREY FLANNEL SHROUD by Henry Slesar (Random House). Also: A DREAM OF FALLING by Mary O. Rank (Houghton Mifflin).

1958 THE BRIGHT ROAD TO FEAR by Richard Martin Stern (Ballantine). Also: THE MAN WHO DISAPPEARED by Edgar Bohle (Random House), NOW WILL YOU TRY FOR MURDER? by Harry Olesker (Simon & Schuster), DEATH OF A SPINSTER by Frances Duncombe (Scribner).

1957 KNOCK AND WAIT A WHILE by William Rawle Weeks (Houghton Mifflin). Also: BAY OF THE DAMNED by Warren Carrier (John Day), ROOT OF EVIL by James Cross (Messner).

1956 REBECCA'S PRIDE by Donald McNutt Douglas (Harper).

1955 THE PERFECTIONIST by Lane Kauffman (Lippincott). Also: IN HIS BLOOD by Harold R. Daniels (Dell), MUCH ADO ABOUT MURDER by Fred Levon (Dodd, Mead).

1954 GO, LOVELY ROSE by Jean Potts (Scribner).

1953 A KISS BEFORE DYING by Ira Levin (Simon & Schuster).

1952 DON'T CRY FOR ME by William Campbell Gault (Dutton).

1951 STRANGLE HOLD by Mary McMullen (Harper). Also: CARRY MY COFFIN SLOWLY by Lee Herrington (Simon & Schuster), THE CHRISTMAS CARD MURDERS by David William Meredith (Knopf), CURE IT WITH HONEY by Thurston Scott (Harper), THE ELEVENTH HOUR by Robert B. Sinclair (Mill).

1950 NIGHTMARE IN MANHATTAN by Thomas Walsh (Little, Brown). Also: THE HOUSE WITHOUT A DOOR by Thomas Sterling (Simon & Schuster), HAPPY HOLIDAY! by Thaddeus O'Finn (Rinehart), STRANGERS ON A TRAIN by Patricia Highsmith (Harper).

1949 WHAT A BODY by Alan Green. Also: THE INNOCENT by Evelyn Piper (Simon & Schuster), THE DARK LIGHT by Bart Spicer (Dodd, Mead), THE SHADOW AND THE BLOT by N.D. and G.G. Lobell (Harper), THE END IS KNOWN by Geoffrey Holiday Hall (Simon & Schuster), WALK THE DARK STREETS by William Krasner (Harper).

1948 THE ROOM UPSTAIRS by Mildred Davis (Simon & Schuster). Also: WILDERS WALK AWAY by Herbert Brean (Morrow), SHOOT THE WORKS by Richard Ellington (Morrow).

1947 THE FABULOUS CLIPJOINT by Fredric Brown (Dutton).

1946 THE HORIZONTAL MAN by Helen Eustis (Harper).

1945 WATCHFUL AT NIGHT by Julius Fast (Farrar).

Best Paperback Original

1988 THE TELLING OF LIES by Timothy Findley (Dell). Also: TRAPDOOR by Keith Peterson (Bantam), PREACHER by Ted Thackrey, Jr. (Jove), A RADICAL DEPARTURE by Lia Matera (Bantam), JUDGEMENT OF FIRE by Frederick D. Heubner (Fawcett).

1987 BIMBOS OF THE DEATH SUN by Sharyn McCrumb (TSR). Also: BULLSHOT by Gabrielle Kraft (Pocket Books), DEADLY INTRUSION by Walter Dillon (Bantam), THE LONG WAY TO DIE by James N. Frey (Bantam), THE MONKEY'S RAINCOAT by Robert Crais (Bantam).

1986 THE JUNKYARD DOG by Robert Campbell (Signet). Also: THE CAT WHO SAW RED by Lilian Jackson Braun (Jove); HAZ-

ZARD by R.D. Brown (Bantam); RONIN by Nick Christian (Tor), SHATTERED MOON by Kate Green (Dell).

1985 PIGS GET FAT by Warren Murphy (NAL). Also: BLACK GRAVITY by Conall Ryan (Ballantine), BLUE HERON by Philip Ross (Tor), BROKEN IDOLS by Sean Flannery (Charter), POVERTY BAY by Earl W. Emerson (Avon).

1984 GRANDMASTER by Warren Murphy & Molly Cochran (Pinnacle). Also: BLACK KNIGHT IN RED SQUARE by Stuart M. Kaminsky (Charter), THE KEYS TO BILLY TILLIO by Eric Blau (Pinnacle), THE SEVENTH SACRAMENT by Roland Cutler (Dell), WORDS CAN KILL by Kenn Davis (Fawcett Crest).

1983 MRS. WHITE by Margaret Tracy (Dell). Also: FALSE PROPHETS by Sean Flannery (Charter), HUNTER by Eric Sauter (Avon), KILL FACTOR by Richard Harper (Fawcett), TRACE by Warren Murphy (Signet).

1982 TRIANGLE by Teri White (Ace/Charter). Also: CLANDESTINE by James Ellroy (Avon), THE MISSING AND THE DEAD by Jack Lynch (Fawcett).

1981 THE OLD DICK by L.A. Morse (Avon). Also: DEAD HEAT by Roy Obstfeld (Charter), DEAD-

LINE by John Dunning (Fawcett), PIN by Andrew Neiderman (Pocket Books), THE UNFORGIVEN by Patricia McDonald (Dell).

1980 PUBLIC MURDERS by Bill Granger (Jove). Also: TOUGH LUCK by L.A. Murray Sinclair (Pinnacle), BLOOD INNOCENTS by Thomas H. Cook (Playboy), LOOKING FOR GINGER NORTH by John Dunning (Fawcett).

1979 THE HOG MURDERS by William L. deAndrea (Avon). Also: THE KREMLIN CONSPIRACY by Sean Flannery (Charter), VORTEX by David Heller (Avon), THE QUEEN IS DEAD by Glen Keger (Jove), THE INFERNAL DEVICE by Michael Kurland (NAL).

1978 DECEIT AND DEADLY LIES by Frank Bandy (Charter). Also: STUD GAME by David Anthony (Pocket Books), THE SWITCH by Elmore Leonard (Bantam), HEARTSTONE by Philip Margolin (Pocket Books), CHARNEL HOUSE by Graham Masterton (Pinnacle).

1977 THE QUARK MANEUVER by Mike Jahn (Ballantine). Also: TIME TO MURDER AND CREATE by Lawrence Block (Dell), THEY'VE KILLED ANNA by Marc Olden (Signet), THE TERRORIZERS by

Donald Hamilton (Gold Medal).

1976 CONFESS, FLETCH by Gregory Mcdonald (Avon). Also: THE CAPTIVE CITY by Daniel Da Cruz (Ballantine), FREEZE FRAME by R.R. Irvine (Popular Library), THE DARK SIDE by Kenn Davis and John Stanley (Avon), THE RETALIATORS by Donald Hamilton (Fawcett).

1975 AUTOPSY by John R. Feegal (Avon). Also: THE ASSASSINATION by David Vowell (Bantam), THE MIDAS COFFIN by Simon Quinn (Dell), CHARLIE'S BACK IN TOWN by Jacqueline Park (Popular Library).

1974 THE CORPSE THAT WALKED by Roy Winsor (Fawcett). Also: FLATS FIXED—AMONG OTHER THINGS by Don Tracey (Pocket Books), THE GRAVEY TRAIN HIT by Curtis Stevens (Dell), JUMP CUT by R.R. Irvine (Popular Library), WHO KILLED MR. GARLAND'S MISTRESS? by Richard Forrest (Pinnacle).

1973 DEATH OF AN INFORMER by Will Perry (Pyramid). Also: THE BIG FIX by Roger L. Simon (Straight Arrow), DEADLOCKED! by Leo P. Kelley (Fawcett-Gold Medal), THE MEDITERRANEAN CAPER by Clive Cussler (Pyramid), STARLING STREET by Dinah Palmtag (Dell).

1972 THE INVADER by Richard Wormser (Gold Medal). Also: NOT DEAD, YET by Daniel Banko (Gold Medal), POWER KILL by Charles Runyon (Gold Medal), THE SMITH CONSPIRACY by Richard Neely (Signet).

1971 FOR MURDER I CHARGE MORE by Frank McAuliffe (Ballantine). Also: THE WHITE WOLVERINE CONTRACT by Philip Atlee (Gold Medal), SPACE FOR HIRE by William F. Nolan (Lancer Books), NOR SPELL, NOR CHARM by Alicen White (Lancer), AND THE DEEP BLUE SEA by Charles Williams (Signet Books).

1970 FLASHPOINT by Dan J. Marlowe (Gold Medal). Also: THE DROWNING by Jack Ehrlich (Pocket Books), O.D. AT SWEET CLAUDE'S by Matt Gattzden (Belmont), AFTER THINGS FELL APART by Ron Goulart (Ace), GRAVE DESCEND by John Lange (Signet), MAFIOSO by Peter McCurtain (Belmont).

Best Short Story

1988 FLICKS by Bill Crenshaw (AHMM, August). Also: BRIDEY'S CALLER by Judith O'Neill (AHMM, May), INCIDENT IN A NEIGHBORHOOD TAVERN by Bill Pronzini (An

Eye for Justice), THE AL-
LEY by Stephen Wasylk
(AHMM, November),
DEJA VU by Doug Allyn
(AHMM, June).

1987 SOFT MONKEY by Har-
lan Ellison (*Mystery
Scene Reader*, Fedora,
Inc.). Also: THE AU PAIR
GIRL by Joyce Harrington
(*Matter of Crime*, No. 1,
HBJ), BREAKFAST TELE-
VISION by Robert Bar-
nard (EQMM, January),
MR. FELIX by Paula Gos-
ling (EQMM, July),
STROKE OF GENIUS by
George Baxt (EQMM,
June).

1986 RAIN IN PINTON
COUNTY by Robert
Sampson (New Black
Mask). Also: BODY
COUNT by Wayne D.
Dundee (Mean Streets,
Mysterious Press),
CHRISTMAS COP by
Thomas Adcock (Ellery
Queen's Mystery Maga-
zine), DRIVEN by Bren-
dan DuBois (EQMM),
THE PUDDLE DIVER by
Doug Allyn (Alfred
Hitchcock's Mystery Mag-
azine).

1985 RIDE THE LIGHTNING
by John Lutz (Alfred
Hitchcock's Mystery Mag-
azine). Also: THERE
GOES RAVELAAR by
Janwillem van de Weter-
ing, translated by Josh
Pachter (EQMM), TROU-
BLE IN PARADISE by
Arthur Lyons (New Black
Mask), WHAT'S IN A
NAME? by Robert Bar-
nard (EQMM), YELLOW

ONE-EYED CAT by Rob-
ert Twohy (EQMM).

1984 BY THE DAWN'S EARLY
LIGHT by Lawrence
Block (Playboy, August/
The Eyes Have It, Myste-
rious Press). Also: AFTER
I'M GONE by Donald E.
Westlake (Ellery Queen's
Mystery Magazine, June/
Levine, Mysterious
Press), BREAKFAST AT
OJAI by Robert Twohy
(EQMM, September),
THE RELUCTANT DE-
TECTIVE by Michael Z.
Lewin (The Eyes Have It,
Mysterious Press), SEA-
SON PASS by Chet
Williamson (Alfred
Hitchcock's Mystery Mag-
azine, October).

1983 THE NEW GIRL FRIEND
by Ruth Rendell (Ellery
Queen's Mystery Maga-
zine, August). Also: THE
ANDERSON BOY by Jo-
seph Hansen (Ellery
Queen's Mystery Maga-
zine, September), BIG
BOY, LITTLE BOY by
Simon Brett (Ellery
Queen's Mystery Maga-
zine, July), GRAFFITI by
Stanley Ellin (Ellery
Queen's Mystery Maga-
zine, March), PUERTO
RICAN BLUES by Clark
Howard (Ellery Queen's
Mystery Magazine,
April).

1982 THERE ARE NO SNAKES
IN IRELAND by Frederick
Forsyth (No Comebacks,
Viking). Also: A DECENT
PRICE FOR A PAINTING
by James Holding (Ellery

Queen's Mystery Magazine), ALL THE HEROES ARE DEAD by Clark Howard (Ellery Queen's Mystery Magazine), TALL TOMMY AND THE MILLIONAIRE by S.S. Rafferty (Alfred Hitchcock's Mystery Magazine).

1981 THE ABSENCE OF EMILY by Jack Ritchie (Ellery Queen's Mystery Magazine, Jan.). Also: A TOKEN OF APPRECIATION by Donald Olson (Alfred Hitchcock's Mystery Magazine, June), THE MIRACLE DAY by Ernest Savage (Ellery Queen's Mystery Magazine, Feb.), MOUSIE by Robert Twohy (Ellery Queen's Mystery Magazine, Nov.), SEEDS OF MURDER by Nan Hamilton (Alfred Hitchcock's Mystery Magazine, Dec.).

1980 HORN MAN by Clark Howard (Ellery Queen's Mystery Magazine). Also: THE MOST DANGEROUS MAN ALIVE by Edward D. Hoch (Ellery Queen's Mystery Magazine), UNTIL YOU ARE DEAD by John Lutz (Alfred Hitchcock's Mystery Magazine), THE CHOIRBOY by William Bankier (Alfred Hitchcock's Mystery Magazine).

1979 ARMED AND DANGEROUS by Geoffrey Norman (Esquire, Dec.). Also: USED IN EVIDENCE by Frederick Forsyth (Playboy, Dec.), SCRIMSHAW by Brian Garfield (Ellery

Queen's Mystery Magazine, Dec.), THE BOILER by Julian Symons (Ellery Queen's Mystery Magazine, Nov.), THE IMPERIAL ICE HOUSE by Paul Theroux (Atlantic, April).

1978 THE CLOUD BENEATH THE EAVES by Barbara Owens (Ellery Queen's Mystery Magazine, Jan.). Also: GOING BACKWARD by David Ely (Ellery Queen's Mystery Magazine, Nov.), STRANGERS IN THE FOG by Bill Pronzini (Ellery Queen's Mystery Magazine, June), THE CLOSED DOOR by Thomas Walsh (Ellery Queen's Mystery Magazine, May), THIS IS DEATH by Donald Westlake (Ellery Queen's Mystery Magazine, Nov.).

1977 CHANCE AFTER CHANCE by Thomas Walsh (EQMM, Nov.). Also: THE LAST RENDEZVOUS by Jean Backus (EQMM, Sept.), JODE'S LAST HUNT by Brian Garfield (EQMM, Jan.), THE PROBLEM OF LI T'ANG by Geoffrey Bush (Atlantic Monthly, Aug.), THE JOHORE MURDERS by Paul Theroux (Atlantic Monthly, March).

1976 LIKE A TERRIBLE SCREAM by Etta Revecz (EQMM). Also: NOBODY TELLS ME ANYTHING by Jack Ritchie (EQMM), LAVENDER LADY by Barbara Callahan

(EQMM), CRAZY OLD LADY by Avram Davidson (EQMM), PEOPLE DON'T DO SUCH THINGS by Ruth Rendell (THE FALLEN CURTAIN by Ruth Rendell, Doubleday).

1975 THE JAIL by Jesse Hill Ford (Playboy, March). Also: THE FALL OF THE COIN by Ruth Rendell (EQMM, June), THE MANY-FLAVORED CRIME by Jack Ritchie (MD Magazine, Dec.), OLD FRIENDS by Dorothy Salisbury Davis (EQMM, Sept.), NIGHT CRAWLERS by Joyce Harrington (EQMM, Jan.).

1974 THE FALLEN CURTAIN by Ruth Rendell (EQMM). Also: THE CABIN IN THE HOLLOW by Joyce Harrington (EQMM), THE GAME by Thomasina Weber (Killers of the Mind, Random House), THE LIGHT IN THE COTTAGE by David Ely (Playboy), A NIGHT OUT WITH THE BOYS by Elsin Ann Gardner (EQMM), SCREAMS AND ECHOES by Donald Olson (EQMM).

1973 THE WHIMPER OF WHIPPED DOGS by Harlan Ellison (Gallery). Also: DO WITH ME WHAT YOU WILL by Joyce Carol Oates (Playboy), THE GHOSTS AT IRON RIVER by Chelsea Quinn Yarbro (Men & Malice, Doubleday), THE O'BANNON BLARNEY FILE by Joe Gores (Men & Malice, Doubleday), FIFTY YEARS AFTER by Anthony Gilbert (EQMM).

1972 THE PURPLE SHROUD by Joyce Harrington (EQMM). Also: CELESTINE by George Bradshaw (Ladies' Home Journal), FRIGHTENED LADY by C.B. Gilford (Alfred Hitchcock's Mystery Magazine), HIJACK by Robert L. Fish (Playboy), ISLAND OF BRIGHT BIRDS by John Christopher (EQMM).

1971 MOONLIGHT GARDENER by Robert L. Fish (Argosy). Also: SARDINIAN INCIDENT by Evan Hunter (Playboy), MY DAUGHTER IS DEAD by Pauline C. Smith (Alfred Hitchcock's Mystery Magazine), THE SPIVVLETON MYSTERY by Katherine Anne Porter (Ladies' Home Journal).

1970 IN THE FORESTS OF RIGA THE BEASTS ARE VERY WILD INDEED by Margery Finn Brown (McCalls, July). Also: MISS PAISLEY ON A DIET by John Pierce (EQMM, Feb.), DOOR TO A DIFFERENT WORLD by Anthony Gilbert (EQMM, March).

1969 GOODBYE, POPS by Joe Gores (EQMM). Also: DOUBLE ENTRY by Robert L. Fish (EQMM), DEATH'S DOOR by Robert McNear (Playboy),

POISON IN THE CUP by Christianna Brand (EQMM), PROMISE OF ORANGES by Duveen Polk (Good Housekeeping).

1968 THE MAN WHO FOOLED THE WORLD by Warner Law (Saturday Evening Post, Aug. 24). Also: THE LAST BOTTLE IN THE WORLD by Stanley Ellin (EQMM, Feb.), CROOKED BONE by Gerald Kersh (Saturday Evening Post, Aug. 10), SUCCESS OF A MISSION by William Arden (Argosy), MOMENT OF POWER by P.D. James (EQMM, July).

1967 THE OBLONG ROOM by Edward D. Hoch (The Saint, July). Also: TWIST FOR TWIST by Christianna Brand (EQMM, May), DARE I WEEP? DARE I MOURN? by John le Carré (Saturday Evening Post, Jan. 28), THE SALAD MAKER by Robert McNear (EQMM, June).

1966 THE CHOSEN ONE by Rhys Davies (New Yorker, June 4). Also: MASTER OF THE HOUNDS by Algis Budrys (Saturday Evening Post, Aug. 27), THE HOCHMANN MINIATURES by Robert L. Fish (Argosy, March), THE SPLINTERED MONDAY by Charlotte Armstrong (EQMM, March).

1965 THE POSSIBILITY OF EVIL by Shirley Jackson (Saturday Evening Post, Dec. 18). Also: FOXER by Brian Cleeve (Saturday Evening Post, Dec. 18), THE CASE FOR MISS PEACOCK by Charlotte Armstrong (EQMM, Feb.), WHO WALKS BEHIND by Holly Roth (EQMM, September).

1964 H AS IN HOMICIDE by Lawrence Treat (EQMM, March). Also: A SOLILOQUY IN TONGUES by William Wiser (Cosmopolitan, May), THE PURPLE IS EVERYTHING by Dorothy Salisbury Davis (EQMM, June).

1963 MAN GEHORCHT by Leslie Ann Brownrigg (Story Magazine). Also: THE CRIME OF EZECHIELE COEN by Stanley Ellin (EQMM, Nov.), THE BALLAD OF JESSE NEIGHBORS by William Humphrey (Esquire, Sept.).

1962 THE SAILING CLUB by David Ely (Cosmopolitan). Also: THE TERRAPIN by Patricia Highsmith (EQMM), AN ORDER by Carl Erik Soya (Story #8).

1961 AFFAIR OF LAHORE CONTOMNENT by Avram Davidson (EQMM). Also: The CHILDREN OF ALDA NUOVA by Robert Wallston (EQMM), Ellery Queen's 1962 Anthology (Collection) by B.G. Davis.

1960 TIGER by John Durham (Cosmopolitan). Also: A

REAL LIVE MURDERER by Donald Honig (A.H.M.M.), SUMMER EVIL by Nora Kaplan (A.H.M.M.), A VIEW FROM THE TERRACE by Mike Marmer (Cosmopolitan), LOUISA, PLEASE by Shirley Jackson (Ladies' Home Journal).

1959 THE LANDLADY by Roald Dahl (New Yorker). Also: THE DAY OF THE BULLET by Stanley Ellin (EQMM).

1958 OVER THERE, DARKNESS by William O'Farrell (Sleuth).

1957 THE SECRET OF THE BOTTLE by Gerald Kersh (Saturday Evening Post). Also: AND ALREADY LOST by Charlotte Armstrong (EQMM).

1956 THE BLESSINGTON METHOD by Stanley Ellin (EQMM). Also: THE GENTLEST OF THE BROTHERS by David Alexander (EQMM), THE LAST SPIN by Evan Hunter (Manhunt).

1955 DREAM NO MORE by Philip MacDonald (EQMM). Also: INVITATION TO AN ACCIDENT by Wade Miller (EQMM).

1954 THE HOUSE PARTY by Stanley Ellin (EQMM).

1953 SOMEONE LIKE YOU by Roald Dahl (Knopf).

1952 SOMETHING TO HIDE by Philip MacDonald (Doubleday).

1951 FANCIES AND GOODNIGHTS by John Collier (Doubleday). Also: TWENTY GREAT TALES OF MURDER edited by Helen McCloy and Brett Halliday, THE MEMOIRS OF SOLAR PONS by August Derleth, HANDBOOK FOR POISONERS edited by Raymond T. Bond, FULL CARGO by Wilbur Daniel Steele.

1950 DIAGNOSIS: HOMICIDE by Lawrence G. Hochman (Lippincott). Also: Q. Patrick for general excellence.

1949 Ellery Queen. Also: Q. Patrick, William Faulkner.

1948 William Irish (Cornell Woolrich). Also: Q. Patrick, Ellery Queen.

1947 Ellery Queen.